Y0-EGD-889

The Couple Next Door

The Couple Next Door

collected short mysteries

MARGARET MILLAR

edited by Tom Nolan

Crippen & Landru Publishers
Norfolk, Virginia
2004

For Mary, without whom
—Tom Nolan

ACKNOWLEDGMENTS

All quotations from unpublished letters by Margaret Millar and from unpublished letters and other unpublished materials by Kenneth Millar are used with the kind permission of the trustee of the Margaret Millar Charitable Remainder Unitrust, owner of the books, copyrights, and materials related to the collected works of Margaret Millar and Kenneth Millar (Ross Macdonald).

Permissions to quote materials from cited archives, collections, and libraries have been granted by the University of California, Irvine; and by Brigham Young University.

TABLE OF CONTENTS

INTRODUCTION

A good many books, even pretty competent ones in other ways, seem to have been written with pale gray typewriter ribbon. They may play tricks with situations and names and places but their animation is essentially mechanical. They may divert one mildly (or, more often, supply a dull gray stretch of print) but they drift past remembrance without ever lodging there.

That is, in part, why one is grateful for the tales of Margaret Millar, realized with a sharp and pricking immediacy eliciting excitement and concern. ... Margaret Millar has very few peers in the wide and various range of mystery and suspense.

—James Sandoe, *New York Herald Tribune Book Review*, November 6, 1960

No woman in twentieth-century American mystery writing is more important than Margaret Millar ...

—H. R. F. Keating, *Whodunit? A Guide to Crime, Suspense and Spy Fiction* (Van Nostrand Reinhold, 1982)

Not many mystery readers in the twenty-first century, it seems, are familiar with the byline of Margaret Millar, who died in 1994. But during her nearly fifty-year career, this unique author—a forerunner of such psychologically sophisticated contemporary genre figures as Ruth Rendell, Minette Walters and P. D. James—helped shape the nature of modern mystery and suspense fiction.

Margaret Ellis Sturm Millar, born in Canada in 1915 and an American resident since 1941, earned an international reputation in the 1940s, '50s, and '60s as a superb storyteller and a master of her craft. Most of her books were published in translation throughout Europe and Asia; several still are. She won an Edgar Allan Poe Award in 1956 (and was nominated over the years for two more), was elected president of the Mystery

Writers of America that same year, in 1983 was named an MWA Grand Master, and in 1986 was given the Crime Writers of Canada's Derrick Murdoch Award.

Her earliest books were light-comic murder mysteries (though they featured one of the earliest psychiatrist-sleuths in detective fiction). But soon Margaret Millar turned more serious, with a string of memorable novels that pioneered the field of "psychological suspense." Later she returned to a semi-comic mode, mixing satire into her stories of homicide and psychosis.

She paid equal attention to plot and character, and she tried to make every word count. Her works, full of surprises and streaked with wit, were admired by all sorts of knowledgeable readers: from "Golden Age" star Agatha Christie to hard-boiled master Raymond Chandler, from expert reviewers Anthony Boucher and Anatole Broyard to European critics including Alfred Andersch and Julian Symons. It was said that Truman Capote, with whom for years she shared a publisher, asked Random House for copies of her novels as soon as they came out.

In today's mystery-reader magazines and Internet discussion groups, those who remember Margaret Millar often bemoan her having labored for the last twenty years of her writing life in the shadow of her betterknown husband Kenneth Millar, also a mystery writer, who used the pseudonym Ross Macdonald. Rarely mentioned are the twenty years before those, when Margaret Millar's success and reputation greatly outpaced her husband's.

Margaret Millar's own literary choices contributed to her relative eclipse in the mystery field. In art as in life, "Maggie" Millar went her own way. She abandoned two popular series characters in favor of doing mostly one-of-a-kind, "stand-alone" novels. Often she wrote books outside the genre: mainstream novels, a nonfiction work about birds. At the start of the 1970s, she said she'd retired—then returned in 1976 to do five more books.

Throughout all phases, her husband was her great champion. Kenneth and Margaret often suggested plots to one another, and they read each other's work with pleasure—each claiming the other was the better writer. The Millars had such different styles and sensibilities, it seemed possible that they might start with the same story premise and produce quite dissimilar novels (and, once or twice, they did just that).

She was the first to publish a book, but he was first to break into paid print (through magazines). For a remarkable four decades, they complemented one another's personal and professional ups and downs. Leading a seemingly bland existence— whether living frugally in Ontario, Canada, where both began writing in the late 1930s; or living frugally in wealthy Santa Barbara, California, their home from 1946 until their deaths— they were the strikingly talented, mutually diligent, far-from-ordinary couple next door.

Though bestknown for her novels, Margaret Millar wrote a handful of mystery and suspense short stories highly prized (for their quality as well as scarcity) by anthologists: "published, republished, and *re*republished," as their creator acknowledged. This volume collects those stories for the first time, along with two early novelettes never before between book covers. In these tales, a reader can trace the author's development from a competent beginner into an accomplished and highly individual storyteller.

The short story would seem an ideal form for Margaret Millar, who, once she found her mature style, pared her text to the minimum. She combined this lean text with an extreme emphasis on suspense, attempting in some books to have her tale's punchline delivered in the final sentence—sometimes in the final word.

Margaret Millar much enjoyed short stories—Somerset Maugham was a favorite author—and though she didn't write many, she wrote them all through life. Her last published work was a short story; and, nearly sixty years earlier, short-story was the form in which she first saw print—when she and her future husband Kenneth were not yet the brilliant couple next door but only brilliant adolescent classmates in a high school in Kitchener, Ontario, Canada.

* * *

And so—Madrid, vast, cold and unfriendly to young lads like Miguel, fired by ambition, and self-confidence.
—M. Sturm, "Impromptu," *The Grumbler*, Kitchener-Waterloo Collegiate and Vocational School, 1931

The ambitious young investigator, Herlock Sholmes,
yawned behind his false moustache and poured for himself a cocaine-and-soda.
    —Ken Miller (sic), "The South Sea Soup Co.,"
    The Grumbler, Kitchener-Waterloo Collegiate and
    Vocational School, 1931

Margaret Sturm and Kenneth Millar (pronounced "Miller")
were from opposite ends of the Kitchener social scale—her father was the town's mayor, his father had years ago left Ken
and Ken's unwell mother to fend for themselves—but they had
things in common. Both loved detective stories (and all sorts of
other prose and poetry); Margaret, because of the copies of *Black
Mask, Detective Fiction Weekly*, and other magazines she found
hidden under her siblings' mattresses: "I've been an avid reader
of mysteries since the age of eight," she later said. "Having two
older brothers with catholic literary tastes, I was practically
weaned on South American arrow poisons and Lunge's reagent."
    Both Ken Millar and Margaret Sturm were conscious of being
"young" and "ambitious," qualities mentioned by each in stories
they wrote for their high-school yearbooks: the first published
work under any byline by either of these two budding authors.
And they both wanted to be writers.
    As literary editor of the Kitchener Collegiate Institute's
Grumbler, Ken Millar had the pleasure of accepting Margaret
Sturm's Somerset Maugham-inspired sketch for publication,
along with his own parody of Sherlock Holmes-via-Stephen
Leacock. He knew Margaret at school, of course (they were each
on a debate team), and he often bumped into her at the library.
He admired her looks and brains, and secretly followed her to
choir practice. But he kept a shy distance from the mayor's
daughter, who—with her top grades, student office-holding, clas-
sics studies, and piano-playing on the radio—was probably the
outstanding girl at KCI.
    It was after they'd graduated high school that Ken got to know
Margaret better; after his father and then his mother died, and
he was on his way to Europe for several months' sabbatical from
his studies at the University of Western Ontario. He ran into
Margaret on the street; she was attending the University of

Toronto. He took her to tea, and invited her to accompany him to Ireland. ("Yes, he was serious," she affirmed nearly sixty years later. "He was *always* serious.") Margaret said no: nice Canadian girls didn't go to Ireland on the first date.

When Kenneth saw her next, in 1937, Margaret was reading Thucydides (in the original Greek) in the London, Ontario, public library. Her own mother had died, and she'd dropped out of university. She was studying psychiatry and other subjects on her own, and more determined than ever to become a writer. She and Kenneth began keeping close company.

The day after he graduated with honors from UWO, they were married: on June 2, 1938. (A decade later, Ken Millar, writing as the pseudonymous Macdonald, would give his private-eye character Lew Archer June 2 as a birthdate.)

After marriage, the Millars moved for a year to Toronto, where Kenneth earned the teaching certificate needed to become a high-school instructor. Despite her attempts to avoid becoming a mother, Margaret recalled, "I got pregnant three months after we were married. We were both so dumb. I knew all about murder but nothing about sex." In June of 1939, Margaret gave birth to the couple's first and only child, Linda Jane.

Needing cash for the maternity-ward bill, Ken Millar wrote a batch of stories and poems aimed at the Toronto and New York magazine markets, which Margaret typed for submission on an Underwood portable he'd won from a radio quiz program. Ontario publications bought several of his pieces, making Ken Millar a pro.

Margaret, who'd wanted a writing career too, was less than delighted with the turn her life had taken.

"Probably," she said in 1990, "if we'd each had a lot of money, maybe we would have gotten a divorce; I don't know. *He* wouldn't have wanted to, but I would have, because—a woman feels funny, when she's married; especially a very independent type, like me. You feel *trapped*, you know? 'Here I am, what have I done with my life? I haven't done anything.' And especially then because I had a child in just a little over a year, and *that's* when you really feel—the entrapment. You know: 'Here I am—*stuck*.' "

* * *

A great many women feel trapped after they have their
first child, especially talented and ambitious women like
Rose. Most of them eventually adjust themselves, in one
way or another ...
  —Margaret Millar, *Rose's Last Summer* (Random
  House, 1952)

Things got worse when Ken Millar took a job teaching at their
old high school in Kitchener. He liked the work well enough,
but Margaret felt more isolated than ever.

"I think the greatest satisfaction of being a teacher," Ken Millar
said many years later, "is that it allows you to relive your adolescence in a sense and do something about it which will help
other people ... The trouble was I spent all my time teaching
and had very little time to spend with my wife, which was one of
the things that made her into a writer that first year."

Margaret sought creative outlets. She proposed writing movie
reviews for a Toronto newspaper, but the paper turned her down.
She wrote some humor pieces, some of which may have been
bought by the same "Sunday-school" magazines that took Ken
Millar's first efforts; but there was no real future in doing more
of the same.

When a doctor diagnosed her as having what Margaret later
called "an imaginary heart ailment," she took to her bed for
weeks. Ken brought her books to read from the public library,
twenty or thirty at a time: mostly mysteries, which were having
a publishing heyday in 1940. "One day I was reading one of
these," she later recalled, "and it suddenly occurred to me, 'I can
do better than this.' "

With her husband's encouragement, and still working in bed,
Margaret wrote a 60,000-word mystery in fifteen days, then
rewrote it twice, with Ken's editorial help.

The Invisible Worm, by Margaret Millar—a comic murder
mystery with a psychoanalyst-detective, the six-foot-five
Dr. Paul Prye—was published by Doubleday Doran in 1941.
Margaret Millar never looked back.

*   *   *

In a recent column it was reported that Mignon Eberhart, a writer of detective fiction for many years, saw her first fingerprint outfit recently when she made a flying trip to Jamaica ...

Since that item appeared Mrs. Kenneth Millar, formerly Miss Margaret Sturm, who is our own local writer of mystery stories, has discovered just how her famous contemporary felt.

Preparing to leave late in June for the United States, where her husband, Mr. Kenneth Millar of the local collegiate staff has been awarded a fellowship at Ann Arbor, Mrs. Millar discovered that being finger-printed was one of the routines to which she had to submit in order to be permitted entry into the republic ...

Not much time is required for the process but every minute is grudged by Mrs. Millar these days as she wants all possible time for her second book, on which she is now at work, and which she plans to name "The Weak-Eyed Bat."

Her first book ... which is to be available by July 11 is entitled "The Invisible Worm" and Mrs. Millar's third book, which she is already planning is to be called "The Raven Is Hoarse."

She reports that all her books will have titles in which the name of some animal or bird is mentioned and that all of them will be quotations from famous poets. "The Invisible Worm" is from Blake's "The Sick Rose," "The Weak-Eyed Bat" from Browning's "Andrea Del Sarto" and the title of the new book not yet started is from Shakespeare's "MacBeth."

—"Pieces of Eight," *Kitchener Daily Record*, May 28, 1941

As Margaret Millar's life underwent drastic change, so did her husband's. The A-plus average Ken Millar had earned in summertime graduate-school courses at the University of Michigan won him a fellowship at that American school. Margaret's new career allowed Ken to quit his Kitchener high-school teaching job, move the family to Ann Arbor in 1941, and teach there while working full-time towards a doctorate.

Maggie meanwhile lost no time writing a second Paul Prye mystery, then a third. Her books attracted a growing number of readers, and praise from the top U.S. detective-story reviewers (including the *New York Herald Tribune's* Will Cuppy, who dubbed Margaret Millar "a mystery find of considerable voltage" and "a humdinger, right up in the top rank of bafflers, including the British").

A piece about her in the Ann Arbor newspaper, in August of 1941 (four months before America entered World War II), reported that the 26-year-old author's handwritten labors had been so intense in the preceding year that she now suffered from writer's cramp. Maggie didn't let that pain slow her down. She wasn't about to lose momentum in the career she'd worked so hard to get started.

The same article said that, between writing two of the novels, "she turned out a novelette for the editors of *The American* magazine, who had read her first book and had liked it." In fact, two novelettes were apparently written by Margaret Millar around this time – neither of which was published by *The American*.

"Last Day in Lisbon," a tale of murder, espionage and romance amongst wartime refugees, seems custom-cut to the cloth of *The Americans*'s table-of-contents pattern; but it didn't see print (in Dell's *Five-Novels Monthly*) until 1943.

"Mind Over Murder," a mystery featuring Dr. Paul Prye, might be the story Maggie wrote with *The American* in mind – or it could be a final, shortened version of that alluded-to, third Paul Prye adventure, "The Raven Is Hoarse."

In any case, the 20,000-word novelette "Mind Over Murder," included in the November, 1942, issue of *Street & Smith's Detective Story Magazine*, seems to have been Margaret Millar's first published mystery-fiction short story of any consequence.

* * *

At its lightest the mystery novel declines into an exercise in shadow-boxing and deserves the pejorative name whodunit. It is a pleasure to play drop-the-handkerchief with Mrs. Christie … but it doesn't bring us into contact with life.
　　—Kenneth Millar, "The Scene of the Crime," University of Michigan lecture, 1953

"Did Mr. Storm admit that the bloodstained handkerchief was his? Where is it, by the way?"

"Where is it?" Prye repeated. "You picked it off the floor, didn't you?"

"No. I … I completely forgot to. It must be here some place."

—Margaret Millar, "Mind Over Murder," *Street & Smith's Detective Story Magazine*, November 1942

In 1941, when "Mind Over Murder" seems to have been written, perhaps the best-selling detective-story writer in the world was Agatha Christie, whose intricately-choreographed puzzle-plots epitomized the first "Golden Age" of mystery fiction. Anyone writing in the genre at this time, especially a woman author, would be well aware of Christie as a point of comparison or departure. Whether as positive or negative inspiration, Agatha Christie was a presence to acknowledge in detective fiction in the 1940s. "Mind Over Murder" both evokes and parodies the Christie pattern.

As "Mind Over Murder" begins, ten people—an assortment of "mildly neurotic" patients, their doctors and attendants— are delivered by boat to a remote island in Lake Huron. This parallels the opening of Christie's popular 1939 book, *And Then There Were None* (made into a 1944 play, *Ten Little Indians*, and a 1945 film), in which ten people unknown to one another are invited to a lonely island and become targets of an unseen killer.

The people killed in "Mind Over Murder" are described as looking in different ways like Indians: one is crudely scalped; another is "very dark, almost as dark as an Indian." This too seems an intentional nod to Christie's work. When the second corpse in Millar's story is found, Dr. Prye thinks, "And now there are two"—another echo of *Ten Little Indians*.

The "Golden Age" device of a monogrammed handkerchief-as-clue, used in *Murder on the Orient Express* and other Christie books, is played with in "Mind Over Murder," which ventilates the cozy mystery's "closed environment" with forensic details and psychiatric symptoms more graphic than Mrs. Christie was wont to employ. Uncozy too is the blunt way Margaret Millar's hero counters irrelevant sentimentality with harsh reality. When someone faced with a corpse asserts, Pollyanna-like,

"There's no death," Prye says with distaste: "Then this is the next thing to it."

Margaret Millar, in the vanguard of the post-Agatha Christie generation of mystery writers, was eager to create a more realistic thriller. At the same time, she was building on a genre whose conventions and popularity Christie had done much to create.

Another author, it seemed, was being responded to in "Mind Over Murder": Ernest Hemingway, recently parodied by Ken Millar's future inspiration Raymond Chandler in the 1940 novel *Farewell, My Lovely* (which also included a phony-talking "noble savage" Hollywood Indian).

In *Farewell*, Chandler's detective Philip Marlowe dubs a cop "Hemingway" and makes fun of his repetitive dialogue. "Mind Over Murder" has a character actually named Hemingway: a strongly-built, simple-thinking type who runs into trouble when he applies brute force to the matters at hand. Ken (and maybe Maggie) Millar felt Ernest Hemingway was a modern equivalent of the American frontier male: self-aware enough to be ironic but isolated from society's more civilizing influences.

"Murder"'s Hemingway is juxtaposed with his dissipated charge, a man from the opposite end of the social-aesthetic spectrum: John Ross Prince III, who seems a caricature of hard-drinking Princeton alumnus and Ernest Hemingway friend-rival Francis Scott Key Fitzgerald. J. R. Prince tells his keeper, "You're no gentleman, Hemingway. You have never worked your way through Princeton. Princeton," Prince jokes to Paul Prye, "was named after me."

"Mind Over Murder," despite its sophisticated touches, is a product of Margaret Millar's beginning style; and its tagged-on romantic element falls flat. By the time "Mind Over Murder" found a home in *Street & Smith's Detective Story Magazine* the following year, Margaret Millar was using a new detective hero, and writing a much different sort of book.

*   *   *

Honesty is practically the whole thing in writing, accuracy of perception and memory. At least it's the *sine qua non*. To return to your own question of not being able to describe a wartless nose, I think it's essentially because you're a romantic, enamored of the strange. A literary critic would call you a decadent romantic, decadent in a literary sense: you frequent the alley rather than the main street, the attic and cellar rather than the living room, the cemetery rather than the Sunday School, the doctor's office rather than the country club, evil rather than virtue. Don't be offended: the best of modern poets, Baudelaire, was the same; the best playwright we have, O'Neill; maybe the best novelist, Faulkner. ...

One thing I hope you do: get inside (your book's female character) in words, show her thinking and acting from the inside out if you can: don't, in a word, be reticent: you're so reticent that you plunge into the depths of horror in order to avoid the statement of a bare and simple fact; it is infinitely less harrowing for you to describe a man killing a woman than making love to her, or a woman contemplating suicide than contemplating her natural feelings. Reality is more horrifying, perhaps, but not more terrifying, when hopped up. ... But this argument is ... not so much a description or criticism of your writing as an attempt to define your motivation as a writer. Don't change, of course. (You won't (you can't)).

—letter from Kenneth to Margaret Millar, June 12–13, 1945

As much as they delighted newspaper reviewers and lending-library patrons, the light-comic mysteries Margaret Millar had written no longer satisfied their author. She hoped to create something more artful and substantial, and her critically astute husband assured her she had the talent to do it.

One notion was to write something that drew on the colorful aspects of her Kitchener childhood; and Ken helped her sketch out a possible play, with scenes involving her piano accompaniment for a radio pitchman and the like. Eventually Margaret wrote instead some nostalgic first-person prose vignettes, one of which, "Grandpa and the Weather," was published in *Woman's Day* magazine.

Instead of further exploring mainstream possibilities now, Margaret Millar went back to mystery fiction—but with a new seriousness.

The change was made with subtlety, in a third book with Dr. Paul Prye. At the start of *The Devil Loves Me*, a sardonically comical opening scene leads the reader to expect the Millar formula as before. But when series hero Prye's intended wedding is interrupted by a poisoning death, the murder is investigated by a new protagonist: a drab Toronto police detective who's everything the suave, smooth-talking, sharp-dressing Prye is not.

The nondescript Detective-Inspector Sands is small, with pale gray eyes and a pleasant, mild voice. There's a stillness in his face and movements, "as if he has been dead a long time and is only going through the motions." Outwardly calm, Sands is inwardly appalled (in the few glimpses the author allows of his interior state) by the world he investigates: "*Indignity*, Sands thought, *the death of anything is an indignity*. He walked on, swinging his arms savagely through the fog."

With Paul Prye neatly married off, Inspector Sands was the sole investigator in Margaret Millar's next novel manuscript, *Wall of Eyes*. In this somber and ambitious work, the focus was much more on the book's supplemental characters and their emotional and social worlds; the police detective didn't appear until page seventy-four, and then he seemed more enigmatic than ever:

> He had no strong sense of identity. He lived alone with no wife or child or friend to call attention to himself or to look up or down at him. Because he lived in a vacuum he was able to understand and tolerate and sometimes to like the strange people he hunted. As insidiously as a worm burrows into an apple he burrowed into the lives of criminals and lay at the core, almost a part of it, yet remaining secretly and subtly himself.

Wall of Eyes, with its complex personalities and interesting settings (including a seedy Toronto night-club), was a major artistic departure and achievement for Margaret Millar.

But this radical-seeming manuscript struck her Doubleday

editors like a bucket of cold water, and they threw it right back at her. The verdict from Doubleday's Crime Club chief Isabelle Taylor was unequivocal: the book didn't work. This wasn't what Mrs. Millar's readers (or publisher) wanted. Try again.

But Margaret believed in *Wall of Eyes*—and so did her at-home Ann Arbor editor, Kenneth. She didn't want to scrap the best book she'd ever written. What to do?

An influential reader came to her rescue. Margaret had dropped the name of popular romance-novelist Faith Baldwin into her second book, *The Weak-Eyed Bat*; and Baldwin, a mystery addict, had begun a correspondence. When Margaret wrote her of Doubleday's action, Baldwin advised she get an agent (the Millars had done without one for three books) and recommended her own: Harold Ober, one of the best in the business. The Ober Agency took Margaret Millar as a client and right away placed *Wall of Eyes* with Random House: one of the two or three top publishers in the country. An apparent career setback became a triumph.

*   *   *

WALL OF EYES. By Margaret Millar. Random House. 243 pp. $2.

One goes along reading mysteries, thinking they are, on the whole, pretty good, and then, at rare intervals, out comes a real sockeroo, like this one, making the run-of-the-mill tale seem drab, inept and lifeless ... Here is a true, adult novel, with wit, satire, fine characterization—and a beautiful plot of crime and mystery ... one you'll want to keep with your good novels, of mystery and crime or otherwise.

—Elizabeth Bullock, "Sleuths and Slayers,"
The Chicago Sun Book Week, September 26, 1943

THE WALL OF EYES
Margaret Millar
(Random House: $2)
...
Summing Up
Heady mixture of society life,
underworld plots, abnormal
psychology, good detecting,
and better writing.
Verdict
Capital.
—"The Criminal Record," *The Saturday Review*,
September 4, 1943

WALL OF EYES, by Margaret Millar. ... Inspector Sands
works out a very neat solution and, in his quiet way, turns
out to be the kind of detective it would be nice to meet
more often. Highly recommended.
—"Mystery and Crime," *The New Yorker*,
September 4, 1943

Margaret Millar had followed her muse, and critics and readers had come right along with her.

Closer to home, her success was inspiring her husband to
attempt a book of his own. After editing and helping plot
Margaret's first several books (Kenneth and Margaret were listed
as co-authors on the books' contracts, if not on the books
themselves, until 1944), Ken Millar felt he'd learned enough about
mystery technique and structure to try his own hand at a thriller.
Working at night for a month in his small English Department
office on the University of Michigan campus, Kenneth produced
The Dark Tunnel, a spy story which Harold Ober sold to Dodd,
Mead for their Red Badge detective-book imprint. Now both the
Millars were professional mystery novelists.

Their friends in Ann Arbor—including other U of M junior-
faculty couples, and mystery-writer H.C. Branson and his wife
Anna—were thrilled for Ken's and Maggie's successes. The
Millars had a small but interesting circle of acquaintances in
Ann Arbor, including the African-American poet Robert Hayden,

poet Chad Walsh; and Donald Pearce, a classmate of Ken's from the University of Western Ontario, who was also now a U of M grad student (as were Hayden and Walsh).

The great young English poet W. H. Auden, who was teaching at Michigan in the early '40s, came for dinner to the Millars' small rented cottage (actually a converted garage). "And he brought (his companion) Chester (Kallman) to meet us," Margaret remembered nearly fifty years later. "Our (four-year-old) daughter took a great dislike to (Auden's) voice; he had a curious sort of voice ... He read one of my books, and he thought it was terrific. He laughed himself sick about this certain scene I'd written, in *Wall of Eyes*. I was, of course, flattered."

The critic Cleanth Brooks was also teaching at Michigan in the early '40s; he too came to dinner at the Millars'.

Evenings at Ken and Maggie's place could be fun occasions; Margaret sometimes played the piano, and Kenneth in those years could be almost raucously convivial. But the Millars were also difficult friends to have and keep: each of them intense, opinionated, frequently scoffing.

"I think I was always a little bit afraid of her," Anna Branson said of Margaret. "Because, let's put it this way: she called a spade a *spade*, and in no uncertain terms."

Ken also had his problematic side, said Anna Branson: "They were both great hands for explaining things through psychology—oh, great hands! ... I was complaining about this forty-dollar bill for some drugs I had to take; I said, 'You know, I forgot to pay it!' And so Ken, very gravely, said: 'That's because you didn't *want* to pay it.' See? There was always a little ... *explanation* ... something that *happened*, that made me do whatever I did. ... I mean, I got to the point where I just thought, 'Well I'm just gonna be careful what I *say*.'"

* * *

MARGARET MILLAR

Since the publication of her satirically humorous *Fire Will Freeze*, Margaret Millar's smoothly ordered life as the wife of a faculty member of the University of Michigan has undergone a somewhat violent change. Her husband, Kenneth Millar of the English Department, received his commission as an Ensign in the Navy last summer and departed for the first stage of his training at Princeton. Defying the laws of physics, which say you cannot crowd anything more into a space already filled, Mrs. Millar found a furnished house there and, with their five-year-old daughter, established a home for him. On completion of his Princeton training he was sent to Harvard and Mrs. Millar followed, still undismayed by the housing shortage and grimly announcing that on the next shift she would be right there too. "Obviously," she observed, "this cannot go on for long because a naval officer goes to sea." ...

  —bookflap copy, Margaret Millar, *The Iron Gates*
  (Random House, 1945)

It seemed the people Kenneth and Margaret were most at ease with were one another (not that they didn't fight). But not long after selling his first novel, Ken Millar took a step that would separate him from Maggie for a significant period: in 1944, he got a commission in the United States Naval Reserve.

In the autumn of '44, Ken Millar went to Princeton for training, then to Harvard. He was at Harvard when *The Dark Tunnel* was published, to more-than-respectable reviews. In early 1945, he was posted to the Eleventh Naval District in San Diego, California. Margaret, with their daughter Linda, accompanied Ken there (as she'd followed him to Princeton and Boston). Ensign Kenneth Millar was assigned to duty as a communications officer aboard the USS *Shipley Bay*.

Part of the idea of Ken's joining the Navy was to ease him out of the academic life, with which he'd grown disenchanted, and into a career as a full-time writer. Margaret had inspired him. She'd also outpaced him, and would soon have even greater success.

Margaret Millar had followed the well-received *Wall of Eyes* with another farcical nonseries mystery, *Fire Will Freeze*. But her next book was another serious murder story with Inspector Sands: *The Iron Gates*.

Random House had high hopes for this one, which they presented as "a psychological thriller" to differentiate it from more run-of-the-mill mysteries. It was published while Ken Millar was at sea aboard the *Shipley Bay*, and its reviews were spectacular. Dorothy B. Hughes (herself a noted suspense novelist) called it "a fine cut, flawless gem ... one of the finest psychological mysteries of all time ... (and a book that) stands equal with those few studies of murder which reach the status of literature."

The Iron Gates sold into a third printing—and, thanks to the Ober Agency's West Coast rep H. N. Swanson, it sold to Warner Bros., who bought movie rights for fifteen thousand dollars and hired Margaret Millar to write a screenplay of her book at seven hundred fifty dollars a week.

These were enormous sums for the cash-strapped Millars, who one recent winter had borrowed money to buy Christmas presents for their little girl, and had burned packing crates in the fireplace for heat. Now, Maggie wrote Ken, half an ocean away: "when you get out of the navy, you won't have to go job-hunting or asskissing or nothing. You'll just come home & we'll write."

Margaret had fallen in love with Southern California. Even before her movie sale, she'd bought a modest house (with *Iron Gates* book-money) in the beautiful oceanside city of Santa Barbara, ninety miles north of Los Angeles.

Hollywood, though, was another matter. Although Maggie liked the other Warners writers she met during her studio stint (who included William Faulkner, John Collier, Jo Pagano, W.R. Burnett, and Elliot Paul), she didn't approve of the movietown's loose moral climate. ("I'm very square," she said later. "The Hollywood life didn't appeal to me.") And she wasn't keen on how her script was subjected to the judgment of unqualified others.

"I like writing dialogue," she said in 1990, "but I don't like other people to come in and interfere. I don't like people asking the charwoman, 'What do you think of this?' If they ask a jury of my *peers*, then—"

The screenplay Maggie wrote all on her own pleased everyone at Warners, from producer Henry Blanke to the head of the studio. "The last I saw of it," Margaret remembered of her *Iron*

Gates adaptation, "Jack Warner had read it and—this is something I'll never forget—he wrote across the front of it: DO IT NOW. And then they offered it to Bette Davis. She turned it down, because the woman (character) dies three-fourths of the way through. She thought I could rewrite it, to let her live to the bitter end—and have a big *scene* then, you know. And then it went to Barbara Stanwyck; and she turned it down, for the same reason. By that time, I couldn't care less. I was already writing something else: my own books ... I'm a worker. I'm a *serious writer*. And all this folderol was—junk."

Ensign Millar, on leave, got to visit his wife at Warners and meet William Faulkner and the other writers; he was at the studio on August 14, 1945: the day Japan surrendered and World War II came to an end.

Another memorable event, one even more momentous in terms of the Millars' subsequent careers, took place during a later leave, when Maggie rendezvoused with Ken in San Francisco. On an October night in 1945 (in a week when the issue of *Liberty* magazine including a condensation of *The Iron Gates* was on newsstands), Kenneth and Margaret Millar got together for the first time with mystery reviewer and writer Anthony Boucher, for several hours of drinks and enthusiastic conversation. Boucher, already an important genre critic and soon to be crime-fiction reviewer for the *New York Times*, was a fan of both Margaret's and Kenneth's work. ("He often said it was amazing," his widow Phyllis White remembered, "to find so much talent in one family.")

Anthony Boucher reminded the Millars of the short-story contest now being held by *Ellery Queen's Mystery Magazine*, the first in what would become an annual competition. The critic urged both Ken and Margaret to enter. Ken took the suggestion to heart. On returning to his ship the next day, he got right to work and wrote two short stories featuring a Los Angeles detective called Joe Rogers, a private eye who bore a passing resemblance to Raymond Chandler's popular hard-boiled hero Philip Marlowe. (Eventually, Millar/Macdonald would rename his Rogers character Lew Archer and use him as the narrator-protagonist in a long series of novels, starting with 1949's *The Moving Target*.) Ken mailed these two stories to Margaret, who had the Ober Agency submit them to the *EQMM* contest.

Maggie too wrote an entry for the competition, an eighteen-page tale entitled "The Zombie."

"It sounds like the sort of thing that could cop a prize by originality and good writing," Ken commented on Margaret's written description of her contest story (unlocated, in 2004). Could this be the all-dialogue item Margaret Millar years later told writer Ed Gorman she'd once done? ("(Y)ou carry that (all-dialogue, no-prose idea) too far and then it doesn't work either. I did it with a short story once. It was a disaster.") In any case, Ken Millar was inspired to write an all-dialogue story himself, "Shock," which he also entered in the *EQMM* competition. ("Shock" was printed eight years later, as "Shock Treatment," in the debut issue of *Manhunt*.)

"The Zombie" didn't snag an award, but one of Ken's stories did. Ellery Queen named "Find the Woman" a fourth-prize winner and published it in an issue of *EQMM* and in a subsequent book-collection.

It would be several years before Margaret and Ken Millar both entered stories again in the same competition. Then the results would be rather different. By then too there would be many other changes in their lives.

*   *   *

Her first book, *The Invisible Worm*, was an ingenious, elegant, and amusing story which introduced Dr. Paul Prye, an Ontario psychoanalyst-detective much given to "highbrow logic" and quotation from William Blake. *Wall of Eyes* and *The Iron Gates*, more serious (though frequently witty) in tone, were also set in Canada, and featured Inspector Sands, a slightly more orthodox detective. But the majority of Margaret Millar's sardonic and tough-minded psychological suspense novels center on a psychopathic personality and its victims, rather than an idealized investigator.

—*World Authors 1950–1970* (H. W. Wilson Co., 1975), John Wakeman, editor

Many writers who found a formula for a significant success would seize and use it as the template for an entire career, working the same trick over and over. But that wasn't Margaret Millar's way. She never stood still in her work. Her follow-up to the moneymaking Inspector Sands "psychological thriller" *The Iron Gates* was a semi-mainstream 1947 novel, *Experiment In Springtime*, with some suspense elements but no Inspector Sands. After that, Margaret wrote the completely nonmysterious *It's All in the Family*, a charming but plotless collection of vignettes involving a precocious twelve-year-old named Priscilla, which, like "Grandpa and the Weather," romanticized Margaret's own childhood (this time in the third person).

It's All in the Family became a minor bestseller in 1948 and was excerpted in *Ladies' Home Journal*. The author followed it up not with a similar work evoking the joys of childhood but with *The Cannibal Heart*, a novel of modern menace, featuring a troubled married couple and their endangered eight-year-old daughter. This was succeeded by another change of pace, *Do Evil in Return*, billed as "Mrs. Millar's first mystery novel since *The Iron Gates*."

Readers (and publishers) never knew what to expect from Margaret Millar—and neither did the author. Her imagination didn't run to formula. Never again, for instance, would she write a book that involved Inspector Sands.

Her husband encouraged Margaret's explorations and innovations; but he needed to tailor his own output (and income) to accommodate her creativity. After writing three more postwar thrillers under his own name—and trying, and failing, to write a mainstream novel about his own more troubled Kitchener adolescence—Ken Millar resurrected the private eye from his prize-winning 1945 short story, called him Lew Archer, and starred him in *The Moving Target*, a 1949 pseudonym-signed "bread-and-butter mystery" whose modest success encouraged Millar/Macdonald to continue writing Archer novels for what would turn out to be the rest of his life.

"He wasn't indifferent to sales, by any means," said Collin Wilcox, a mystery writer who became friends with Ross Macdonald in the 1960s. "I was moaning one time about, 'Geez, I haven't got a real good paperback deal.' He said, 'Well it's the same with Margaret: she didn't give a damn, she just writes what she feels like writing and—you know, the hell with 'em!' And so he said it was sorta up to him to, you know, bring home the bacon! And he recognized that a series was the way to go."

If Margaret's writing was unpredictable, her output remained consistent; it had to.

"One thing he did tell me," recalled Hugh Kenner, the Canadian academic and critic who knew the Millars in Santa Barbara in the 1950s, "was that the economics of mystery writing really required that you produce two books a year. And between them, they could do that ... So that collaboration of theirs was what kept them in very good circumstances."

Or, as Margaret would put it: "No writee, no eatee."

Working at opposite ends of the house and at different times of the day, Kenneth and Margaret Millar maintained their professional pace for decades.

"I think things would have been very different for both Ken and me had there not been a Depression and had we not been (raised during it)," Margaret said in 1990. "But then, maybe we wouldn't have worked so hard all our lives. Because we never took a day off. Sundays—Christmas—nothing. We just worked."

And, though their writing styles differed, their respect for one another's work was mutual and undiminished.

"(Ken) used to envy—he did, to me—Margaret's writing," said Donald Pearce, a friend of the Millars' for thirty years. "And he said of her that she was a *natural* writer, as compared to himself. And he instanced an example of it; he said, 'Frinstance,' he recited to me a sentence with a simile in it: 'Her question trailed off into the room like a faint cigarette track in the air,' or something like that ... The comparison between the question and the ... smoke trailing off, was so perfect ... The ear is so fine, and the tuning is so good there, that it *is* a successful piece of writing."

"I know that Ken said that Margaret could write better than he could," agreed Lydia Freeman, another friend of the Millars' throughout the 1950s and '60s.

Margaret was equally appreciative of Kenneth's work. "I remember running into (author) Glenway Westcott I think, at some station or other," she said years later. "He said, 'You know,

I think your husband's a better writer than you are.' And I said, 'I agree—absolutely.' And I *did* agree, and I was very very happy about it. (Ken was simply embarrassed.)"

Mystery writer William Campbell Gault bumped up against Margaret's high opinion of her husband's prose when he first encountered the Millars at a party in San Diego in the early 1950s. Ticked off by Ken's opening remark to him, Gault recalled responding: "'Are you Ken Millar? ... I'll tell you something ... your wife writes better than *you* do.' I thought she did. Maggie's in the toilet and overhears me. When she comes out, she says, 'Some little son of a bitch out there says I write better than Ken!'"

"They were a great mutual admiration society," *Los Angeles Times* critic Charles Champlin said of the Millars, whom he met several times during the 1960s and '70s. "They both liked each other's work a whole lot, which I thought was interesting—perhaps more from her direction than from his."

"Of course the thought you always had with Margaret and Ken was: who was the dominant personality?" said Claire Stump, another friend of the Millars' in the '50s and '60s. "And in a way, you kinda felt that Margaret was. But Margaret kind of felt that people thought she was stronger but she really wasn't, that Ken was. So maybe they each found strength in each other.

"But I would say that Ken would be inclined to ... acquiesce to Margaret's wishes; at least, that was my feeling."

Saul David, an editor at Bantam Books, cast his professionally curious eye on the Millars when he visited them in Santa Barbara in the 1950s, during a brief period when Ken and Margaret were both being published in paperback by Bantam. "As I remember it, she was sort of the head of the household, or so it would seem," David said. "But not like a Hollywood head of the household; I mean, there was nothing driven about it. It was very easy, familial ... I was interested in the way they worked. She advised him on his books; she used to criticize and advise. Ken was a very gentle kind of guy, very soft-spoken. Maggie was really rather more the pro than he was; she was very well-established. But they were so different. And (their books were) so different, that it made a very interesting contrast."

"If I wanted him to, he was eager to read (my manuscripts)," Margaret Millar said after her husband's death. "But ... we both liked to go our own way; and then if we goofed, go back and correct. But I think if you're really born to be a writer—and I think both of us were—you sort of *know* when you're goofing.

"We used to call it 'the one-third blues' and 'the two-third blues.' If you were lucky, you got to two-thirds before you got the feeling that, 'Geez, this is terrible! How did I get stuck with this ghastly plot? What am I gonna *do*?' And *then* I might ask Ken to read it. And he might ask me to read his.

"And you got out of it, someways, always. Maybe that's the whole secret of writing mysteries: paint yourself into a corner, and then get yourself out."

*   *   *

There is an atmosphere in some of M. Malraux's novels that is reminiscent of the mystery novel and there is characterization in the mystery novels of Margaret Millar that takes you right into the novel proper. ... At any rate, Mrs. Millar told us the other day that she was *not* a mystery writer, though many people would disagree.

When we asked her *what* she was Mrs. Millar said she was a novelist with a mystery element in her work. "I care," she told us both firmly and affably, "about creating human beings, not about intriguing and meshing situations." What, we asked with a forcing inflection, about Agatha Chrystie? "She's a mystery writer," Mrs. Millar declared peremptorily. "I happen to be able to *write* rings around her and she happens to be able to *situate* rings around me."

—Harvey Breit, "In and Out of Books," *The New York Times Book Review*, August 4, 1957

I read contemporary detective stories, of course. There's a very good American writer called Elizabeth Daly. Michael Gilbert's early ones were excellent ... Another American, Margaret Millar, is very original.

—Agatha Christie to Francis Wyndham, *The Sunday Times Weekly Review*, February 27, 1966

Short stories were engaging Margaret Millar's originality often in 1954, a year which saw publication of three of her efforts in the form.

First of this trio in print was "Wimbi's Wedding Dress," a *Woman's Day* story involving an American woman botanist and a young Witoto Indian girl in the Brazilian jungle. Margaret, who'd never been near Brazil, was inspired to write it after reading an article in the *National Geographic*.

Of more likely interest to Margaret's usual readers was "McGowney's Miracle," a chilling tale which her husband thought "a humdinger." First published in *Cosmopolitan*, "McGowney's Miracle" combined suspense, horror, and black comedy in a concise manner which was becoming a hallmark of Margaret Millar's work. "McGowney's Miracle" would be anthologized many times over the years. Prolific mystery short-story writer Edward D. Hoch would call it "a gem of a story."

Margaret's third short tale of 1954 was written for the ninth annual *Ellery Queen's Mystery Magazine* contest. Although both Ken and Maggie had entered the original *EQMM* competition in 1945, Margaret's entry then had not been officially acknowledged, allowing the Millars now to claim disingenuously this was the first time they'd both submitted stories in the same year.

In any case, John Ross Macdonald's Lew Archer adventure, "Wild Goose Chase," took a third prize—and Margaret trumped him with her second-prize winner, "The Couple Next Door." This was a classic story of detection with a twist; and its detective was none other than Margaret's old fictional friend Inspector Sands, not encountered by readers since her 1945 book *The Iron Gates* (and never to be met again). The Toronto police detective was retired now; in his post-police years, he'd made his home (like the Millars) in Southern California.

"The Couple Next Door" was a notable effort. With it, Margaret Millar abandoned the short-story form for several years. She had bigger fish to fry.

* * *

For my own part, it's taken me 4 months' rest to get over writing the book (*Beast in View*), & I still jump a foot in the air when the phone rings. Well, it's a novel way of exercising, anyway—mental trampoline?

... It might interest you to read the condensed version in *Cosmo* this coming month. I had a lot of fun with it, maintaining my central theme (which I was instructed to change) while pretending not to, in fact, adding another one.

    —Margaret Millar to James Sandoe, May 7, 1955

The most artistically important period of Margaret Millar's writing career, it could be argued, were the seven years between 1955 and 1962. In that productive span, she wrote five novels: one of which won the Mystery Writers of America's Edgar Allan Poe Award, the next of which was published while she served as president of the MWA, and the final three which readers and fellow writers admire for the craft with which they conceal and reveal their plots' solutions. Of this last trio, the accomplished Edward D. Hoch would write: "they are, in a special sense, the peak of the mystery writers' art."

Beast in View, Margaret's Edgar-winner, limned with memorable intensity the behavior of an emotionally disturbed woman. The story grew out of Maggie's longstanding interest in abnormal psychology, including the Beauchamps case: the first documented instance of schizophrenia in America.

As commentators have noted, elements of *Beast in View*'s innovative structure have since been used in several other stories, somewhat diminishing the book's surprise. In fact, a Gore Vidal TV play the author saw while writing *Beast in View* seemed so close to her book's intentions that she was ready to scrap her work-in-progress before it was even finished. Her husband, though, suggested a final twist that salvaged the novel and made it even more effective. "He saved the book," she wrote in 1983, "from becoming what would have been by this time a cliché."

Beast in View was bought for condensation by *Cosmopolitan*. The author elected to do her own abridgment. "You could either do it yourself," she recalled, "or have one of the editors do it. Well—some choice." Maggie enjoyed reshaping her own text. "It's difficult to cut a book down to 25,000 words, unless you really know how to do it. And it just came natural to me." So much so, she was sometimes able to work variations on her original work, as she indicated to critic James Sandoe regarding her *Beast in View* job.

Given her active participation, the abridgments Margaret made of her novels might almost be considered part of her short-fiction oeuvre. Other books she condensed for *Cosmo* were *An Air That Kills* (which the magazine called "The Soft Talkers," the book's UK title) and *The Listening Walls* ("Listening Walls").

Several Ross Macdonald books were also bought by *Cosmo*, and Margaret Millar tutored Ken in doing their abridgments. At first, she said, "Ken would go through, and he'd look *laboriously* ... thinking he could *spare* that deft line, *spare* this one—you *can't do* that; you have to cut out the whole shebang. You know. And then, when he learned it, he became very proficient at cutting his own work."

At the time the Edgar Allan Poe Award was being given to *Beast in View*, its author and her family were undergoing a terrible series of events relating to the Millars' sixteen-year-old daughter: Linda Millar was involved in a fatal hit-and-run automobile accident in Santa Barbara. After months of front-page publicity, Linda admitted responsibility for the incident and was sentenced to eight years' probation. In the wake of this calamity, the Millars moved to Northern California for a year. Kenneth and Margaret returned to Santa Barbara in late 1957.

Margaret Millar nonetheless kept writing. In 1957, she published *An Air That Kills*, a book some reviewers thought nearly as good as *Beast in View*; and her colleagues elected her president of the Mystery Writers of America.

Maggie went to New York that year to officiate at the Edgar Awards dinner at Toots Shor's. There she had the singular pleasure of calling upon in public a crucial figure from her past whom she'd never met in person.

After telling her Edgar-dinner audience the "Cinderella story" of how the head of Doubleday's mystery unit sent her a telegram in 1940 accepting her first book for publication (she omitted mention of *Wall of Eyes'* later rejection), President Millar announced from the rostrum: "I understand that the editor who sent that telegram is in the audience tonight. Will Mrs. Isabelle Taylor of the Crime Club please stand up?"

The Millars endured another family crisis in 1959, when daughter Linda disappeared for ten days while attending college at UC Davis. She was found in Reno, Nevada, and eventually resumed studies at UCLA.

Also in 1959, Margaret Millar published *The Listening Walls*, the first of what Edward D. Hoch would call her "special trio of novels," each of which "withholds the key element of its solution until the very end of the book." It was followed in 1960 by *A Stranger in My Grave* and in 1962 by *How Like an Angel*.

"Just as the success of her early novels helped launch her husband, Kenneth Millar (Ross Macdonald), on his career as a mystery writer," Ed Hoch wrote, "there is some evidence in *A Stranger in My Grave* and her following novel that she has been influenced by the California tradition of sleuths like Lew Archer," in that the answer to these mysteries "lies in the past, in tangled family relationships."

Few families' relationships had seemed more tangled than the Millars' own. In 1962, with her daughter Linda newly and happily married, Margaret Millar wrote a remarkable short story which seemed to deal, at least symbolically, with some of the events and issues of her only child's earlier years.

Children of writers may have special problems. Linda Jane Millar suffered a number of them.

As a youngster of seven or eight years old, in postwar Santa Barbara, Linda Millar had trouble fitting into (or not intruding on) her parents' routines. Mother and father both worked at home, and each needed privacy. Where was Linda supposed to be? For a while, she attached herself to the family of a postman living nearby.

As Linda grew older, her parents' brilliance intimidated her. At the same time, all three Millars were isolated—by work, by intellect, by choice—from the community. At school, Linda was too brainy and odd to be accepted by the popular crowd. Often the friends she found were reckless ones.

Linda Jane was a source of inspiration for her writer-parents, especially Margaret, several of whose books included smart, willful, emotional little girls who resembled her own. After Linda's awful troubles (her fatal car accident, her disappearance), Margaret Millar and Ross Macdonald each used fiction

to explore and perhaps exorcise family patterns that may have
contributed to Linda's fate.

In Margaret Millar's story "The People Across the Canyon,"
we meet Paul and Marion Borton, a couple not unlike Ken and
Margaret Millar. The Bortons' eight-year-old only child Cathy
seems to have picked up many ways and moods from the Millars'
blue-eyed Linda. Like the Millars, the Bortons cherish their
privacy—for which their daughter pays a steep price.

As Linda once did, Cathy becomes attached to another
family in the neighborhood: the blandly-named, romantic-
seeming Smiths, who seem much happier and more exciting
to Cathy than her own bristly parents. The lonely eight-year-
old's wistful claim about her plans with the Smiths seems
heartbreaking: "I'm going away with them to dance and play
baseball."

"The People Across the Canyon" shifts point of view several
times in the course of its pages: from the watchful, wary mother's;
to the cautious, knowing child's; to the cheery but discouraged teacher's. The tale too switches mood and shape: Is it a mystery? A
ghost story? A fantasy? Or some sort of muted modern tragedy?

However labeled, Margaret Millar's short work was haunting,
at once poignant and chilling. It seemed worthy of keeping company with the fables of any number of notable contemporaries,
from Ray Bradbury to Shirley Jackson to John Cheever.

The Ober agents did their best to place this special story somewhere outside Margaret's usual markets; they sent "The People
Across the Canyon" in early 1961 to *The Atlantic, Cosmopolitan, Good Housekeeping, Harper's, Harper's Bazaar, Hudson
Review, Ladies' Home Journal, Mademoiselle, McCall's, The New
Yorker, Redbook, Virginia Quarterly Review,* and *Woman's Day.*
In the end, though, it was only *Ellery Queen's Mystery Magazine*
who wanted it. Maggie the pro was happy to give it to them, for
two hundred and fifty dollars.

* * *

The most striking thing about the *Trivialroman,* or
"trivial" novel, is its immortality ...

... we find, particularly in Simenon, Highsmith and (Margaret) Millar, carefully developed and solidly-based psychology, and a tenacious pursuit of themes. The fictional technique is nearly always faultless; it is constantly varied and elaborated. Very often these books achieve a magical homogeneity ...
    —Alfred Andersch, "How trivial is the trivial novel?",
    Times Literary Supplement, October 8, 1971

"Some days, I'll write a sentence ten times. If I knew a lot of mystery writers who did that, then I think I'd read more of them. I can't stand sloppy writing and sloppy structure. I miss some of the older writers: Elizabeth Sanxay Holding, Helen McCloy, Charlotte Armstrong. I consider Christie an excellent plotter. When I read *Witness for the Prosecution*, I knew she really had a twisted little mind. I wished I had thought of it."
    —Margaret Millar, quoted in Dilys Winn's *Murderess
    Ink: The Better Half of the Mystery* (Workman, 1979)

Margaret Millar's nineteenth novel, *The Fiend*, was published in 1964. Its jacket copy (probably written, as was most of Margaret's bookflap text throughout her career, by Kenneth) called the book "simple and shocking ... a searching and scathing inquiry into the guilty relations of adults with children." In 1976, Ross Macdonald named *The Fiend* one of his three favorite books by his wife (the other two being *Beast in View* and *A Stranger in My Grave*.)

Her twentieth work, which took four years to research and write, was Margaret Millar's most surprising effort yet, in a career of surprises that delighted her husband and kept readers and publishers alert: *The Birds and the Beasts Were There*, a nonfiction account of Maggie's birdwatching activities in and around Santa Barbara.

The book was charming, fascinating, humorous, informative, and beautifully-paced. Its centerpiece, a vivid account of a huge wildfire that menaced much of Santa Barbara (including the Millars' house) in 1964, was as gripping and suspenseful as a Margaret Millar novel. An excerpt from this book was printed in (of all surprising places) *Sports Illustrated*.

Margaret Millar returned to fiction in 1970 with *Beyond This Point Are Monsters.*

Then, late in 1970, the Millars' only child Linda died, at the age of thirty-one. It was the heaviest of blows. Margaret, who'd kept writing all during her daughter's adolescent crises, now put down her pen, she said for good.

It was in these years that Margaret Millar the writer slipped most into the shade of her husband Ross Macdonald, who'd become a bestselling author in 1969 with his fifteenth Lew Archer novel, *The Goodbye Look.*

"I hope she comes back to writing eventually," Ken Millar wrote Julian Symons late in 1974, "but at the present time she's just beginning to *read* again." In early 1975, Kenneth told their young friend William J. Ruehlmann: "Margaret is well and active but not working. She claims she's had her say. But I kind of wish a book would overtake her."

* * *

The numbers game

Jon Carroll's article, *Ross Macdonald in Raw California*, June, was most informative. Especially to me. I did not know that Macdonald's wife, Margaret Millar, had "numberless" wrinkles. I thought she only had 3,796.

Thanks. Sort of.
MARGARET MILLAR
Santa Barbara, Calif.
—*Esquire*: August 1972

Canadian Mysteries

Sir: It was generous of Jack Batten to mention my work in his article about Canadian mystery writers (January) even though, as he points out, I am not exactly a Canadian. I was born in the United States of Canadian parents, got most of my education in Canada, did my first paid writing for *Saturday Night*, and married a Canadian girl.

This girl, no longer quite a girl except in attitude, and since 1961 no longer a Canadian, is the missing person in Mr. Batten's otherwise comprehensive article. For under the name of Margaret Millar she has written sixteen or seventeen mystery novels, half-a-dozen of which are laid in Toronto. She has been given the Edgar Allan Poe Award by Mystery Writers of America, and served as president of that organization. In 1971, in the *Times Literary Supplement* of London, the German novelist and critic Alfred Andersch listed Margaret Millar, with Patricia Highsmith, Graham Greene, Eric Ambler, John le Carre, Giorgio Scerbanenco, and Georges Simenon, among the leading mystery writers of our time. I long ago changed my writing name to Ross Macdonald for obvious reasons.

Kenneth Millar
Santa Barbara, Calif.
—*Toronto Saturday Night*: March 1973

But then, in a move no more surprising than many others in her career, Margaret Millar began writing again—gripped, she said, by a plot that wouldn't let her go.

The result was *Ask for Me Tomorrow*, a 1976 novel which reviewers and faithful readers were most happy to greet. It featured as investigator a Hispanic lawyer named Tom Aragon, who returned in the more lighthearted 1979 book *The Murder of Miranda* and once more in *Mermaid* (1982). "Reports of my retirement," Maggie sometimes inscribed her new books, "have been greatly exaggerated, mostly by me."

By 1980, though, Ken Millar was showing symptoms of what was later diagnosed as Alzheimer's disease. (The last Ross Macdonald novel, *The Blue Hammer*, was published in 1976.) Margaret meanwhile was experiencing the onset of macular degeneration. After caring for Kenneth at home as long as she was able, a legally-blind Maggie Millar had her husband moved into a private rest home in December 1982.

In April of 1983, the Mystery Writers of America gave Margaret Millar its Grand Master Award. "I don't know whether I deserve this award," she said at the Edgar dinner in New York, "but I do know I worked like hell for forty-three years to get it. I wish my husband were here with me right now."

Ken Millar died three months later, at the age of sixty-seven.

And later that year, Margaret Millar published another book: *Banshee*. Her final completed novel, *Spider Webs*, was printed in 1986.

The year after that brought one last Margaret Millar short story, "Notions": an almost Zen-koan tale about love and loss that might be read as a sort of private p.s. to the most enduring relationship in its author's life. "Notions" was published by *Ellery Queen's Mystery Magazine* in December: the birth-month of Kenneth Millar.

Margaret Millar was seventy-nine when she died in 1994.

A decade after her death, all but a few of her books were out of print in America (though many were republished regularly in Europe). It seemed as if her entire life's work might, like the work of so many other past masters, be almost completely forgotten in her own adopted country.

Yet why shouldn't Margaret Millar's career, so full of surprising plot twists, yield a final surprise in the form of a posthumous revival? Why couldn't readers—weary of grisly forensics, o.d.'ed on books stuffed with what Maggie called "padding," hungry for inventive stories of ageless dilemmas—once more discover the unique novels of (to quote critic Marilyn Stasio) this "subtle and ... genuinely original writer"?

In the last words of Margaret Millar's last story: "It was a lovely notion."

Notes

"to hard-boiled master Raymond Chandler": In the spring of 1949 (two days after writing a letter to reviewer James Sandoe critical of Macdonald's debut novel *The Moving Target*), Chandler wrote another correspondent he thought the most intriguing character in mystery fiction might be the night-club master of ceremonies in Margaret Millar's *Wall of Eyes*.

"It was said that Truman Capote": "Interview with Margaret Millar," Diana Cooper-Clark, *Designs of Darkness* (Popular Press, 1983)

"once or twice, they did just that": Mystery expert Marvin Lachman has noted ("The American Regional Mystery: Southern California," *The*

Armchair Detective, October 1977) the parallels between Margaret Millar's *How Like an Angel* (1962) and Ross Macdonald's *The Moving Target* (1949): "Though similar in bare-bones outline, the books are distinctive and both excellent."

"Somerset Maugham was a favorite author": "I think the most influential writer in my life was Somerset Maugham," Margaret Millar told Ed Gorman (*Mystery Scene*, May 1989), "who didn't have anything whatsoever to do with mysteries except if you reread his best stories, they all had a kind of mystery plot to them. Not in wondering who did it, but in wondering what happened. He's the best in short stories ... Ever since I found out what a terrible son of a bitch he was I've tried not to think so highly of him but, that's separate, that's quite separate."

" 'I've been an avid reader of mysteries since the age of eight' ": *World Authors 1950–1970*, edited by John Wakeman (H.W. Wilson, 1975).

" 'Yes, he was serious' ": Margaret Millar to TN. Unless otherwise indicated, all MM quotes are from interviews with TN.

" 'I got pregnant three months after we were married' ": Sally Ogle Davis, "Murder, fatalistic humor and a three-Edgar family," *Toronto Globe and Mail*, July 16, 1983.

" 'I think the greatest satisfaction of being a teacher' ": Kenneth Millar interview with Arthur Kaye, The Kenneth Millar Papers, Special Collections and Archives, UC Irvine Libraries.

" 'an imaginary heart ailment' ": Wakeman, ibid.

" 'One day I was reading one of these' ": "The Writing Life," *Canadian Author & Bookman*, Fall 1988.

" 'a mystery find of considerable voltage' ": "Mystery and Adventure," *New York Herald Tribune Books*, July 20, 1941.

" 'a humdinger' ": "Mystery and Adventure," *New York Herald Tribune Books*, February 22, 1942.

" 'Princeton ... was named after me.' ": And the bibulous John Ross Prince may have been named after Margaret Millar's youngest brother Ross.
    When Ken Millar's first pseudonym "John Macdonald" (his own father's first and middle names) drew a complaint from the young writer John

D. MacDonald, Millar changed it for a time to John Ross Macdonald; then eventually to Ross Macdonald.

" 'Mind Over Murder' found a home in *Street & Smith's Detective Story Magazine*": The novelette was later reprinted in the 1943 edition of *All Fiction Detective Stories*.

"Honesty is practically the whole thing in writing": Kenneth Millar to Margaret Millar, K Millar Papers, UCI.

"Grandpa and the Weather": *Woman's Day*, March 1943.

" 'I think I was always a little bit afraid of her' ": Anna Branson to TN.

"a fine cut, flawless gem": *Albuquerque, N.M. Tribune*, May 11, 1945.

" 'when you get out of the navy' ": Margaret to Kenneth Millar, February 25, 1945, The Margaret Millar Papers, Special Collections and Archives, UC Irvine Libraries.

"the issue of *Liberty* magazine": October 13, 1945. The magazine reported erroneously that the novel would soon become a movie "with Lauren Bacall and Humphrey Bogart."

" 'He often said it was amazing' ": Phyllis White to TN, May 31, 1990.

" 'It sounds like the sort of thing that could cop a prize' ": Kenneth to Margaret Millar, November 4, 1945, K Millar Papers, UCI.

" '(Y)ou carry that (all-dialogue, no-prose idea) too far' ": Gorman, ibid.

"excerpted in *Ladies' Home Journal*": May 1948.

" 'He wasn't indifferent to sales' ": Collin Wilcox to TN.

" 'One thing he did tell me' ": Hugh Kenner to TN.

" '(Ken) used to envy' ": Donald Pearce to TN.

"Her question trailed off into the room like a faint cigarette track in the air": Or perhaps (from *An Air That Kills* (Random House, 1957)): "He gave her a cigarette and lit it for her. The smoke curled up from her mouth in a quiet smile."

" 'I know that Ken said' ": Lydia Freeman to TN.

" 'Are you Ken Millar?' ": William Campbell Gault to TN.

" 'They were a great mutual admiration society' ": Charles Champlin to TN.

" 'Of course the thought you always had' ": Claire Stump to TN.

" 'As I remember it' ": Saul David to TN.

"a *Woman's Day* story": *Woman's Day*, January 1954.

"For my own part": Margaret Millar to James Sandoe, May 7, 1955, The James Sandoe Collection, MSS 317, L. Tom Perry Special Collections, Harold B. Lee Library, Brigham Young University.

" 'they are, in a special sense, the peak of the mystery writers' art' ": *Twentieth-Century Crime and Mystery Writers*, editor John M. Reilly (St. Martin's Press, 1980).

" 'He saved the book' ": Afterword, *Beast in View* reissue (International Polygonics, Ltd., 1983).

" 'I understand that the editor who sent that telegram' ": *The Third Degree* (MWA newsletter), April 1957.

"special trio of novels": *Crime and Mystery Writers*, ibid.

"In 1976, Ross Macdonald named *The Fiend*": Macdonald interviews with Paul Nelson, UCI.

"(of all surprising places) *Sports Illustrated*": "A Career of Spying," April 15, 1978.

"I hope she comes back to writing eventually": Ken Millar letter to Julian Symons, September 10, 1974; copy sent by JS to TN.

"Margaret is well and active but not working": Ken Millar letter to William Ruehlmann, January 31, 1975; typed copy, UCI.

" 'I don't know whether I deserve this award' ": *The Third Degree*, June/July 1983.

" 'subtle and ... genuinely original writer' ": "A Sweep Through the Subgenres," *The Sleuth and the Scholar: Origins, Evolution, and Current Trends in Detective Fiction*, edited by Barbara A. Rader and Howard G. Zettler (Greenwood Press, 1988).

ABOUT THE AUTHOR:
MARGARET MILLAR

ABOUT THE AUTHOR: MARGARET MILLAR
Preface by Tom Nolan

"My life is remarkable only for its omissions," Margaret Millar claimed to the *Wilson Library Bulletin* in 1946. "I have never broken a limb, been divorced or arrested, never had anything stolen, and the only thing I ever lost was a phonograph needle."

The author was being modest—and a bit disingenuous. Even by 1946, her professional and personal lives were full of remarkable things.

Maggie Millar, as a storyteller or an autobiographer, was adept at using prose to conceal as well as reveal. Her spare and elegant sentences told only what she let them.

Such was the case in 1950, when she sketched this self-portrait for the *Unicorn Mystery Book Club News*. Her charming account of her life-to-date was accurate as far as it went; but an equally "truthful" and darker silhouette of the author emerged between the lines of her novels, works populated with anxious and neurotic characters who were anything but unremarkable. Her tenth volume, *Do Evil in Return*, prompted this stylish self-assessment.

Notes

" 'My life is remarkable only for its omissions' ": Miriam Allen Deford, "Margaret Millar," *Wilson Library Bulletin*, Volume 21, Number 4, December 1946.

"this stylish self-assessment": Margaret Millar, "About the Author: Margaret Millar," *Unicorn Mystery Book Club News*, Volume 3, number 3, 1950.

Do Evil in Return was the second Margaret Millar title to be chosen as a Unicorn selection. The very first Unicorn volume, in 1945, included her book *The Iron Gates*.

About the Author: Margaret Millar

When, at the age of four, I fell over a twenty-foot banister and landed on my feet unhurt, my mother decided that I must be a genius. She wasn't sure what I was a genius at, however, so I was forced to play the field. During the next ten years I did monologues, imitations, readings; played the clarinet; danced in amateur reviews; sang in a choir, contralto, tenor, or soprano, wherever sheer volume was needed. I went from choir to choir as utility infielder. But it was the piano that led me, in a backhanded way, into writing.

After playing at banquets, dancing classes and funerals for considerable time, I persuaded the manager of the local radio station to let me have a program of my own. In a few weeks it became painfully clear that no fan mail was forthcoming unless I wrote it myself. This required intense cunning, since the manager possessed a suspicious nature. Not only was a change of handwriting, ink, and paper necessary for each letter, but I was compelled to develop various styles of writing to fit the various characters I had dreamed up. I'm still dreaming them up, and still developing various styles. I no longer write my own fan mail, though I sometimes wish I did.

Since the last war I've been living in Santa Barbara with my husband (or husbands: Kenneth Millar and his pseudonym, John Ross Macdonald), our sixth-grader daughter Linda, a collie, a cocker spaniel, and two female hamsters who can teach us all a lesson in serenity. We swim a great deal, ride some, go dancing when the spirit (me) moves Ken, and root fervently, though at a distance, for the Tigers and the Dodgers. Mostly, however, we just write. It seems to agree with us. Once in a while I play the piano, for old time's sake. Mercifully, the clarinet has disappeared.

During the war, while Ken was at sea literally, I was at sea figuratively, in Hollywood, doing the script for my *Iron Gates*, which has yet to see film. Before that, we lived in Ann Arbor, before that in Canada. University of Toronto. Before that—but this is where I came in.

MIND OVER MURDER

MIND OVER MURDER
Preface by Tom Nolan

Neither Margaret nor Ken Millar based their fiction closely on truth, but both drew on real-life experience to lend credence to made-up tales.

"Mind Over Murder," written circa 1941, takes place on an island in Lake Huron quite like the one on which the Millars honeymooned in 1938.

"It was a private island in Georgian Bay, south of Lake Huron," Margaret Millar remembered in 1990. "Georgian Bay is noted for these private islands—so private, that you couldn't see anything. So private, that the johns only had three sides. Uh huh.

"A friend of Ken's—actually, his dentist—had offered his cottage; and the way he described it, it was a pretty nice place. Well, we had to take a boat, of course—and the boat had to go back. Suddenly, there we were, the two of us—alone! Alone, with about 500 million cockroaches, and a lotta poison ivy. It was really quite an experience ... Fortunately we were only there for eight days ... I do know that when the boat came, I decided that I intended to get a divorce, as soon as I hit *land* ..."

Kitty Tyler, the blond, hormone-driven female prowling "Mind Over Murder"'s island, bears little resemblance to the brunette writer who dreamed her up—except in one regard: her proud penchant for truth-telling. This was a virtue (if virtue it be) the bluntspoken Margaret Millar had in spades, said Donald Pearce, a teacher and writer who knew both the Millars for thirty years, in Canada, Michigan, and California.

"Margaret has this wonderful quality about her," he said in 1990, when he and she were still alive. "It's something that Alexander Pope said about himself: 'I can't be silent, and I will not lie.' And that was the way it was with her."

And that's the way it is with this story's Kitty, who boasts:

"I'm no liar. Even if the truth is devastating, and it often is, I tell it."

Note

" 'Margaret has this wonderful quality about her' ": Donald Pearce interview with TN.

MIND OVER MURDER

I

The island rose out of Lake Huron like a huge bloated ghost.

"There she is!" cried the fat man in the bow of the motor launch to the tall young man beside him. "Magnificent, eh?"

Dr. Prye looked bored as he always did when he was seasick. "You are not seasick," he told himself silently. "The concept is impossible because this is not a sea but a lake, a cute, harmless lake, and you've only been on it for half an hour."

He still felt very bad. He said: "Choppy today, isn't it?"

"Not nearly as choppy as usual," Dr. Haller said vigorously. "You know, Prye, this scheme of ours might revolutionize the whole science of psychiatry."

"Yours, not ours."

Haller paid no attention. "I've thought of everything. I've chosen my subjects carefully and they are all enthusiastic. They want to be cured. That's half the battle with neurotics. It was most fortunate that you were available, Prye."

"Fortunate," Prye asked faintly, "for whom?"

"For my subjects, for me, for the world. With you to assist me, I shall turn the minds of these poor creatures inside out, expose them to the sun and the air and the elements, let them struggle with the fundamentals of life."

"Struggle. Yes. How?"

Haller's cherubic pink face glowed. "Let them prepare their own meals, do their own work, grow their own vegetables."

Prye shaded his eyes against the late-afternoon sun and squinted in the general direction of the island. "Looks like rock to me."

"Oh, yes, it is. Solid rock. The growing of vegetables was purely a figure of speech. Actually, the food is in cans, two hundred dollars' worth of cans for a start."

"I have never seen two hundred dollars' worth of cans," Prye said. "It will be an interesting sight."

"Excuse me. I must superintend the landing." Haller disappeared into the small cabin.

From the rear, a female voice said loudly and with no trace of sympathy: "Seasick? Too bad."

He turned to behold a blond young woman in a pale-blue slack suit. She was extremely pretty, but seemed to be either unaware of the fact or so well aware that she didn't think of it. A cigarette drooped from her red lips.

"Are you one of us? Or one of him"—she cocked her head in the direction of the cabin. "In brief, are you crazy or are you a genius?"

"I alternate," Prye told her.

"That's fine," she said warmly. "So do I. Let's be friends. My name is Kitty Tyler. I am twenty-five and I have a deep-seated neurosis which defies psychiatrists to unseat it. Are you a psychiatrist?"

Prye said, "Yes."

"All right. It defies you, too. The trouble is, I'm swarming with hormones. Oh, there you are, Johnny. And smoking, too! Didn't Dr. Haller tell you that nicotine is a noxious toxin?"

The fair young man with the halfback physique smiled and said: "Sure, but I'm crazy about noxious toxins."

"Just think," Kitty mused. "Another five minutes and we'll be saying good-by to all these degrading pleasures, cigarettes, meat, alcohol." She turned to Prye again and remarked in a sibilant whisper: "Johnny's going to go mad without alcohol. He's just getting over his second attack of D.T.'s."

"Third," Johnny said mildly. "My name is John Prince." He held out his hand to Prye.

"Glad to know you, Prince," Prye said. "I'm Dr. Paul Prye, Dr. Haller's assistant."

"Haller's batty," Johnny said. "He's got a fixation. He thinks I'm batty. Ah, here comes my faithful keeper. Hello, Hemingway. Looking for me?"

"You know damned well I was looking for you," Hemingway said. He was a middle-aged man with a pleasant face and long, powerful arms. He put one of them around Johnny's shoulder in a friendly fashion. "Come on, Johnny. I want to search you."

"Search me? What for? You're no gentleman, Hemingway. You

have never worked your way through Princeton. Princeton," he added confidentially to Prye, "was named after me. Go ahead, Hemingway. Strip me and I'll throw you into the lake."

"Come on, Johnny," Hemingway said with a smile, and Johnny followed him down to the cabin from which Dr. Haller was just emerging.

Kitty Tyler bent down hastily and drew a long rectangular package from one leg of her slack suit.

"You take this," she told Prye. "Keep it for me." She thrust the package under his coat.

"But I—" Prye began.

"Stool pigeon," she hissed. She whirled around to greet Dr. Haller with a beautiful, candid smile. "Why, Dr. Haller! We were just talking about you. I was telling Dr. Prye what a perfectly marvelous idea your Colony for Mental Hygiene is."

Haller beamed on her. "Thank you, Miss Tyler. Did I see you give Dr. Prye a package a minute ago?"

"No, indeed," Miss Tyler replied. "I hardly know the man."

"Throw it overboard, Prye," Haller ordered. "We must assist Miss Tyler to overcome her fleshly weaknesses, in this case, cigarettes. Cast the carton upon the waters, Prye."

Miss Tyler let out an anguished cry as the carton hit the water.

Haller looked at her reproachfully. "May I remind you, Miss Tyler, that you are a voluntary member of this colony, that you are expected to obey the rules, and that this is the third carton of cigarettes you have secreted upon your person?"

"You have an evil eye," Miss Tyler said, and walked away with a great deal of dignity.

"They're children really," Haller said with a benign smile. "I have purposely kept the age grouping below forty, as you will see. They are all in perfect physical health, although Mr. Prince's constitution is not at present up to par. Mr. Prince, I may say, is not exactly a volunteer. His father recommended the treatment. But we don't have to worry about Prince. Hemingway will act as his special attendant and he's a good man."

The launch had glided into a small bay beneath the rocky shore of the island and stopped beside a flat rock which jutted out into the water, forming a natural landing stage. Several men and women had come on deck carrying crates and suitcases. A small, dark woman detached herself from the group and approached Dr. Haller.

"I didn't have time to search Tyler's luggage again," she said wearily.

"Quite all right," Haller said. "Miss Eustace, this is Dr. Prye. Miss Eustace is my nurse."

Miss Eustace offered a sad smile. "I saw the boat pick you up, doctor. I hope you will like the colony." Her voice expressed grave doubt.

Prye murmured politely that he was sure he would, he was fond of all children under forty. Miss Eustace picked up the crate she had been carrying and walked down the deck, shouting to the rest of the group.

Miss Tyler appeared, carrying nothing at all.

"Share and share alike, Miss Tyler," Haller called to her across the deck. "We must all do our bit. This is a co-operative colony."

Miss Tyler nodded pleasantly, waved her handkerchief at him, and disembarked.

"Miss Tyler is going to be a trouble," Haller said sadly. "I was not altogether anxious to bring her in the first place."

"What's the matter with her?" Prye asked.

"Well"—Haller took Prye's arm and led him toward the cabin—"we'd better collect our own luggage. As I was saying, Miss Tyler shows some symptoms of … ah … nymphomania."

Prye let out his breath with a long whistle. "That's dandy. How many men are there in the colony? I want to know my chances."

"Well, besides Prince and Hemingway and ourselves, there's Mr. Jenkins. He is here with his wife. They're the keenest of the lot. They live on raisins and peanuts and plan to sleep outdoors when it's warmer. Then there's Mr. Storm. Storm is thoroughly inhibited and seems to have a number of interesting phobias. Those are the men."

Five minutes later, Prye stumbled onto the island. It appeared to consist, as Haller had said, of huge rock formations which sloped up to form a rough flat plateau. At the summit stood two long low buildings made of logs, and bordered on two sides by screened verandas. A lone tree had fought its way out of the rocks in front of the south building, but the only other foliage visible was masses of dark-green leaves clinging to the rocks like ivy.

From the veranda of the south building came a loud cry of rage. Dr. Haller dropped his luggage and scrambled up the rocks like an adipose mountain goat. Prye followed as best he could.

On the veranda they found Hemingway.

"So!" he said ominously.

"Why, Hemingway," Haller said in a soothing voice. "Is anything wrong?"

Hemingway waved his hand toward the vast expanse of rock to the south. "Do you know what that green stuff is? It's poison ivy. I repeat, it's poison ivy!"

"Of course, it's poison ivy," Haller said. "If we accept the wonders of nature, we must be prepared to accept its mistakes also, Hemingway."

"I am allergic to poison ivy. Look!" He held out his arm and both doctors examined the small reddish blisters beginning to form.

"It couldn't possibly be poison ivy," Haller said heartily. "We just arrived and poison ivy symptoms don't appear until twelve to twenty-four hours after exposure. It must be something else."

Hemingway smiled bitterly. "Something else such as what? Measles? I want to get off this island here and now."

"Sorry," Prye said. "There goes the boat."

The launch was pulling away from shore. Hemingway let out a groan. "How far is the mainland?"

"Ten miles," Haller replied. "But you needn't worry, Hemingway. The boat will be back the day after tomorrow with fresh milk."

"I won't see the day after tomorrow. How about the other islands we passed?"

"They're uninhabited," Haller said. "Later on, when the season begins, perhaps some more people will arrive. That's why I chose the beginning of June to come up here. It will give us a chance to get started in strict privacy. Come inside, Hemingway, and we'll fix your arm with a good scrubbing of yellow soap, and tomorrow we'll eradicate the poison ivy."

They went inside, and Prye sank wearily into a deck chair.

A short stout woman came out of the door of the lodge carrying a pail in her right hand. Her left arm was extended at a right angle from her body and the tears were streaming down her cheeks.

"I must get water," she sobbed. "I must get some water in this pail and my arm is paralyzed again. Look at my poor arm. Oh, the horror of it!"

Prye got to his feet and said: "Come now, sit down and tell me about it, Miss—"

"M-M-Miss S-S-S-Studd."

"Sit down, Miss Studd."

Miss Studd sat down, still sobbing vigorously. "I'd put up my hand to wave good-by to the boat and I couldn't get it down again and Miss Tyler was very nasty about it. She said I was just pretending so I wouldn't have to bring up any water."

"Shall I help you lower your arm?"

Miss Studd stopped crying immediately. "If you think you can do it without breaking it off. I'd much rather have a paralyzed arm than no arm at all."

"And you're quite right," Prye said. "There now, down we go." The arm was lowered very gently.

Miss Studd briskly wiped the tears from her eyes and, without speaking, picked up her pail and walked down the veranda steps. Prye watched her thick dumpy figure bobbing up and down among the rocks.

In five minutes she was back again with the pail full. As she passed Prye, she said in a hurried whisper: "Oh, my dear, I hope you don't catch anything from me."

Prye said: "Wait a moment, Miss Studd," but she was already inside the building. He heard Miss Eustace's thin weary voice: "Thank you, Miss Studd. Your arm is better again. I see."

Miss Studd said: "Yes. It's the air."

II

Dinner was served at seven o'clock in the north building. Dr. Haller had reserved the north building for eating and recreation, the south for sleeping. They ate at a rough pine table covered with a gay tablecloth and illumined by four kerosene lamps.

Mrs. Jenkins had cooked the meal and Mr. Jenkins was serving it. He was clad in a pair of khaki shorts and a red turtle-neck sweater. Between courses, he stood beside a maplewood buffet and nibbled raisins and peanuts, humming to himself. At intervals, Mrs. Jenkins, a tall, thin vigorous woman of thirty-five, would insert her head into the dining room and ask jovially:

"How is it? Good?"

"Wonderful," Prye said. The meal wasn't bad, in fact, except that the drinking water seemed slightly murky.

Dr. Haller was explaining how he had conceived his idea for the colony. "I saw the advertisement in the *Herald*—island with double lodge for sale, cheap. So I hired a boat—same boat that brought us today—and came over to take a look at it."

At this point Mr. Jenkins withdrew his hand from the bowl of raisins and peanuts and applauded heartily.

The small, wizened man wedged between Miss Studd and Miss Tyler pushed aside his plate.

"I can't eat with all this noise going on," he said querulously. "My food curdles before it hits my stomach. I shall retire."

"Well, go ahead," said Miss Tyler in a matter-of-fact voice. "I can do without you, Mr. Storm."

"Now, children." Dr. Haller rose to his feet and beamed around the table. "Mr. Storm, you will learn to eat in a crowd if you're patient. Agoraphobia is most difficult to cure—"

"Difficult," Mr. Storm said with a snort. "It's impossible."

"—without the fullest co-operation."

"Maybe I could eat in an ordinary crowd, but not in this crowd. They're all crazy."

"Crazy!" Miss Studd cried. "Well, I like that!"

Dr. Haller thumped a pudgy fist on the table. "Crazy is a word which the colony deplores. It is a word you must all strike from your heads, your hearts, and your vocabularies."

Kitty Tyler said, "How about crazy as in 'I'm crazy about Johnny'?"

Johnny blushed and studied the plate in front of him intently. "Oh, Kitty," he mumbled. "I wish you wouldn't. I've got a wife and two kids back in Omaha."

"Liar," Kitty said. "That's one thing you can't say about me. I'm no liar. Even if the truth is devastating, and it often is, I tell it. Don't I, Miss Eustace?"

"You certainly do," Miss Eustace said absently.

Mr. Jenkins gamboled into the room with a bowl of canned peaches in one hand and a pile of fruit dishes in the other.

"Anybody want some of my raisins or nuts?" he asked affably. "Raisins for iron and nuts for—"

"Nuts," said Miss Tyler, and Mr. Jenkins roared with mirth, slapping his bare thighs.

Prye bent his head toward Miss Eustace. "Mr. Jenkins is in very high spirits this evening. Is he always?"

"He has been since I first met him yesterday," Miss Eustace replied.

"You mean that some of these people aren't Dr. Haller's patients!"

"Dr. Winthrop sent Mr. and Mrs. Jenkins and we got Mr. Prince from a private sanitarium for alcoholics. But, of course, we have their case histories. Actually, we know a great deal about them, but—" Her words trailed off in a sigh. "Frankly, doctor, I don't care for nature in such large slabs, and I feel that a co-operative colony would be difficult to manage under the best of conditions."

On the other side of Miss Eustace, Hemingway was contemplating his poison ivy in morose silence.

"May I touch it, Hemingway?" Johnny asked.

Hemingway frowned at him almost tenderly. "Now, Johnny, behave yourself and I'll let you wash the dishes."

"I'll help you, Johnny," Kitty Tyler said. "I love washing dishes."

Dr. Haller regarded her coldly. "Tomorrow night, Miss Tyler. Tonight you may help Miss Studd fetch the water from the lake."

"You damn ape," Kitty said under her breath. "Get your own water."

Her head disappeared under the table for a moment, and when it reappeared there was a lighted cigarette in her mouth. She inhaled dreamily.

"Give me one, Kitty," Johnny said.

"Ya, ya!" said Miss Tyler. "Bow down, minions. I've got a whole package."

"Absolutely no smoking," Dr. Haller said firmly. "Do you hear me, Miss Tyler?"

Miss Tyler heard him but she preferred to run for it. In an instant, she was out of the door and bounding over the rocks toward the water.

Mr. Jenkins swallowed a peanut, yelled, "Come on, Josephine!" and dashed out with Mrs. Jenkins after him. Miss Studd's arm became paralyzed as she reached out for more peaches. Hemingway's poison ivy began to itch. Johnny wanted a drink and Miss Tyler wanted Johnny. Mr. Storm shut himself in his room, and Dr. Prye and Miss Eustace washed the dishes and exchanged bitter reflections on the nature of nature.

Undressing for bed at nine thirty under the bored gaze of two cockroaches, Dr. Prye contemplated his position and found it wanting.

He sighed and turned down the wick of the kerosene lamp. For half an hour, he lay in bed listening to the roar of the water on the rocks. When he woke up, he could still hear the water roaring, but another noise sounded above it, the high, thin wail of a woman in anguish.

It was Miss Studd he found first. She was lying face down across a rock about a hundred yards south of the sleeping lodge. One of her hands clutched a clump of poison ivy. There was a gash in her forehead from which blood was flowing, and she was unconscious.

Prye raised his eyes from Miss Studd and saw Dr. Haller, also in his pajamas, bounce around the corner of the north building and cover the hundred yards to Miss Studd with flying feet.

"What's happened?" he shouted. "Miss Studd, are you hurt? Miss Studd!"

"She's fallen," Prye said. "Wait till I move her hand out of that damn ivy. You'd better tell Miss Eustace, and I'll carry Miss Studd back to her room!"

Haller turned to go back to the lodge. Ten yards from Prye he stopped short and his eyes widened in horror. Close to his foot lay another foot, naked and swollen and red.

Hemingway was no longer allergic to poison ivy. He had been lying face down in a bed of it for some time, and his expression had not changed at all.

Dr. Haller was emitting small squeaks like a clarinet in the hands of an amateur. "He's naked!" he gasped.

Prye, teetering under Miss Studd's considerable weight, stopped and demanded impatiently, "Who's naked?"

"Hemingway. He's dead and naked and he's been scalped. He's been scalped," Haller repeated in a daze.

Miss Studd changed hands.

"You take her," Prye said. "Keep the others inside the lodge until I can look around."

"I think I'm going to faint," Haller said weakly.

"All right. I'll carry both of you." With Miss Studd hanging over his right shoulder and Dr. Haller clinging to his left hand, Prye made the trip to the lodge in five minutes. Mr. Jenkins was just coming out of the door with two pails.

"Hi-ho," he said briskly. "What's happened here? The little lady faint?" He dropped the pails, put a hand to his mouth and roared, "Oh, Josephine! Oh, Josephine!"

Mrs. Jenkins, a ghastly vision in green shorts, pranced out, took a look at Miss Studd, and smiled indulgently.

"Tenderfoot," she said tolerantly. "Righto."

"Righto," Mr. Jenkins replied.

The word was apparently the Jenkins' signal for prompt action. In less than a minute, they were whisking Miss Studd into her bedroom.

"I'd better superintend," Haller said faintly.

"Do," said Prye.

In his room, Prye struggled into a pair of gray flannels, a long-sleeved sweater, and his heaviest socks and shoes. He drew on an old pair of pig-skin gloves, picked up a yard ruler in the kitchen, and went back to Hemingway.

It was shortly before seven o'clock and the sun was not yet strong enough to dry the dew on Hemingway's broad smooth back. From the top of his head a neat circle had been cut and it lay beside him sprouting black hair like a strange plant.

The scalping didn't kill him, Prye thought, and the poison ivy couldn't have killed him.

Prye slashed away at the ivy with his yardstick and then leaned over and dragged the body onto a section of bare rock. He noticed that the limbs were rigid as he turned Hemingway on his back. Beneath the left breast there was a short, straight incision, its outlines marked by dried blood.

Probing among the leaves of the poison ivy, Prye found a butcher knife encrusted with blood. The knife was familiar to him. He had washed it the night before, and Miss Eustace had cautioned him to be careful. She had taken it from him, dried it, and put it in a drawer of the kitchen cabinet. But somebody had taken it out and put it in Hemingway.

Nobody had any reason to kill Hemingway, Prye thought. Haller had said he was an experienced and skillful attendant. All the patients liked him and went to him for advice and sympathy. Old Mr. Prince was paying him an additional salary to look after Johnny and Johnny had liked him right off the bat.

Judging by the type of wound, there should have been a great deal of blood but the only stains Prye found were small. One was on the leaves on which Hemingway had been lying, and the other was where the knife had been thrown.

"He was killed with his clothes on," Prye said aloud. "The murderer soaked up the blood with Hemingway's clothes. Then where are the clothes? Probably in the lake. Why isn't Hemingway in the lake, too? Why undress a corpse, throw away the clothes and leave behind the more damning evidence, the corpse itself?"

He heard a shout from the direction of the lodge and turned to see Miss Eustace running toward him. She had evidently flung herself into her uniform, for she was still buttoning it as she ran, and her long black hair was streaming along behind her. From a distance she looked like a maenad hurrying to an orgy, but when she came up Prye saw that she was the same tired and slightly bored Miss Eustace.

"Dr. Haller told me," she said, puffing a little. "Is there anything I can do? Where is he? Where—Oh!"

She glanced at Hemingway briefly and turned back to face Dr. Prye.

"What did I tell you?" she said, sighing. "I knew this scheme of Dr. Haller's would lead to trouble. Poor Hemingway. I was very fond of him."

Prye studied her, puzzled. "You don't seem as upset as I am."

"No," Miss Eustace said. "Violence doesn't upset me any more. I've been a psychiatric nurse for ten years. I was in the next ward when my sister was beaten to death with a chair. I guess I felt like quitting then, but I didn't. I've been at this work for so long that I feel odd, out of place, when I go into the outer world where people are supposed to act like reasonable beings and don't."

Watching her, Prye said: "You have the case histories of all the people in the colony. Has any of them a tendency to be violent?"

"Of course not. Dr. Haller would have refused to bring them if that were so. They are all mildly neurotic with the exception of Miss Studd, whose condition seems more serious to me. She's a hypochondriac, according to Dr. Haller. According to me, she's a hypochondriac plus, but harmless and very easy to manage."

"How about Johnny?" Prye said.

"Well, of course, Johnny was violent when he had his attacks of delirium tremens but that's the usual thing. All delirious patients are potentially violent, but the violence is general and not directed against people but against any instrument of restraint. Johnny is a lovable boy. His is a case of too much money and too much idleness."

"And Miss Tyler?"

"Miss Tyler," Miss Eustace said thoughtfully, "is a puzzling case. She came to Dr. Haller's office about a month ago and said she believed she was on the point of going insane and that she wanted to be psychoanalyzed. Well, as you know, Dr. Haller does no psychoanalytic work at all, but he was interested in the girl and invited her to join the colony. She seems to have a great deal of money. She has never been institutionalized. In fact, Johnny is the only one who has."

Her eyes went back to Hemingway. "What shall we do about Hemingway? There is no place to bury him."

"We'll have to get in touch with the authorities," Prye said. "It's murder, you know."

"I know. But how are you going to get in touch with them? Dr. Haller gave orders to the boatman to come back tomorrow afternoon, and no sooner."

"Flag a ship," Prye suggested.

"What ship? There are no ships in this part of Lake Huron in early June. If the boatman doesn't come, I'm afraid we may have to bury poor Hemingway at sea."

"What sea?" Prye said coldly.

Miss Eustace's glance was full of reproach. "We must all try to keep our heads and our tempers, Dr. Prye."

She turned to go back, stepping delicately around the poison ivy. Prye was bending over Hemingway again when he heard her shout:

"Stay back, Miss Tyler! Go and get your breakfast."

Miss Tyler shouted back: "There is no breakfast and I never eat it, anyway."

Miss Eustace put a firm hand on Miss Tyler's arm, but Miss Tyler was equally firm in removing it.

"I'm exploring," she said brightly.

"You can explore after breakfast."

"But I just said there is no—Why, there's Dr. Prye. Yoo, hoo, Dr. Prye!"

"Yoo, hoo," Prye said. "Beat it."

But Miss Tyler had already arrived. She saw Hemingway, gave a husky cackle, and sat down abruptly on a rock. With her eyes tightly closed she said: "It has happened. I am now crazy. I have just had a visual hallucination of a most repellent nature. Pad my cell." Her voice broke. "Oh, it's terrible to be crazy. Miss Eustace! Are you there, Miss Eustace? I'm scared to open my eyes."

"If you're crazy," Miss Eustace said practically, "so am I. Now get up and come back to the lodge. You are not having hallucinations, Miss Tyler. Somebody has murdered Hemingway. Take my arm and in Heaven's name open your eyes. I don't intend to carry you."

Miss Eustace's unexpected severity shocked Miss Tyler into mobility. She got up and walked away without any assistance.

"Miss Eustace," Prye said. "Tell Dr. Haller to come and help me get Hemingway back to the lodge. We can't leave him out here; Miss Tyler makes that clear. Get everyone else in the north building for breakfast and we'll put Hemingway in his own room."

It was half an hour before Hemingway's body was placed on his bed and covered with a sheet. Prye locked the door, and with the key in his pocket, walked over to the north lodge with Dr. Haller.

Dr. Haller didn't want any breakfast, but he took his place at the head of the table.

"What's going on here this morning?" Mr. Storm asked. "Who was doing that yelling?"

Miss Tyler opened her mouth to reply, but Dr. Prye put his hand over it. By that time all attention was fixed on Dr. Haller who had risen to his feet.

"Guests," he said, "Mr. Hemingway has met with an accident."

Mr. Storm said: "Ha. About time. That's one less to bother me."

Johnny's face was wrinkled with concentration. "What do you mean, accident? I didn't really throw him in the lake. I was just kidding. I like Hemingway."

"Shut up, Johnny!" Miss Tyler cried.

"Mr. Hemingway," Haller said gently, "is dead."

Johnny sat motionless, staring into space. Miss Tyler ran over to him and flung her arms around his shoulders.

"Oh, Johnny, don't feel badly. If you feel badly I'll c-cry and I haven't got a h-h-handkerchief. I'll l-look after you, Johnny. That's one thing you c-can say ab-b-bout—" Miss Tyler gave it up.

Mr. Storm was pressing his hands tightly over his ears. He took one down, reached in his pocket tossed a handkerchief at Miss Tyler, and hurried out of the room.

Miss Tyler's sobs were immediately translated into giggles. "Why, it's a d-d-dirty handkerchief. It's got b-b-b-blood on it!"

Prye was out of the door in five seconds. Mr. Storm was not in his room in the south lodge. Prye went around to the small icehouse at the back of the lodge.

"Hey, Mr. Storm! What are you doing in there?"

Mr. Storm's quavering voice came through the door: "Just sitting."

"Where did you get that handkerchief you gave to Miss Tyler?"

"From my pocket."

"Is it your handkerchief?"

Mr. Storm unlocked the door and stuck his head out. He tried to be dignified, but his small wizened face looked more than ever like a monkey's.

"I am not in the habit of using other people's handkerchiefs. I think I shall retire to my room."

"I'll retire with you," Prye said pleasantly. "I'd like to have a private talk."

Mr. Storm replied that he had done and heard quite enough talking that morning, that the whole human race sickened him, that he wanted to be alone and the only place he could be alone was the icehouse because his room didn't have a key.

Prye guided him firmly into the back door of the south lodge and down the hall. From the room beside Hemingway's, Mrs. Jenkins' voice could be heard assuring Miss Studd that her cut was a "teeny-weeny scratch," and Miss Studd's voice replying with sad simplicity: "I am dying."

"Go on to your room, Mr. Storm," Prye said. "I'll be with you shortly."

He rapped softly on Miss Studd's door and Mrs. Jenkins caroled: "Come in, come in, whoever you are!"

Miss Studd was sitting up in bed. Her head had been lavishly bandaged and one eye was completely hidden. The other eye surveyed Prye with infinite sorrow.

"I want to make peace," she said. "I ask forgiveness of my enemies and I bestow blessings on my friends however undeserving. My time has come."

"Isn't she a card?" Mrs. Jenkins said with delight. "If you ask me, the only trouble with her is that she's overweight and the strain of carrying around fifty pounds too many has affected her mind. Fat people are never good-natured. If you ask me—"

"I'll certainly ask you, Mrs. Jenkins," Prye said, "but later. I want to talk to Miss Studd alone."

Miss Studd was outraged. "Fifty pounds too many! Oh!" She sank back among her pillows, letting out asthmatic little snorts. Mrs. Jenkins moved gracefully to the door, humming contentedly under her breath.

Miss Studd folded her arms on her chest and waited for the end.

Pyre said: "Hemingway was murdered, you know. You fainted this morning because you found him, is that it?"

Miss Studd nodded.

"Why were you up so early this morning, Miss Studd?"

Miss Studd replied: "I knew it was to be my last day on earth and I wanted it to be as long as possible."

"You have insomnia?"

"I never sleep a wink. I never close my eyes."

"Your room is next to Hemingway's. Did you hear Hemingway go out last night after we had all retired?"

"I heard him talking."

Prye kept his voice casual. "Talking to himself or to someone else?"

"He was talking to someone else."

"Who was it?"

"I don't know," Miss Studd said angrily. "The other person was whispering. I couldn't understand a thing he said."

"It was a man?"

Miss Studd's one eye looked thoughtful. "Now that I come to think of it, it couldn't have been a man. Hemingway called her Myrtle."

"What did he say to Myrtle?"

"Oh, he talked for a long time. I only understood a little of it."

"Tell me what you understood."

"Well, Hemingway said right at the first: 'I found it and half of it's mine.' Then Myrtle whispered a lot and then Hemingway said: 'We can get away together, Myrtle. You can't keep it up long.'"

Prye had taken out a small notebook and was writing down Miss Studd's words. "Did Hemingway seem angry?" he asked.

"Oh, yes!" Miss Studd cried. "That was what made me listen in the first place. Mr. Hemingway was such a good-natured man usually. He swore at Myrtle and I think … I think once he called her a … a girl dog, you know."

"I know," Prye said. "You're sure of that?"

Miss Studd certainly was sure of it.

"What did Hemingway appear to be talking about, Miss Studd?"

"Dope," she said tersely.

"You actually heard the word 'dope'?"

"I certainly did. Mr. Hemingway said: 'I've got the dope on you, Myrtle.'"

Prye's smile was pained. "Dope in that sense might mean information. It's like saying, 'I know all about you, Myrtle.' Did he mean that, do you think?"

"Both," Miss Studd replied in a triumphant voice. "He meant that he had information, that is the dope, that Myrtle was a dope fiend. That covers everything. I have quite an analytical mind."

"You have indeed," Prye said. "Can you remember anything else that Hemingway said?"

Miss Studd thought hard, but her analytical mind had deserted her. All she could remember was a door opening and closing and the sound of feet going down the hall.

"How many feet?" Prye asked.

Miss Studd was very acid. "Two feet. No one would hop on one foot in the middle of the night."

"How about four feet?"

"Two feet," Miss Studd persisted. "Two feet went down the hall and outside."

"You actually heard the feet go outside and not into another room?"

"They went outside. I heard the front door creak twice, opening and closing."

"After the front door opened, did you hear Hemingway in his room?"

"I did. Then I went to sleep."

It was useless to remind Miss Studd that she hadn't slept at all. Prye said he would look in on her later, told her to hang onto life as long as possible, and went out.

The hall ran the full length of the building and the bedrooms opened on it in pairs. On the south side were Dr. Haller at the front, then Mr. Storm, an empty room, Johnny Prince and Miss Eustace. Across from Haller was Hemingway, then Miss Studd, Miss Tyler, Mr. and Mrs. Jenkins, and Dr. Prye.

Prye made a small diagram in his notebook, then he rapped on Mr. Storm's door and waited. Mr. Storm could be heard removing his barricade of furniture. When he opened the door, he was puffing violently.

"The icehouse is simpler, isn't it?" Prye said. "May I come in?"

Mr. Storm observed tartly that he had every intention of coming in anyway, so he might as well come in, providing he didn't accuse an innocent man of stealing other people's handkerchiefs.

Prye sat down in a wicker rocking chair. "All right, Mr. Storm, it's your handkerchief. Perhaps you'll be able to tell me how the blood got on it."

"What blood? Whose blood?"

"Hemingway's blood, probably. Hemingway was stabbed to death sometime last night."

Mr. Storm licked his dry lips and began swallowing very fast.

Prye said: "I thought you knew he was dead, Mr. Storm. But you didn't know he was murdered?"

Mr. Storm muttered something about responsibility. His face was the color of ashes.

"What do you mean?" Prye asked.

"My fault. All my fault. If I'd gone with him when he asked me—my fault he was killed. The blood on my handkerchief is a sign from Heaven."

"It's nothing of the sort," Prye said briskly. "Mr. Hemingway asked you to go outside with him last night. When was this?"

Storm had pulled himself together somewhat, but his voice was still shaking. "The others had gone to bed. I was in my room undressing when Hemingway rapped on the door. He said he wasn't sleepy, that he wanted to take a walk. He had something to tell me, he said. I told him—"

"I can imagine what you told him," Prye said dryly. "It wasn't pleasant."

Storm was rapidly becoming normal again. "Why should it be pleasant? Is anyone ever pleasant to me? It was after eleven o'clock. I was tired. Why should I take a walk when I'm tired?"

"You're perfectly right. Did Hemingway hint at what he wanted to tell you?"

"No, he didn't. He just said he'd changed his mind anyway, that he could handle the situation himself. Then he went out."

"Out of the lodge?"

"Out of my room. I don't know whether he went out of the lodge or not. The man was nothing to me. Why should I listen to where he went?"

Prye got to his feet and went to the door. "As far as you know, then the handkerchief you gave to Miss Tyler this morning was the same one you had in your pocket last night, but at that time it was perfectly clean?"

"Yes."

"All right. That's all for now."

Prye walked thoughtfully back to the south lodge and entered the dining room. Miss Eustace and Dr. Haller were still sitting at the table, looking completely unhappy.

"Where are the others?" Prye asked.

"Miss Tyler and Mr. Prince are washing the dishes," Miss Eustace replied, sighing. "Mr. Jenkins and his wife are swimming, I think. Sit down, doctor. Dr. Haller and I are trying to settle something."

Prye sat down, reached in his pocket for a cigarette, found none and scowled in Haller's direction.

"Have you any noxious toxins?" he asked coldly.

Haller said: "No. I wish I had."

"So do I," Miss Eustace said.

They regarded each other glumly. Prye broke the silence with: "Do you suppose Miss Tyler would have any?"

"We can't ask Miss Tyler," Haller said in a spirited voice. "Think of the loss of face!"

"I don't mind losing a little face in a good cause," Prye said and walked into the kitchen.

Miss Tyler was very sweet about it. "I'm sure I'd love to give you some cigarettes, Dr. Prye, but the fact is, I don't think they're good for one. One should not surrender to one's fleshly temptations."

"Female Scrooge," Prye said.

"That's not it at all," Miss Tyler said virtuously. "I am simply helping you preserve your own ideal—mind over matter. It's quite different with Johnny and me. Our ideal is matter over mind."

"Oh, Kitty, give him one," Johnny said.

Miss Tyler removed her hands from the dish water and dried them with exasperating slowness.

"Close your eyes," she said. Prye closed his eyes. "All right, open your eyes."

Miss Tyler held out a package of cigarettes and Prye took three and carried them back to the dining room.

Miss Eustace inhaled deeply and remarked that there was a great deal to be said for Miss Tyler.

"Something, anyway," Haller conceded. "Prye, what are we going to do about Hemingway?"

"He's all right where he is at present," Prye said. "It's too late to help Hemingway. The thing is to protect ourselves."

A shocked silence greeted this speech. Prye went on: "When a man is stabbed, stripped, scalped and placed in a bed of poison ivy, two interpretations are possible—either the murderer is mentally ill or he is a sane man pretending to be mentally ill. In this situation both are plausible. In the case histories of the patients we have with us, there are no evidences of violence. But you realize that this is not conclusive, Dr. Haller?"

Haller shifted in his chair and said defensively: "It's not conclusive, no. It would be fairly so if the case histories had been compiled at an institution and covered a long period of time. My case histories were prepared from my own observations of the people, from those of their close relatives and in some instances by other doctors."

"Given a certain set of circumstances," Prye said, "any man is capable of murder, whether he is sane or insane, a millionaire or a flagpole sitter. Miss Eustace, what are your given names?"

"Dorothy Adelaide," Miss Eustace replied.

"And Miss Studd's?"

"Rita Agnes."

"Miss Tyler's?"

"Catherine Elizabeth."

Miss Eustace reeled off the names of the others: Henry H. Jenkins and his wife, Josephine; Albert Storm; John Ross Prince, 3rd; Dr. Paul Prye, and Dr. Homer Virgil Haller.

Dr. Homer Virgil Haller blushed and said crossly: "Why do you want to know our first names?"

Prye took out his notebook and read Miss Studd's statement aloud.

"There's no Myrtle here at all," Miss Eustace said, frowning. "You cannot always believe what Miss Studd tells you."

Haller bristled at this. "Miss Studd's lies are always connected intimately with her own condition. She exaggerates her symptoms in the same way that others of her type do. But she is not an indiscriminate liar. I believe her statement. It may contain some inaccuracies, but I believe that in the main it is true."

"Unless she happens to be guilty herself," Prye said quietly.

"She was fond of Hemingway," Miss Eustace protested. "We all were."

"Still, he's dead, isn't he?" Prye's eyes met Miss Eustace's over the table. "Nurses are very light sleepers as a rule. Are you?"

She was extremely pale. "I heard nothing last night, if that's what you mean. I went to bed at nine thirty. I slept soundly. I guess … I suppose it's the air. I was—" She got up quickly. "I think I hear Miss Studd calling. Excuse me."

Prye noticed that her step was unsteady as she went to the door.

"Miss Eustace has very sharp ears," Haller said complacently. "Sharper than mine anyway."

"She's an efficient nurse, the best I've ever worked with. She has a real concern for her patients no matter how exacting and unpleasant they are. Miss Eustace is a gem."

Gems, Prye thought cynically, are subject to the same temptations as other people. He was certain that Miss Eustace had heard something in the night, or that she preferred to conceal the reason why she did not hear something. A light sleeper would have heard the front door creak as Miss Studd did, and psychiatric nurses slept lightly for the sake of their own survival.

Why hadn't Miss Eustace admitted the truth? Had she been out of the lodge herself at the time?

Dr. Haller was talking again. "Did Mr. Storm admit that the bloodstained handkerchief was his? Where is it, by the way?"

"Where is it?" Prye repeated. "You picked it off the floor, didn't you?"

"No. I … I was trying to soothe Miss Tyler. I completely forgot to. It must be here some place."

It wasn't, however. After fifteen minutes of searching, Haller sat down again and wiped his forehead.

"It's p-preposterous!" he spluttered. "Somebody around here is crazy."

Prye smiled thinly. "Strike the word from your vocabulary, Haller."

"It was right there on the floor where Storm threw it! I saw the bloodstain on it myself before Miss Tyler shouted."

"Who was in the room?"

"There was Miss Eustace, myself, Miss Tyler and Johnny. Mr. Jenkins came in after you left. He managed Johnny while I managed Miss Tyler. An amazing man, Jenkins. He cheered Johnny up in five minutes."

"Amazing is putting it mildly. What's the matter with Jenkins and his wife?"

"So far as I can tell, nothing. Winthrop sent them to me when he heard of my idea for the colony. Their case histories are startlingly similar. They went to Winthrop in the first place complaining of a general maladjustment to the world. The only suspicious fact in their histories is a superabundant vitality and energy which led me to look for manic depression. I found no signs of it at all."

"Maybe," Prye said, "the world is maladjusted to the Jenkinses. I've just been talking to Mr. Storm."

"Now there's an interesting case for you," Haller said with enthusiasm. "Storm is a retired teacher. He came to me about a month ago. He'd had to give up his job because he developed rather a severe case of agoraphobia, and could no longer tolerate the sight of his pupils. This, of course, developed into an unreasoning fear of all people in groups, not merely his pupils. Teachers do occasionally suffer from this. But Storm's case is unusual because he has also a terrible fear of wide open spaces, of eternity, of time and space."

"I have met with it," Prye said, "but I usually found it was an occupational neurosis. I had a retired jail warden a year ago with an extremely serious case of it. He refused to go out of doors at all."

The discussion was interrupted by the entrance of Miss Tyler. She was looking very virtuous.

"I have been slaving over a hot stove," she said. "That I do not mind. Honest labor never hurt anyone. But I do object to the onslaught of a mechanized unit of cockroaches and the lack of utensils with which to cut bread."

Prye yelled, "What?"

"Bread knife," Miss Tyler explained. "There is no bread knife. Do we tear the bread apart with our hands like noble savages or—"

Prye was already out in the kitchen, making a frantic search of the cabinet drawers.

"There was one last night," he kept saying. "A large knife with a wavy edge." He closed the last drawer and shouted to Haller: "Get everybody in the dining room right away, including Miss Studd. Everybody!"

Miss Tyler and Johnny made an enthusiastic dash for the back door.

"Come back here, you two," Prye said. "Get into the dining room and sit down."

"I've never been so insulted in my life," Miss Tyler declared.

"I'm bigger than you are," Johnny said gently, "and you insulted a lady."

Miss Tyler had Johnny by the arm. "Don't be silly, Johnny. I'm no lady. I'll bet you two toxins I can beat you at double Canfield. Come on."

Prye stared thoughtfully at Miss Tyler's shapely blue linen back as it disappeared through the door. Then he walked out of the lodge by the back way to find Mr. Storm. It was not difficult, as Mr. Storm was once more ensconced in the icehouse.

Mr. Storm did not want to come to the dining room; in fact, he would be damned if he would. However, he was a reasonable man when he was not contemplating eternity, and Prye was most persuasive. They walked back to the dining room, arm in arm.

"About this handkerchief of yours," Prye said. "I noticed when you got off the boat yesterday you were wearing one in your breast pocket. Did you change it this morning?"

"No, I didn't. I didn't have any reason to. It hadn't been used."

"You went to bed shortly after eleven last night. Did you barricade your door?"

Mr. Storm looked surprised. "No. Why should I?"

"You did this morning."

"Oh, that's different. I don't like to be annoyed by people. But last night nearly everyone was in bed, so I wasn't afraid of being annoyed."

"I thought perhaps you had something valuable in your room and were protecting it from thieves."

"Thieves!" Mr. Storm snorted. "I'm not afraid of the biggest thief who ever lived. It's these jabbering tongue-waggers I can't stand."

In the dining room, Miss Tyler and Johnny were playing double Canfield to the tune of enthusiastic cheers and promptings from Mr. and Mrs. Jenkins.

"Eight of clubs, Johnny, old boy!" Mr. Jenkins was shouting. "Beat her to it!"

Mr. Storm clapped his hands over his ears and made for a corner.

"Oh, Josephine!" Mr. Jenkins cried. "Mr. Storm looks lonesome."

"Righto," Josephine said affably, and went into action. She

approached Mr. Storm with all her large white teeth showing in what she considered a friendly smile. Ignoring his violent frown, she removed Mr. Storm's hands from his ears.

"Get more out of your life, Mr. Storm," she urged. "Play games! Sing! Be merry! Burn up your calories!"

Mr. Storm groaned.

"That's the way," Josephine cried. "Try again. That was a little flat. All together. One—two—three—go. 'For he's a jolly good fellow, for he's a jolly good fellow, for he's a jolly good fell-*ow*, which nobody can deny.'"

While Mrs. Jenkins was collecting her energies for a second chorus, Prye said in a loud distinct voice: "Myrtle!"

Everyone turned and regarded him with astonishment. Everyone, Prye thought gloomily, not just Myrtle. If there were a Myrtle.

Mrs. Jenkins flashed Prye a smile. "Sorry, I don't know any piece called 'Myrtle.' How about 'I'm Forever Blowing Bubbles'?"

"Forever," Mr. Storm said hollowly, "and ever and ever."

Josephine slapped him playfully on the bald spot at the top of his head and burst into song. When Dr. Haller appeared, Josephine was still singing.

Dr. Haller gave the others a painfully reassuring smile and walked over to Prye. In a voice almost drowned by Josephine's bubbles he said: "The knife has been found. Come outside a minute."

Miss Tyler's sharp blue eyes stabbed at Prye. "Anyone dead?" she inquired.

"Now, Miss Tyler," said Haller, "you go right on with your game. Nothing at all has happened."

"Then I guess there's nothing to keep me here," said Miss Tyler with an air of sweet reasonableness. She rose and yawned, and strolled to the door.

Prye strolled after her. "I think you'll stay here," he said pleasantly. "We'll be wanting lunch at one thirty and it's after twelve now. You and Johnny can strong-arm a few cans. I'd let Johnny do it by himself, but I'm afraid he'd cut his hand and die of septic poisoning."

"I couldn't get blood poisoning," said Johnny with a smile. "My blood is a ten percent solution of alcohol."

"We won't discuss alcohol," said Miss Tyler firmly. "Johnny hasn't had a drink for a month."

Johnny looked at her, puzzled. "How do you know? I haven't known you that long."

"Hemingway told me." Miss Tyler's cheeks were pink but her words came glibly enough. "I'm interested in alcoholics because my great-uncle Frederick was one."

"Very clear," said Prye.

Haller was beckoning Prye from the doorway. Once outside the building, the two men quickly walked over to the south house and down the hall to Miss Studd's room.

III

Miss Studd was lying almost buried among her pillows, her unbandaged eye glaring up at the ceiling in a fixed stare. She did not turn her head when they entered.

Outside the covers on Miss Studd's stomach was a long bread knife with a wavy edge. She was not touching it; she seemed to be unaware that it was there. It rose and fell with her breathing.

"Miss Studd," Prye said. She did not reply, but her eye blinked.

"Is your head bothering you?" he asked.

Miss Studd shook the head in question.

"Have you been out of bed, Miss Studd?"

She shook her head again. Prye turned to Dr. Haller, who was sitting by the window wiping his forehead. "Did you find the door of this room unlocked?"

"Yes."

Prye said, "Miss Studd, I heard you lock this door after I left you this morning. Have you had any other visitors?"

Her hands began to pluck at the covers. "Myrtle," she said. "Myrtle was talking to me."

Prye's voice was without expression. "Myrtle was here talking to you? You saw her?"

"You mustn't hurt Myrtle," Miss Studd said. "You mustn't try to catch her. She lives on the rocks like the ivy."

Haller was clutching the arms of his chair, his knuckles white.

He said in a strangled voice, "Miss Studd, you mustn't be frightened. You must tell us exactly what Myrtle said."

"I am not frightened," Miss Studd said. "I have no reason to be frightened. I am Myrtle."

Prye repressed a shudder and said evenly, "You killed Hemingway?"

"Myrtle killed Hemingway. He was going to kill the ivy where she lives. She has been here for a million years, waiting for me to come."

"It's no use," Haller said, but Prye waved him to silence.

"Miss Studd, did Myrtle tell you these things?"

"Yes." Miss Studd turned her head and her pale eye regarded Prye steadily. "You are next."

"Myrtle wants to kill me, too?"

"You are next," Miss Studd repeated. "Myrtle is going to kill you. No one will find her, for she is the color of the rocks where she lives."

Prye looked out of the window and saw the rocks like huge cysts on the shoulders of the island. A cancerous island, he thought. A lonesome ghost of an island.

"I'll get Miss Eustace," Prye said.

As he went out, he looked back at Miss Studd. "She's flabby and pale and fat," he thought, "like a white slug under a rock. A fat, white worm living under a rock. Maybe Hemingway was stripped so he'd look like a white slug—"

He tapped lightly on Miss Eustace's door and waited. As there was no response, he opened the door and stepped inside. Miss Eustace was lying on the bed asleep. Her closed eyelids were red and transparent and the tip of her small straight nose was red. She had evidently cried herself to sleep.

Miss Eustace was a gem whom violence didn't upset, but she had cried into her pillow until she was exhausted and fell asleep. Prye touched her arm and she was awake in an instant.

"Oh," she said, "I'm sorry. I was so tired. I'm terribly sorry."

She scrambled to her feet, straightening her uniform and patting her hair into place. When she saw the knife in Prye's hand, her eyes widened, but she said calmly, "What are you doing with that?"

"Holding it," Prye replied. "I found it on Miss Studd's bed."

Miss Eustace wrinkled her brow. "But that's silly. What would Miss Studd want with a bread knife?"

"She'll tell you," Prye said grimly. "We'll have to take shifts watching her. You may go there now and I'll relieve you after lunch."

"You mean she has confessed to the murder?"

"I mean that whatever Miss Studd confesses will never be used against her. She is disturbed."

To a psychiatric nurse that word meant a great deal. Her mouth tightened, and the muscles of her jaw moved up and down rhythmically as she clenched and unclenched her teeth. She said through her teeth: "I knew it. I knew this would happen."

She swept out of the room, her small sturdy body stiff and militant. Prye heard her enter Miss Studd's room and say in the jovial but firm voice peculiar to nurses, "Well, and how are we now, Miss Studd?"

A minute later Dr. Haller came from the room and joined Prye in the hall.

"I didn't dream this was possible," he muttered as they left the building. "There was nothing at all in her symptoms to suggest this terrible change in her."

"Nothing at all," echoed Prye.

By lunch the news of Miss Studd's condition was floating through the air with the greatest of ease. It had a depressing effect on the other colonists. Johnny sulked into his plate and Miss Tyler became even more acid than usual. Mrs. Jenkins was least affected; the only change in her was a decrease in the volume of her voice so subtle that it passed unnoticed by Mr. Storm. He set the tempo for the meal by calling Mrs. Jenkins an unfeeling, insensitive monster of a woman.

Prye studied his dish of spinach carefully, with the detached interest of a scholar, as if the dish contained stewed papyrus leaves that might throw light on ancient Egyptian civilization. He ate one forkful, decided that they were papyrus leaves, and asked Miss Tyler for a cigarette.

But Miss Tyler, it seemed, had no cigarettes. She had lost them to Johnny at double Canfield, and Johnny had smoked them one right after another. The others stared at Johnny in righteous disapproval.

"My nerves were bad," he said, flushing.

"Hog," Mr. Storm said distinctly. "Unprincipled hog."

Miss Tyler fixed Mr. Storm with a cold eye. "Johnny may be a hog, but he's not unprincipled. I'm beginning to dislike you savagely, Mr. Storm."

"I have disliked you from the first, Miss Tyler," Mr. Storm said politely.

"Such talk!" Mrs. Jenkins cried with an indulgent laugh. "After all, we're all brothers in the colony. Love thy neighbor, you know."

"I know," said Miss Tyler, "but I reserve the right to choose my neighbors, and I don't choose him."

"Well, I didn't choose you," Mr. Storm replied.

"I," said Prye, "didn't choose either of you, but here I am and here I stay, at least until the boat comes tomorrow. Meanwhile, we have a murder to investigate."

Johnny raised his head and looked at Prye. "I thought Miss Studd had confessed. I mean, why investigate when she's confessed?"

"I'll illustrate," Prye said, "just so my point will be clear. There once was a silver spoon which disappeared from the main dining hall of a mental hospital I was connected with. Of the fifty people in the room, nine confessed to removing the spoon and each of the nine gave some compelling reason for the theft. You can't divide a silver spoon by nine."

"But nine of us haven't confessed," said Miss Tyler. "There are only nine of us."

"That's true," Prye said. "Eventually the silver spoon was found, but not on any of the nine who confessed. The man who had it had not confessed."

"I see," Miss Tyler said pensively. "You can't accept Miss Studd's confession until you get some more evidence to support it."

"And so," Prye continued, "I am going to question you all separately after lunch. While I am doing this, I want you to go down to the lake in pairs and watch for a passing ship. Mr. Jenkins, you're an expert at building fires, I suppose?"

"None better," Mrs. Jenkins said loyally, while Mr. Jenkins hung his head modestly in his dish of raisins.

"In that case, we should have a fire built ready to light on the high rock behind the lodge."

The Jenkinses moved in concert to the door.

"Wood in kitchen," Mrs. Jenkins sang.

"More wood piled behind the lodge," sang Mr. Jenkins.

"Righto!"

The Jenkinses disappeared, and Mr. Storm said nastily, "Thank God! What a dreadful pair!"

"*You* should talk," Miss Tyler said significantly.

Dr. Haller leaned toward Prye. "If you want to take them in alphabetical order, I'll relieve Miss Eustace now."

"Good," said Prye.

"Not, of course, that we could suspect Miss Eustace in any way. Miss Eustace is a gem."

"I have heard so," Prye said, as Haller went out.

In about five minutes, Miss Eustace appeared in the doorway, looking cool and unperturbed.

"You wished to talk to me, doctor?" she said to Prye.

"In the sitting room. While I'm gone, Miss Tyler, you might wash the dishes."

"I'm always washing dishes," Miss Tyler said coldly. "Have the rest of you got hydrophobia?"

"It's better than doing nothing," Johnny said.

Miss Tyler disappeared into the kitchen with a contemptuous snort. Noises of intense activity ensued, the clank of silver, the shattering of a plate, and a vigorous "Damn!"

Miss Eustace smiled as she led the way into the sitting room. She sat down rather stiffly on a settee of knotty pine upholstered in blue leather.

She said, "Is my interview with you purely a formality or am I actually under suspicion?"

"Miss Studd has confessed," Prye said.

Miss Eustace sighed. "Please don't try to deceive me. I've heard too many patients confess to too many things to believe Miss Studd's confession, at least until something substantiates it."

"All right then. I will tell you that you are under the same suspicion as the rest of us." Prye took out his notebook and pen. "Tell me a little about yourself, Miss Eustace."

Her eyebrows arched in surprise. "The story of my life? What bearing could that have on the murder of Hemingway?"

"Probably none at all, but I'll hear it anyway."

"Very well," Miss Eustace said in a resigned voice. "I am thirty-one years old, the oldest of a family of four. I went into training at seventeen, and three years later I took a postgraduate course in psychiatric nursing at Holloway Hospital. Dr. Haller was chief resident psychologist there. When he left three years ago to go into private practice and treat the lighter types of neurosis, I left with him."

"And Hemingway?" Prye prompted.

"Hemingway came to Dr. Haller from a private sanitarium for alcoholics about two years ago."

"You scarcely need an attendant for mild neurotics," Prye said.

"Dr. Haller preferred to have one handy. Besides, Hemingway helped him conduct tests and even acted as chauffeur occasionally. He was a kind man and a first-class attendant. I know nothing of his private life except that he was unmarried and planned to retire and buy a farm when he had saved enough money."

"Attendants don't usually earn enough money to buy farms."

"Hemingway was quite well paid, and saved his money. And, of course, when he took on an extra job like looking after Johnny, he was paid extra for that. Dr. Haller sometimes loaned him out for D. T. cases that didn't require hospitalization."

"He never mentioned any love affairs?"

"Never," Miss Eustace said firmly.

"Did he swear much?"

"Swear?" she repeated. "I never heard him swear."

"Still," Prye said, "when you work with a man for two years you pile up a lot of conversation, don't you?"

"You do, but the conversation isn't necessarily personal. We discussed the patients and things like that. Hemingway was very much interested in psychiatry, and he followed new developments closely. He even wanted to offer himself as a control subject in the frozen sleep experiments in cases of schizophrenia, but Dr. Haller couldn't spare him because we were coming up here." Her voice shook slightly. "But he got his sleep. And all for the sake of a few members of the idle rich class who haven't the courage to face their difficulties the way the rest of us have to."

"Neurosis isn't a class disease," Prye said.

"The hell it isn't," Miss Eustace said bitterly.

Prye changed the subject. "Do you go to sleep easily, Miss Eustace?"

"Yes, very easily." Her voice was flat and expressionless again.

"And wake up easily?"

"Yes."

"Did you wake up last night?"

"No. I went to bed at nine thirty and slept soundly all night. It's the air."

"The phrase has a familiar ring. I didn't believe it this morning and I don't now. Did you disobey Dr. Haller's orders and take a sleeping capsule last night?"

"Yes," Miss Eustace said eagerly, "that's it."

She seemed very uncomfortable. She uncrossed and recrossed her legs and tugged at the collar of her uniform.

"That isn't it at all, Miss Eustace, and you know it."

"All right," she said finally. "I'm lying. But you can boil me in oil and I won't change my story."

"It won't be necessary to boil anybody in oil. It seems obvious that you recognized the person you heard last night and that you're trying to protect him. Now whom would you try to protect? Miss Tyler? Hardly. Miss Tyler protects other people. Mr. Storm? No, indeed. Mr. and Mrs. Jenkins? Emphatically, no. Do you know where that's leading us, Miss Eustace? I see you do. But why protect Johnny if you think he's innocent?"

"Johnny wouldn't hurt a fly!" she cried. "Johnny was terribly fond of Hemingway. Johnny—I knew you'd all pick on him! Somebody's got to look after him now that Hemingway's gone."

"Miss Tyler's doing all right," Prye said.

Miss Eustace flushed. "Yes, and you know why."

"Why?"

"She'd walk a mile for a camel if it had pants on."

"You've seen a lot of nymphomaniacs," Prye said. "Does Miss Tyler seem the garden variety?"

"No," Miss Eustace said sulkily. "But if that isn't what's wrong with her then there's nothing wrong with her, and if there's nothing wrong with her, what is she doing here?"

Prye bent over his notebook for a moment. He felt Miss Eustace's eyes burning into the paper. So he wrote: "Nuts to you, Miss Eustace!" and looked up quickly. She turned her head away, blushing.

"So you heard Johnny last night?" Prye said softly. "Did he go out of the lodge?"

"Yes."

"How did you know it was Johnny?"

"I looked out into the hall to see. I heard him moving around in the room next to mine. Then I heard his door open and close again. When I looked out, he was just going out the back door of the lodge. I went back into my room and and watched him from the window. The moonlight was shining on his hair—" She closed her eyes, and saw the moonlight on Johnny's hair, Johnny's lovely bright hair.

"She's got it bad," Prye thought, "and probably for the first time." Aloud he said, "Where did he go?"

She opened her eyes slowly, reluctantly. "I couldn't see him for very long. But he was walking in the direction of the landing rock."

"Did you notice what time he went out?"

"It was about one o'clock. He was just gone for fifteen minutes. There wasn't time enough, you see," she said. "He couldn't have done that to Hemingway in fifteen minutes; he couldn't possibly."

"Did you stay at the window while he was out?"

"Yes."

"You heard nothing?"

"Nothing but the booming of the lake. I don't like this lake. It's not friendly. It's like the sea." She paused. "I saw lights."

"You saw what?"

"Lights. They looked like flashlights. They kept going on and off over there." She pointed through the window toward the northeast shore of the island.

"Near the spot where we landed yesterday?"

"Just about there. That's where Johnny went. And Hemingway was found on the other side of the island. That's how I'm so sure Johnny didn't do it. It must have been Johnny down there at the landing rock with two flashlights."

"There were *two* flashlights?"

"Yes."

"What would Johnny be doing with two flashlights?"

"He's just a boy," Miss Eustace said hastily. "It was his first night here, and he probably wanted to explore. You know what boys are."

"Johnny is twenty-five. A protracted boyhood, is it not, Miss Eustace?"

"Hemingway was murdered on the other side of the island," she repeated.

"We have no proof of that and we have no proof that Johnny went to the landing rock. And when I think of two flashlights I don't think of one man playing with two flashlights but of two men each with a flashlight."

Miss Eustace began to cry.

"Damn the moonlight on Johnny's hair!" Prye thought.

"You're picking on him!" she sobbed.

Miss Eustace did not cry prettily, and Prye turned and looked out of the window. He saw the Jenkinses putting the finishing touches on what appeared to be a funeral pyre. Then he saw them gambol over the rocks to the lake, hand in hand, yelling, "Ship ahoy!"

Prye shuddered and turned back to Miss Eustace, whose sobs had degenerated into sniffles.

"Forget Johnny," he said. "Tell me about Miss Studd."

Miss Eustace's professional instincts were aroused. "Miss Studd is having auditory hallucinations," she said, frowning. "Her symptoms suggest schizophrenia of some sort, but there are so many contradictory factors, aren't there, doctor? For one thing she's too old, thirty-eight. For another, the change in her was very sudden. Also, she is well aware of her environment, and remembers all our names and how she came to be here. Her case history is completely free of hallucinations of any kind. She had delusions, of course, but they were mild."

"Odd," Prye agreed.

Miss Eustace continued. "At first I thought her hallucinations were the result of the shock of finding Hemingway. But she was perfectly natural when I helped her bandage her forehead. Shock would have affected her immediately, wouldn't it?"

"I believe so. You were in your room when she heard Myrtle. Did you hear any voices?"

Miss Eustace smiled. "No, I didn't."

"But you were crying, of course."

She nodded.

"You cry vigorously, Miss Eustace. I don't suppose you heard Miss Studd go out of the lodge and get the knife?"

"Did she do that?"

"She had it, and it was stolen from the kitchen. Besides, her door was unlocked. When I left her earlier, she locked the door behind me. But when Dr. Haller went to see her the door was open and the knife was lying on her bed."

It was Miss Eustace's turn to stare out of the window. But in a moment her jaw dropped and her eyes widened.

"What on earth is Mr. Jenkins doing?" she asked.

Prye looked out. For one thing, Mr. Jenkins was removing most of his clothes. He was also shouting in the direction of the lodge. Josephine was jumping up and down, waving her arms.

"What the hell?" Prye said, and strode out, with Miss Eustace at his heels.

"It must be a ship," Miss Eustace said, as they walked rapidly toward the lake. "It would be just like Mr. Jenkins to try to swim out to it."

"Look closely," Prye said. His voice was tired, and Miss Eustace glanced at him sharply. Then she turned her eyes to the lake. Something was bobbing up and down in the water. Occasionally, a wave swept over it and hid it from view, but it always came up again.

By this time Mr. Jenkins had stripped down to his shorts and was poised on a rock ready to dive. He hit the water with a great splash and his arms began to move up and down rhythmically.

Mrs. Jenkins on the shore was going through the motions of an enthusiastic baseball fan during a home run. When she saw Prye and Miss Eustace she dashed toward them, shouting: "A man! A man!"

"Eureka," Prye said. He didn't want to see a man; he especially didn't want to see a dead man.

Mr. Jenkins had reached the thing bobbing up and down in the water. He had put one hand underneath the thing's chin and was swimming backward, propelled by his other hand and his feet.

"And now there are two," Prye thought. "Wouldn't it be funny if Mr. Jenkins died, then I'd go out and put my hand under *his* chin and then there'd be three. And then Mrs. Jenkins could grab my chin—"

He stood silently on the shore, nodding at whatever Josephine was saying, at whatever the wind blew out of her mouth and carried across the lake.

IV

The water was deep at the shore. Prye pulled the dead man out of the water by his arms and Mr. Jenkins scrambled out after him. He looked as if he felt he ought to get a medal.

Josephine said: "You ought to get a medal. You were wonderful."

Miss Eustace was staring at the swollen face of the dead man. "I have never seen him before," she said.

The man was still wearing his clothes, khaki trousers and shirt and rough work boots. He was quite young, with the hands and muscles of a workingman. His skin was deeply tanned.

Prye turned him over on his face. His khaki shirt was slit between the shoulder blades and revealed the wound in his back, gaping like a fish's mouth.

"Where did he come from?"—Prye thought. "There are no ships and no inhabited islands. He's been in the water for a long time, fifteen hours perhaps."

Prye said: "We'll have to take him up to the lodge, Jenkins."

"I can take him alone," Jenkins said.

Prye was a little tired of Mr. Jenkins. He said: "Don't swing in any trees on your way up."

Mr. Jenkins looked blank. Miss Eustace swallowed a giggle and a sob, and the procession started back to the lodge in single file. The water from the dead man's clothes and hair trickled steadily down Mr. Jenkins' back.

"Where to?" Jenkins asked.

"The sitting room," Prye said. "I want everyone to get a look at this man."

Miss Eustace stumbled. When she regained her balance, she

said: "Why? Why must they? He's a stranger. He probably just fell out of a boat and drowned. He wasn't murdered."

"Maybe not," Prye said. "Maybe he was swimming backward and stabbed himself on a swordfish. Please go on ahead and tell the others to remain in the dining room."

Miss Eustace hesitated, but she had obeyed doctors for too many years to rebel now. A couple of minutes later Prye heard her voice floating out the window in the dining room: "There has been a man found in the lake. Dr. Prye wants you to try and identify him."

He heard Miss Tyler's little shriek and Mr. Storm's groan.

Josephine arranged the settee where half an hour before Miss Eustace had been sitting, and Mr. Jenkins laid the young man on it.

Josephine glanced at him and said softly to herself: "There's no death."

Prye said with distaste: "Then this is the next thing to it. Sit down, Mrs. Jenkins."

"Oh, no, thank you. I prefer to stand."

"Well, do you mind if I sit down?" Prye asked.

"Not if you really want to. Although I think you coddle yourself too much. All this sitting when you could be standing and standing when you could be walking. Live, Dr. Prye. Live!"

"Look at it this way, Mrs. Jenkins—I'm sitting when I could be lying down. Mr. Jenkins, you may go out, closing the door behind you."

Mr. Jenkins said jovially: "Ha, ha. You won't get far with Josephine. Josephine can take care of herself."

"Ha, ha," said Josephine. "You bet I can."

"Ha, ha," said Prye. "Beat it, Mr. Jenkins."

Mr. Jenkins went out, and Mrs. Jenkins stood by the window taking deep breathing exercises.

"Do you know this man?" Prye asked.

"I do not. I have never seen him before. He is a complete and utter stranger to me, and to Mr. Jenkins as well."

"We'll let Mr. Jenkins speak for himself."

"That won't be necessary," Mrs. Jenkins said firmly. "We are one."

"When did you first meet Hemingway?"

"In Dr. Haller's office a couple of weeks ago. I didn't actually meet him; I merely saw him. I remember him because he had such a perfectly developed chest."

Josephine's own chest was hardly memorable, but she thumped it to emphasize her words.

"When did you actually meet him?"

"On the boat. He was already on the boat when it picked some of us up at Port Innis."

"What time did you retire last night?"

"Early to bed and early to rise," Josephine said archly. "We retired at nine. It is our custom to retire at nine and rise at six. Just like the chickens, you know."

"I don't know much about chickens," said Prye. "Do they sleep soundly? Or do they wake up at the slightest noise?"

"Sound as a bell," said Josephine. "Eat right and you'll sleep right."

"True," Prye said, sighing a little. It was useless to go on with Josephine, he felt. Whether she was innocent or guilty, her answers would be the same. Her actions were all of a piece; either she was extremely innocent, or doing a fine job of appearing so. In either case, questioning was futile.

"That's all," he said. "You may go."

Her face fell. "You mean that's all?"

"That's what I mean."

"Aren't you even going to ask me who murdered Hemingway?"

"No."

"Not even if I know?"

"You don't know," Prye told her.

"Miss Studd," Josephine said. "Miss Studd."

Prye opened the door for her, and she walked out rather huffily. Miss Tyler was at the door in an instant, demanding, "Is it true? Is someone really dead?"

She peered around Prye's arm into the sitting room and saw the lonely young man lying on the settee. She put her hand to her mouth.

"Come in," Prye said.

"No, tha-anks," Miss Tyler said shakily.

"I invite you to come in," he repeated.

She walked unsteadily toward the settee, glanced at the young man, and closed her eyes.

"I don't know him," she said.

"Look again. Make allowance for the fact that his face is bloated by the water."

"I did," Miss Tyler said weakly. "I always m-make allowances. I think I'll go out now."

"For the love of Heaven, Miss Tyler, open your eyes. Don't you realize that this man has been in the water for some fifteen hours, that he couldn't have come off a ship because there was no ship, that his death took place about the same time as Hemingway's, and that the other islands in this part of the lake are uninhabited?"

Miss Tyler opened her eyes with extreme care. "I still don't know him," she said.

She did not go back into the dining room. Instead, she went out the front door. She was breathing hard and her face was very pale. Prye went to the door and looked out after her. She was running down toward the lake and the wind was whipping her hair into a yellow froth.

Prye turned away thoughtfully. "Who killed you?" he said to the lonely young man.

"Suppose he answered me?"—Prye thought. "I think I'd die too. I am very sure he won't answer me. But if he did, or if I thought he did—

"That would make me like Miss Studd. Did Miss Studd only think she heard Myrtle? Or did Miss Studd hear Myrtle?"

The door opened, and Mr. Jenkins came in, looking almost serious.

"I've been thinking," he announced. "It's all very well for you to question us, but who questions you, Dr. Prye?"

"I have examined my own conscience and found it clear," Prye replied.

"Still, don't psychiatrists frequently develop mental disease? Isn't that a fact?"

"Life is full of facts, but they don't all have a bearing on this particular situation. If you want to question me, Mr. Jenkins, go ahead."

"I don't want to question you, Dr. Prye, but I feel it's only fair that you and Dr. Haller suspect each other if you're going to suspect us. Have you interviewed Dr. Haller?"

"No."

"Would you like me to get him?"

"I should like you to sit down."

It was an anticlimax, but Mr. Jenkins sat down.

"All right," Prye said. "You didn't know Hemingway, you'd never met the other colonists, you have no motive for murdering anyone, and you don't know anyone called Myrtle, and you heard nothing suspicious last night."

"That's right," said Mr. Jenkins in some surprise. "How did you know?"

"I have heard it before," Prye said. "You went swimming this morning, Mr. Jenkins. You returned to the dining room and found Miss Tyler in hysterics and Johnny in the doldrums, and you cheered Johnny up. You also picked up a handkerchief from the floor."

"Did I?" Mr. Jenkins said, frowning.

"Where is it?"

"Well, this is embarrassing," Mr. Jenkins said. "I don't even remember picking one up."

"I can easily search your room and your clothing."

Mr. Jenkins smiled. "I don't think you'd find anything and I wouldn't want you to waste your time; honestly, I wouldn't."

"Whose handkerchief was it?"

"I don't recall seeing it, so I couldn't say whose it was."

"It had bloodstains on it," Prye said. "I saw you pick it up and put it in your pocket."

"You couldn't have! You were out of the—" Mr. Jenkins' jaws jerked shut.

"Sucker," said Prye.

"You think you're smart," Mr. Jenkins said hotly.

"I don't have to be smart. Why pick up a handkerchief belonging to Mr. Storm?"

"Mr. Storm! That handkerchief was Josephine's. I saw the initial J in the corner and the blood on it, and I knew right away somebody was trying to implicate Josephine."

"You're pretty smart yourself."

Mr. Jenkins beamed. "Oh, I can add two and two."

"What did you do with the handkerchief?"

"Wrapped it around a stone and threw it into the lake."

"You're sure it was Josephine's, and not, for instance, Johnny's? J for Johnny. The handkerchief was a large one, as I remember it."

Mr. Jenkins' mouth fell open. "He's coming up for air," Prye thought. "I've given him a revolutionary idea."

"I never thought of that," Mr. Jenkins said at last.

"Call Johnny in here, will you?" Prye said.

Mr. Jenkins went to the door and called, and in a minute Johnny came in. He stopped on the threshold when he saw the body on the settee and said, "Gosh."

"Do you know him?" Prye said. "Come a little closer."

Johnny approached the settee, his face red except for a white line around his mouth. He had his hands in the pockets of his gray flannel slacks and Prye could see his fists clenched beneath the cloth.

"I don't know him," Johnny, said.

"The phrase," said Prye, "is becoming irksome."

Johnny paid no attention. "I should know him. I think I should know him. I think it is not putting too much strain upon the laws of probability to assert that I should know him. His face gives me a familiar twinge of familiarity, if you know what I mean. 'Oft in the stilly night.'"

"Come here, Prince."

Johnny took his hands out of his pockets and smiled. His gait was not quite steady when he walked in Prye's direction, and he seemed to have difficulty in focusing his eyes.

"Blow," Prye said.

Johnny blew.

"That's a mighty pungent breath you're sporting," Prye said.

"You're cute," Johnny said. "I knew I couldn't fool you."

"Where did you get it?"

"Get what?" Johnny said, injured. "I ask you, where did I get what?"

"Miss Tyler might know. I'll ask her."

Johnny's hands grasped Prye's coat. "No. Don't ask Kitty. Please don't tell Kitty. I couldn't bear it if you told Kitty. You've got to promise."

Prye removed the hands from his coat and said, "I'll promise nothing. Where did you get the Scotch?"

"Under the water," Johnny said in a sulky voice. "I found it. I dived into the lake and there it was."

"Very convenient," Prye said. "You must be one of Mother Nature's favorite children."

"I dived in," said Johnny, "and there it was."

"A bottle?"

"A case. A whole damn case. It was a most pleasant surprise."

"When did you find it?"

"This morning."

"And where?"

"Well, gosh, you can't expect me to tell you that. You'd take it away from me."

"It's a question of taking it away from you or taking you away from it. How would you like to be strapped to your bed?"

"You couldn't strap me to a bed," Johnny said pleasantly. "Nobody can do anything with me except Hemingway."

"And he's dead."

"Yes," Johnny said.

Prye took out his notebook and flicked over the pages. "Shall I tell you almost the last words Hemingway said before he was killed, Johnny? Miss Studd heard him say, 'I found the stuff and half of it's mine.'"

"He didn't find it!" Johnny shouted. "I found it."

"Where?"

"Over there." He pointed through the window toward the rock where they had disembarked the day before. It was there that Miss Eustace had seen the two flashlights.

"You left it there?" said Prye.

"Yes. Except just one bottle. I needed one bottle; you can see that for yourself. I'm a sick man. My nerves are shot. Now I need another bottle, too."

"All right," Prye said. "Let's go and get it."

Johnny's feet were difficult to manage, and it was ten minutes before they reached the landing rock. They found Kitty Tyler sitting there, staring out over the lake. She seemed not to hear them coming. Her chin was resting in her hand and her blue eyes were thoughtful.

"Don't tell Kitty," Johnny whispered to Prye. His foot slipped and he fell beside Miss Tyler. She turned with a start and eyed him coldly.

"You big souse," she said distinctly.

Johnny was struggling to his feet. "Oh, Kitty, honestly I haven't had a drop. Ask Dr. Prye."

"Not a drop more than one bottle anyway," Prye said.

Miss Tyler had not taken her eyes from Johnny's face. "You're so plastered you can't lift your feet. You'd better sober up."

Miss Tyler rose calmly, extended her hand, and pushed. There was a terrific splash, followed by a series of spluttering shouts from Johnny: "You ... nasty ... little ... fiend! You ... you—"

"He can't even swear properly," Miss Tyler said contemptuously.

"While you're immersed," Prye yelled, "bring up that case of Scotch."

Johnny's head disappeared under the water.

"So that's it," Miss Tyler said.

Prye sat on the ledge peering down into the water. He didn't see the rope two inches from his hand until Miss Tyler said, "What's that rope there for?"

The rope looked like a piece of dirty clothesline. It was fastened around the rock and tied in a double knot. It had been cut about a foot from the knot and the cut end was rust-colored.

"That's funny," Miss Tyler said. "Isn't that where the boatman tied the launch yesterday? But his rope was much thicker."

"Yes," Prye said, "his rope was much thicker and it didn't have bloodstains on it."

Miss Tyler had grown very pale. "Blood? That's not blood. It doesn't look in the least like blood. I'm quite sure you're mistaken."

"I wish I were," Prye said.

She drew in her breath and said, "Dr. Prye, listen—"

Johnny's head appeared at the surface. "I need help!" he shouted.

"You were saying, Miss Tyler?" Prye prompted.

"Nothing," Miss Tyler said flatly.

Prye leaned over and took the case of whiskey from Johnny and set it down on the rock. Johnny emerged from the water, his trousers clinging to his strong legs, his hair plastered across his forehead, and shook himself like a huge St. Bernard.

"Take the case up to Dr. Haller," Prye said to him. "I'll be up shortly."

"I can't take it to Haller," Johnny protested. "He'll take it away again. Let's just keep it a secret among the three of us."

"A secret!" Miss Tyler said nastily. "An anosmic butterfly could smell your breath at twenty paces. Come on. I'll see that you don't get lost."

Johnny slung the case over his shoulder and started to walk. It seemed that the dip had sobered him. Miss Tyler walked behind him, prodding him none too gently.

When they had gone, Prye tugged at the rope until it slipped off the rock. That it had been used to moor a boat was obvious; a small boat, for the rope was thin. No one had heard a motor during the night so probably it had been a rowboat. And it must have come during the night because the rope had not been there yesterday.

But why cut the rope? Why not untie it?

"Someone must have been in a hurry," Prye thought. "A really frantic hurry, or the rope would have been slipped off the rock as I slipped it off, or else untied. It has been cut with a sharp knife and unless I miss my guess, the same sharp knife that was found beside Hemingway. There was blood on it; it had just been used to stab Hemingway and the boatman—"

Where had the boat come from and why?

"It was no pleasure cruise," Prye thought. "The lake was rough last night. So the boat had come to the island for a purpose. It had come in the dead of night so its purpose must have been a shady one. And who was in the boat, who was at the oars?"

The lonely young man.

He closed his eyes and pictured the young man. He was very dark, almost as dark as an Indian. His expression, too, was the tight-lipped sullenness of an Indian. There were a lot of Indians at Port Innis, and the motor launch had picked up the colonists at Port Innis yesterday. Someone in the colony had probably talked to the dead young man yesterday, had paid him money to row out to this island last night. Why? Was the young man bringing something to this island, or was he taking something off the island?

Prye put the rope in his pocket and walked back toward the lodge.

Prye slipped quietly into the sitting room by the front door. He stood above the settee, staring down at the quiet, untroubled young man who had come in a boat in the dead of night.

He had tied up his boat, he was standing on the shore a little tired from the row, and someone had crept up behind him and stabbed him in the back. There were no bloodstains on the rocks; he must have fallen directly into the water.

But why kill a man who's going to do you a favor, who's going to take something off the island that you want taken off?

The answer is: You wouldn't. He was bringing something, and when he had brought it he was killed and the rope of his boat was cut. The boat and the young man had been scuttled.

Prye went into the dining room. Haller was standing in the middle of the floor talking, and Johnny was sitting in a corner listening. No one else was there.

"Now what?" Haller said, frowning.

"I want to borrow Johnny for a while if you can spare him," Prye said.

Johnny looked up, startled. "What for?"

"Dr. Haller and Miss Eustace have enough work to do," Prye said. "I thought I'd ask you to help me with the two autopsies."

Johnny's face was as green as an olive. "My God! You ... you can't—I'm not—My God, no!"

"It's a little messy, of course," Prye said. "But you'll live. Chalk it up to experience. Come along. Oh, yes, better get a couple of pails."

Haller was about to protest, but Prye waved him to silence. "We can't have our Johnny growing up to be a cissy. Come on, Johnny. If you feel sick, take some long deep breaths."

Johnny was pushed unceremoniously into the sitting room.

"Go on over and take another look at the man before we start," Prye said. "He's a hell of a lot prettier than Hemingway. That's why we'll start with him, to break you in. You were quite fond of Hemingway, weren't you?"

Prye was a little unsteady himself, but he walked over and put his hand on the young man's hair. "See how young he is, Johnny? Look at his face. He couldn't be more than twenty-one. He's even younger than you are, Johnny, and I bet you're not ready to die. See the calluses on the palms of his hands? He's been rowing, I think."

Johnny's knees folded and he sat down on the floor, covering his face with his hands. His body was shaking.

"Why, Johnny, what's the matter? Have you recognized him?"

"Yes." The word was almost inaudible.

"All right." Prye helped him to his feet. "Come outside and get some air."

They sat on the veranda. Johnny rested his head against the back of the deck chair, breathing hard.

Prye said: "Let's have it."

"I don't know his name," Johnny said in a hoarse whisper. "I was on the dock at Port Innis and I saw him standing there. Hemingway was putting the luggage into the motor launch and he wasn't paying any attention to me. So I—"

"So you went over and gave the young man some money and told him to row out to the island last night with a case of whiskey."

Johnny choked and said, "Yes. I gave him a hundred dollars. He said he knew the island."

"Expensive drinking, Johnny," said Prye. "A hundred dollars and a death."

"I didn't know—"

"Go on."

"That's about all, except that I told him I'd be waiting at the landing rock at twelve thirty. He told me to bring a flashlight down to the shore and flash it on and off five times."

"But you didn't get there at twelve thirty?"

"No. I went to sleep. I was lying on the bed with my clothes on and went to sleep. It was nearly one o'clock when I woke up. I couldn't get out very fast because I was afraid Miss Eustace would wake up and hear me. I took my flashlight down to the rock and flashed it as he told me to, but he didn't show up."

"He showed up," Prye said grimly. "You got there too late, Johnny."

"Then I looked around a bit with my flashlight. I didn't see any sign of the Indian, but I found a flashlight beside the rock and picked it up. I thought maybe one of us had dropped it. But I guess it was his flashlight."

"I guess it was," Prye said.

"I guess, in a way, I killed that man."

"I think so," Prye said. "I think you're a great big beautiful, irresponsible boy, and I think somebody should take a crack at that exquisite pan of yours. I'm strongly tempted to do so myself."

Johnny said nothing, and Prye got to his feet and went back into the lodge. For a long time Johnny sat on the veranda, staring with bleak eyes at the lake.

Miss Tyler found him there at five o'clock, but he refused to talk with her.

"What's the matter with you?" she asked coldly. "Or is something the matter with me?"

"You're all right," Johnny told her.

"What did Dr. Prye say to you?"

"Nothing."

Miss Tyler turned and entered the lodge with an angry twitch of her slacks. She found Prye and Mr. Storm talking in the dining room.

"What did you do to Johnny?" she asked wrathfully.

"What someone should have done long ago," Prye said. "Bounced him over the head with a fact."

"You brute beast," said Miss Tyler.

"I can't stand any more of this excitement!" Mr. Storm shouted. "I can't stand any more of it! I'm going crazy."

"Silver-lining Storm," Miss Tyler said balefully. "Always a cheerful word and a merry smile."

"Beat it," Prye said.

The words were intended for Miss Tyler, but Mr. Storm took them personally. With a shrill cry he whirled, and scurried out of the door.

"He's always running out of rooms," Miss Tyler said. "Where does he go?"

"Why don't you go and find out?" Prye asked.

Miss Tyler went and found out. She returned hastily.

"What an extremely bizarre way to pass the time," she said. "Why does he sit in the icehouse all the time? Has he a phobia or something?"

"He has a phobia all right," Prye said. "He's frightened of the wide open spaces and has an uncontrollable desire to sit in a small inclosed space. It's not a very common type of phobia."

"I should hope not," Miss Tyler said.

"By the way, Miss Tyler, what are you doing up here?"

Miss Tyler had been patting her blond curls, but her hand dropped to her side. "Me? I have a deep-seated neurosis."

"Now that's funny," Prye said.

"Not funny at all. You see, I'm terrified of going batty. I have all sorts of batty aunts and things. My aunt Isabella steals things. We have to buy cheap little gadgets just so she can have the pleasure of stealing them. It's very sad."

"You fooled me completely. Now I should have said you were a perfectly normal young lady, that you were not afraid of going insane at all, that Aunt Isabella is a fictitious figure, and that you joined the colony for a very special reason not connected with nerves. See how you fooled me?"

Miss Tyler turned on her heel and walked to the window. Prye watched her for a minute and then went out. He passed Mr. Jenkins sitting on top of his funeral pyre, watching for ships. He judged from the rattles issuing from the kitchen window that Josephine was opening cans for their evening meal, and he quickened his step.

Miss Eustace answered his knock. "Miss Studd is resting," she said quietly.

"I am not resting," Miss Studd called loudly from the bed. "I am thinking."

Miss Eustace's shrug dismissed resting and thinking as equally unimportant. Prye entered the room and approached the bed. Miss Studd was looking better.

"Want to talk?" he asked her.

"I don't mind talking," she replied, "if it can be done in private."

She flung Miss Eustace a nasty look, and Miss Eustace passed composedly into the hall and closed the door behind her.

"Heard anything more from Myrtle?" Prye asked.

Miss Studd sat up in bed. She was suddenly very dignified. "I've heard nothing more."

"Do you want to?"

"What do you mean? You know—"

"Don't be frightened. I'll be back soon."

He passed Miss Eustace in the hall and went out the back door and around to Miss Studd's window. Taking a handkerchief from his pocket, he tied it around his mouth. The sound that floated into Miss Studd's room was a high-pitched whisper.

"It's Myrtle. I killed Hemingway. I've been waiting for you to come."

He took his pen from his breast pocket, took aim, and tossed it through Miss Studd's window.

When he re-entered her room, she was holding it in her hand and staring at it. Her flabby body was shaking with rage.

"Tricked," she muttered. "Tricked. Tricked."

"That was Myrtle you heard?" said Prye.

"Yes."

"May I have my pen, please?"

He replaced the pen in his pocket and called Miss Eustace in from the hall. She was shocked at Miss Studd's appearance, and gave Prye a reproachful look.

"She'll be all right now," Prye said. "So you didn't hear any voices this morning, Miss Eustace?"

"No," Miss Eustace said, rather angrily.

Miss Studd was regaining her composure. She said, "I've remembered something. It's not very important, but I told you that Hemingway had called Myrtle a ... a girl dog. It wasn't a girl dog. It was another unpleasant word that begins with a b, too. It signifies illegitimacy. You know the word?"

"Yes," said Prye. "I have been called it on occasion."

He was smiling grimly to himself as he went out. He went down to the shore and sat there for some time lost in thought. The sun was beginning to set when Mr. Jenkins' "Hello!" summoned him to dinner.

Mrs. Jenkins had opened cans with reckless abandon. Having lived on raisins and nuts for a number of years, she had only hazy ideas on the diet of ordinary people.

Prye plowed his way through three different kinds of beans and finished up on raisins, much to the delight of the Jenkins family.

But it was a doleful meal. This way madness lies, Prye thought, looking at Miss Tyler's downcast eyes and Mr. Storm's glum face. Perhaps I'll get the Jenkinses to organize some group games. Or perhaps someone might make up a table of bridge.

The question was put to the others.

"Musical chairs!" Mr. Jenkins cried. "Let's have musical chairs!"

"There's no music," Prye said.

"I could sing," Josephine offered. "I'd just love to sing."

"I don't like musical chairs," Miss Tyler said coldly. "Somebody hit me over the head with a musical chair when I was a baby. Can't we be civilized for once and play bridge?"

"Oh, bridge!" Mrs. Jenkins exclaimed with contempt. "There's no zip to bridge. You just sit. There's no real joy in it."

Mr. Storm, too, proved difficult.

"I can't play bridge," he announced.

Miss Tyler, who was an expert, made a heroic sacrifice. "I'll teach you as we go along."

Mr. Storm shook his head obstinately. "I can only play seven-up, and I only played that once."

"Seven-up it is," Miss Tyler said, sighing.

The Jenkinses retired to a corner of the room, to compose a song, they said, and the cards were brought out and the card table set up.

From his chair in front of the fireplace, Prye watched Miss Tyler shuffle the cards with careless ease and distribute them to Miss Eustace, Mr. Storm and Johnny. The others waited patiently while Mr. Storm dropped cards and recovered them and laboriously arranged his hand in suits.

"You must try not to drop your cards," Miss Eustace said in a resigned voice. "I know your whole hand."

"Well, you shouldn't have looked," Mr. Storm said with some acerbity. "I'm not peering into your hand."

"I wasn't peering," Miss Eustace retorted.

"Who has the seven of hearts?" Miss Tyler asked hastily.

No one admitted having the seven of hearts.

"He's got it," Miss Eustace said finally. "I saw it."

"You see? You were peering," Mr. Storm said, looking at her darkly.

The game progressed. Miss Eustace handled her cards slowly and carefully. She probably doesn't play much, Prye thought. Mr. Storm kept on dropping cards. Prye noticed that he shuffled awkwardly, but dealt the cards with the swift proficiency of a teller counting money. Johnny played absently, saying nothing at all.

At the end of the fourth hand, the Jenkinses emerged from their corner in triumph.

"Listen to this!" Josephine cried. "It's a sort of theme song for the colony.

"Oh, it's sweet to go and freely flow
　　From place to beautiful place.
Oh, we live at where we hang our hat
　　For we love extent of space.
We need no tent but the firmament,
　　As free as the birds are we.
With a rollicking shout we wander about
　　With a banjo on our knee!"

Johnny and Miss Eustace clapped politely. Miss Tyler said, "Why a banjo?" Mr. Storm simply walked out.

"Why not a banjo?" Mr. Jenkins demanded.

"It seems silly to me," Miss Tyler replied coldly. "I think I'll go to bed." She, too, walked out.

"There's no joy in her either," Mrs. Jenkins said in a mournful voice.

"It's too late for joy," Prye said. "Why don't we go to bed?"

They filed out. Prye saw them all safely into their rooms. He went to his own room, locking the door behind him, and sat down on the bed.

"A long night," he thought. "It's going to be a long night." He did not undress.

V

A quarter moon, like a thin slice of melon, shone through the windows and gradually floated away again. At two o'clock he was still sitting on his bed, listening, hearing nothing but the water and the wind. He got up at last and stretched his cramped legs. A board in the floor creaked and he jumped at the sound.

"The water makes too much noise," he thought. He went to the window, slung his legs over the sill and dropped to the rocks below.

In the dim light the island was more than ever like an unhappy ghost groaning in protests as the lake tumbled against its sides.

Prye walked around the back of the lodge, keeping close to the wall. Then he saw the flames creeping up the side of Mr. Jenkins' funeral pyre. In the second that he watched, they grew larger, leaping from log to log, roaring as they towered.

He cried, "Fire! Fire!"

He turned his head and saw the figure running toward the lake, a figure with bright-yellow hair in which the flames were caught.

He yelled again: "Fire! Everybody out! Fire!"

From the lodge came the shrill hysterical screams of Miss Studd. Miss Eustace's pale face appeared at the window of her room and as quickly disappeared. Her shouting rose above the noise of the fire and the waves.

Miss Tyler was the first to emerge from the lodge. She came stumbling out the front door, clutching a suitcase. Miss Studd came next, clinging fast to Miss Eustace's arm and half fainting with fright; and then Dr. Haller, a short, squat figure in pajamas. He carried his wallet in one hand and an immense book in the other.

They were all shouting now, but their voices were lost in the roar as the flames mounted higher and higher. The island glared red. In the wavering light they could see Mr. Storm running toward them, his face terrible with fright, and behind him, running with swift, relentless strides, the figure of Johnny Prince. Suddenly, Johnny stumbled forward on one knee, his face anguished as bone struck rock.

Mr. Storm was blubbering like a maniac, the saliva frothing around his mouth and dribbling down his chin. He fell almost at Prye's feet. Prye bent over and set him upright again, holding him by the shoulders.

"He wants to kill me!" Storm said through chattering teeth. "He wants to kill me. Oh, God, save me!"

Miss Tyler screamed, "Johnny!" and ran toward him. Dr. Haller was after her like a shot. "Keep away from him!" he cried. He caught hold of Kitty's hair and they stood struggling for a moment until she collapsed in Haller's arms.

"Save me!" Storm was crying. "Oh, save me!"

Prye slapped him hard across the cheek and he stopped, dazed and swaying in Prye's grip.

Johnny was on his feet again, limping toward them with his shoulders hunched together. The firelight gleamed on the knife he held in his hand.

Mr. Jenkins had emerged from the lodge. "Shall I rush him?" he shouted to Prye.

"Don't be a fool," Prye said. "You can't rush a man with a knife."

Johnny was approaching steadily over the rocks, bent double like a blond ape, clasping his wounded knee in one hand.

"He did it all," Mr. Storm was gibbering. "He killed Hemingway. Don't let him kill me. He killed the man in the boat, and he wants to kill me. Oh, God, save me!"

Prye's hands tightened on Storm's shoulders and shook him back and forth. "*What* man in the boat?"

"The man with the whiskey. He brought a case of whiskey. Johnny killed him and now he's going to kill me. He chased me down to the lake."

Prye shook him again. "Why did he kill Hemingway?"

"Money," Storm whispered. "The money. The money."

Johnny's voice rose above the roar of the flames. "Let me at him. Stand back, all of you. I want Storm!"

Jenkins was tearing off his bathrobe, breathing hard. He crouched like a runner waiting for the starting gun. With a sudden jerk, Prye sent Storm catapulting into Jenkins' rear, and Jenkins fell on his face.

"O. K., Johnny," said Prye.

Johnny straightened up, tossed the knife to the ground, and came limping toward Jenkins. Miss Studd joined Miss Tyler in a dead faint. Jenkins was picking himself up, trying to stanch the flow of blood from the cut on his forehead. Storm sat quietly on a rock, opening and closing his mouth like a fish.

Prye touched his arm. "It's all over, Storm," he said, but Storm didn't hear him. "Get up, Storm."

Jenkins was wiping the blood from his forehead and repeating, "Goodness gracious, what happened? Goodness gracious."

Storm did not move, and Prye took his arm quite gently and raised him to his feet.

Johnny was very pale. "I guess he's just crazy," he said.

"What happened?" asked Mr. Jenkins again.

Mr. Storm said nothing.

"Sure, he's crazy," Prye said. "He thought he was pretending to be crazy, but—"

Mr. Storm began to laugh. "Crazy? Me? Fifty thousand dollars' worth crazy, that's how crazy I am. Fifty thousand dollars, I tell you, fifty thousand dollars!"

"See, Johnny?" Prye said. "He is crazy. He thinks he's got fifty thousand dollars."

"I have got fifty thousand dollars!" Storm screamed. "I've got it and I'm as sane as you are. I'll show you!"

"They all get like that occasionally," Prye said. "Of course, you have it, Mr. Storm; certainly you have. Don't irritate him, Johnny. Pretend you think he has it. Of course, he has it, haven't you, Mr. Storm?"

With a swift motion, Storm shook off Prye's hand, and ran toward the icehouse. "I'm not crazy!" he screamed. "I've got it, I tell you, and I'm not crazy!"

Johnny and Prye followed him into the icehouse. Mr. Jenkins saw the three of them troop into the icehouse and passed his hand across his bloody brow.

"Maybe," Mr. Jenkins said wonderingly, "I'm crazy."

Miss Tyler was returning to consciousness. Dr. Haller chafed her hands briskly and spoke to her in an encouraging bedside voice.

"I love you," she said.

Haller dropped her hands as if they were twin rattlesnakes. "You ... you ... what?" he gasped.

"I love you, Johnny," Miss Tyler said dreamily. "I don't care what you've done. I love you. We'll go to Polynesia."

Mrs. Jenkins was ministering to her stricken mate. "A fine thing," she sniffed. "It wasn't fair play at all. A deliberate trip."

"I could have rushed him," Mr. Jenkins said.

"Certainly you could," Mrs. Jenkins said heartily. "You could have rushed him."

Miss Studd opened her eyes and said, "Myrtle."

"It's all right, Miss Studd," said Miss Eustace. "They've got him."

"Him?"

"Mr. Storm."

"Mr. Storm!" Miss Studd immediately had a relapse.

The three men emerged from the icehouse. Two of them were looking dazed. The third was saying in a triumphant voice:

"Crazy, eh? Crazy! How about that? And that? And that?"

Every time Mr. Storm said "that" he tossed a package of bills to the ground with great emphasis. It was, Prye decided, a most impressive gesture.

Johnny choked. "How ... I mean, where—"

Prye smiled and took Mr. Storm's arm. "Mr. Storm is tired now. He and I are going to have a little chat and then he's going to bed. You may have my room for the rest of the night, Mr. Storm. It has a lock and key. I don't think you'll be bothered by wide open spaces for some time."

Mr. Storm seemed not unhappy at the prospect. He trotted obediently into the lodge. Johnny and Miss Tyler picked up the money and locked it in Miss Tyler's room. Mr. and Mrs. Jenkins put out the bonfire, and Dr. Haller and Miss Eustace took Miss Studd back to bed. It was four o'clock in the morning.

Breakfast was served an hour late the next day. Mr. Storm, of course, was absent, but Miss Studd took his place. The bandage on her forehead had dwindled to a pad of cotton and some adhesive tape. She was herself again, having suddenly developed a severe case of tuberculosis during the night. She coughed happily throughout the meal.

"Really," Mrs. Jenkins said to Prye. "I do think you owe us some explanation for the unwarranted attack on my husband."

"And how you got on to Mr. Storm," Mr. Jenkins said.

Prye put down the piece of toast he was about to eat. He preferred talking to eating, anyway.

"I think I'll answer Mr. Jenkins' question first. I didn't get on to Mr. Storm all at once, but there were a number of things which led me to suspect him—his occupation of the icehouse, his fear of space, the handkerchief episode, and lastly, the way he dealt cards.

"Now Mr. Storm, when he came to Dr. Haller about a month ago, gave his profession as retired teacher. He had two fears—first, fear of people, which is a fear not uncommon among teachers who are not qualified emotionally for their work; and second, fear of space. The fear of people, then, was consistent with Mr. Storm's story of himself, but the second and more powerful fear was not. Fear of space is frequently an occupational neurosis: that is, a man who had worked in a small inclosed area for a considerable time may miss his inclosure when he leaves it to such an extent that he develops an unreasoning fear of open places. This is usually most pronounced when the man has left his job under unpleasant circumstances.

"Mr. Storm was not feigning this symptom. He frequently went and sat in the icehouse, a small inclosed space. But why, I wondered, should Mr. Storm have developed an occupational neurosis which had nothing to do with his occupation as a teacher? Suppose, however, that Mr. Storm had not been a teacher but a bank teller, for instance, who spent his time in a kind of cage in a bank? Suppose he had left his job under unpleasant circumstances? Bank tellers are respectable people. Why lie about the fact that you had been one unless you had something to conceal?

"That was the thin edge of the wedge—the suspicion that Mr. Storm had not told the truth about his profession. That is all I had to begin with, a small and possibly unimportant lie. I felt fairly sure Storm, or Murrell as his name is, had not been a teacher, but something else, maybe a bank teller.

"The second suspicious thing about Storm was the handkerchief episode. He professed to know nothing about the blood on the handkerchief and interpreted it as a sign from Heaven that he had helped to kill Hemingway by not going out for a walk with him the night he was killed. He felt very badly about that. But why? He was an irascible and unpleasant man with no sympathy in him at all. Why the sudden grief? Why, moreover, would Hemingway have chosen to confide in him? I had then two more odd things about Storm—his sudden attack of conscience over Hemingway's death, and his story that Hemingway had planned to tell him something important shortly before Hemingway was murdered. Once again, I suspected Storm of lying if of nothing worse. We come now to the words Hemingway said."

Prye took out his notebook and read aloud: "'I found the stuff and half of it's mine.' 'We can get away together, Myrtle. You can't keep it up long.' 'I've got the dope on you, Myrtle.' The first point that occurred to me was not what Hemingway had found, but when he had the opportunity to find it. From the moment that Hemingway disembarked he was busy unpacking, treating his poison ivy, and looking after Johnny and the rest of you. It was probable, I decided, that whatever he found he did not find on the island.

"When, then, did he find it? When, in fact, had he done any searching? At this point, I remembered the scene on the motor launch shortly before we disembarked. Hemingway took Johnny to the cabin to search his clothes and luggage for contraband. As the male attendant, he was responsible also for searching the other men of the colony, Mr. Jenkins and Mr. Storm. It seemed most likely that this was the time Hemingway found 'the stuff,' and that he had found it in the luggage of either Johnny or Mr. Storm or Mr. Jenkins.

"But what was the stuff? It was something valuable enough to induce Hemingway to give up his job—'We can get away together, Myrtle'—and since it was necessary to get away, the stuff must have been obtained in some shady manner. It couldn't, as Miss Studd suggested, have been dope. Hemingway, as a competent attendant, would have immediately reported it to Dr. Haller because he knew the dangers of dope in a colony of this sort. My first thought was money, although stolen jewels were a possibility.

"But whose money was it? Obviously, Myrtle's. And who was Myrtle?

"There was no one by that name in the colony. It was a woman's name, but was Myrtle a woman? There were two thin pieces of evidence to the contrary—the first was the probability that Hemingway had found the stuff in the luggage of one of the three men. The second was Miss Eustace's report of Hemingway's manners in front of women; he was formal, she said, and he never swore. But Miss Studd heard Hemingway call Myrtle a violent name. Both pieces of evidence were slim but they pointed the way.

"My assumptions added up to this—that Myrtle was a man in possession of illegally obtained money or valuables. I struck Johnny off the list immediately, since he already has more money than he can ever spend. I had left Mr. Jenkins and Mr. Storm.

"The last and most important clue leading to Storm was his method of dealing cards. He was obviously an incompetent player, but he dealt the cards swiftly and easily with a peculiar motion that reminded me instantly of a bank teller counting out money. This, too, was thin, taken by itself, but add to that his phobia, his occupation of the icehouse, his lying about his profession, and the probability that what Hemingway found was money. If Mr. Storm was an absconding bank teller it all fitted perfectly.

"I had no tangible case against the man, so I asked Johnny to help me build one up and I gave him certain instructions. As you all know, Mr. Storm's bedroom window faces south; that is, the funeral pyre built by Mr. Jenkins yesterday afternoon was visible from Storm's window. My idea was this—suppose the pyre was lit and Mr. Storm thought his money or whatever it was—I still wasn't sure, you see—was in danger of being destroyed, he would probably rush out to save it. It's the first thought anyone has under the circumstances, to save what is most valuable. Notice that Dr. Haller brought out his wallet and his autographed copy of 'The Psychiatry of Multiple Personalities.'

"Mr. Storm was not sleeping well, anyway, and as soon as Johnny lit the fire shortly before two o'clock, Storm saw it and climbed out his window. Naturally, he did not raise the alarm. He ran toward the icehouse where he had hidden his money, saw Johnny, and turned back. Johnny had a knife in his hand and he was, as you know, a fearful figure. Mr. Storm, who was firmly convinced that the rest of you were insane, ran down to the lake in terror. Johnny chased him, being careful not to catch him.

"Meanwhile, I came out as arranged and gave the alarm, and everyone came running out of the lodge. Mr. Storm saw us and came back toward the lodge with Johnny still at his heels. By this time Storm was nearly crazy with fright, but not so crazy that he didn't see his opportunity to throw the blame for everything on Johnny.

"When Storm reached us, Johnny conveniently stumbled, giving me a chance to ask Storm two questions. His answers gave him away completely. He said that Johnny had killed the boatman who had brought whiskey, and that the motive for killing Hemingway was the money. But only Johnny and I and the murderer knew that the dead man was a boatman and that he had brought whiskey. As soon as Storm had given himself away, I told Johnny he could quit playing the maniac."

Prye turned to Jenkins. "Sorry I had to trip you, but you would have ruined the set-up."

"I forgive you," Mr. Jenkins said handsomely.

"Certainly. We forgive you," said Josephine.

"Under ordinary circumstances," Prye went on, "Storm wouldn't have fallen for the next bit of horseplay, my pretending that he was crazy. But remember, he had joined this colony for neurotics thinking the rest of you were crazy and that he himself was perfectly sane; and he had just been chased by a maniac with a knife. His one desire was to convince me and himself that he was perfectly sane and that he had killed for a perfectly sane motive—money."

"But why did he have to kill Hemingway?" Miss Tyler asked. "Why didn't he divide the money?"

"He probably would have if he could have been sure Hemingway would never give him away. He had gone to some pains to steal the money and to avoid discovery. He thought the colony would make an ideal hide-out for him until the affair blew over. Dr. Haller's scheme for the colony received some publicity in the newspapers—that is why Murrell or Storm went to him in the first place. The police department of Philadelphia, he figured, wouldn't be looking for an absconding teller in a colony of neurotics headed by a doctor from Detroit.

"The mutilation of Hemingway's body was done to cast suspicion on the rest of you, notably Johnny. His chief attempt to implicate Johnny was thwarted by Mr. Jenkins. Hemingway had apparently borrowed one of Johnny's handkerchiefs and when Storm killed him he found the handkerchief in Hemingway's coat pocket. It had blood on it by this time. Storm put the handkerchief in his own pocket, wanting to make it appear as though it had been planted there. It was an impulsive idea and the whole thing was spoiled anyway by Mr. Jenkins. Thinking the J on it stood for Josephine, Jenkins wrapped the handkerchief around a rock and threw it in the lake, although he ought to have known it was too large for a woman's handkerchief."

"How sweet!" Mrs. Jenkins said, beaming on her mate. "How true-blue!"

Miss Studd began to cough hollowly, and when everyone's attention was fixed on her, she said: "Why did he whisper outside my window and throw the knife into my room?"

"Because," Prye said, "his attempt to implicate Johnny having failed, he decided that perhaps you could be made to believe that you yourself were guilty. He knew you were suggestible. He came out of the icehouse around the side of the lodge, heard Miss Eustace crying in her room and knew she wouldn't hear him whispering outside your window. He had already taken the bread knife from the kitchen as a means of protecting himself if necessary.

"The whole performance took very little time and Miss Studd reacted as he thought she would. At first she leaped out of her bed in terror, unlocked her door and was on the point of running out. But before she got out she heard the voice tell her that she was guilty, that she was Myrtle. Dr. Haller found her in bed, dazed with shock, and quite firmly convinced of her own guilt. That was one of the places where Storm overplayed his hand. Miss Studd's auditory hallucination looked suspicious right from the start. It wasn't in accord with the rest of her symptoms and so I sought another explanation and found it."

Miss Tyler's blue eyes were very thoughtful. "Why did he kill the young man in the boat?"

"Sheer panic," Prye said. "About midnight Storm had left Hemingway's room. Hemingway had demanded half the money and Storm was ostensibly going out to get it. What he actually got was the meat knife from the kitchen. When he didn't come back to Hemingway's room, Hemingway went out to look for him. He found him down near the south shore apparently recovering the money from beneath some rocks. Actually, he expected Hemingway to come after him and Hemingway did. When Hemingway was off guard he stabbed him. It was at this point that he saw the light flashing across the water near the northeast shore. It was the boatman's signal to Johnny. Storm, of course, knew nothing of the business arrangement between Johnny and the boatman.

"Thoroughly frightened, he crept over to the northeast shore, still holding the bloody knife in his hand. By this time the boatman, receiving no answering flash from Johnny, had tied up his boat and come ashore to investigate. He unloaded the case of whiskey and sat down to wait for Johnny."

"I'd promised him another fifty," Johnny said in a low voice.

"Storm was in a panic by this time. The boatman continued to sit, his flashlight turned on beside him. Storm had not yet had time to arrange Hemingway's body or take off the clothes and dispose of them. At any moment someone might come from the lodge to meet the boatman, or the boatman himself might decide to look around the island. And if Storm tried to get back into his room, maybe he'd run into the man or woman whom the boatman was obviously expecting. In a sudden fury, he crept up behind the man and stabbed him and pushed him over into the water. Then he cut the boat loose with the bloody knife.

"This was not done, as I had supposed, because he had no time to untie the rope, but because he saw the case of whiskey and decided that it was Johnny who had arranged for the boatman to come. Therefore, it was Johnny on whom suspicion was most likely to fall. So he deliberately left the bloodstained rope where it was, and put the case of whiskey under the water in a place where it would probably be found. He couldn't leave it on the rocks, you see, because if Johnny were the murderer he would have hidden the whiskey. Storm is a fairly subtle man."

"How did Hemingway know Storm's real name?" Mr. Jenkins asked.

"Probably he read the papers more carefully than I do," Prye replied, "and added two and two. A man named Murrell robbed a Philadelphia bank of fifty thousand dollars. A man of the same description named Storm had fifty thousand dollars in his luggage. Hemingway probably connected the two facts and taxed Murrell with them."

There was a short pause. Miss Tyler rose to her feet suddenly and cried, "There's the boat! Look!"

The launch was approaching the island.

"Oh, dear," Mrs. Jenkins said unhappily. "I don't want to leave. It seems a shame to let all this beautiful fresh air and sunshine go to waste."

"A crying shame," her husband agreed.

"I'm afraid," Haller confessed, flushing, "that I'll have to give up the colony, at least temporarily. But there's no reason why you two shouldn't stay on."

"Oh, joy!" Mrs. Jenkins shouted.

Prye smiled. "True children of nature," he thought, "of which I am not one. I wonder if the boatman on the launch will give me a cigarette."

Miss Tyler drew Johnny out to the veranda, and they sat down on the steps.

"Johnny," Miss Tyler said.

"Yes," Johnny said.

"I've got a confession."

"Have you?"

"I'm not really crazy."

"Of course you aren't."

"Not even a little crazy. I just came up here because of you."

Johnny blushed. "How could you? I mean, I never even saw you before I came here."

"I saw you, though. I saw you playing polo twice. I fell in love with you right away. I've always been crazy about horses anyway."

"I like horses, too," Johnny said.

"I read about the colony in the papers, about you going along, I mean. I thought I'd come, too, and look after you."

"Oh."

"You won't need looking after any more, Dr. Prye said, but just the same—" She paused and added dreamily: "I think love is wonderful."

"It's fine," Johnny said.

LAST DAY IN LISBON

LAST DAY IN LISBON
Preface by Tom Nolan

Unlike her husband, who wrote fiction almost exclusively in the first-person voice, Margaret Millar favored third-person narrative for nearly all her work. An exception was "Last Day in Lisbon," a tale of a young American woman in wartorn Europe. No doubt the first-person mode gave a more immediate feel to this story of Elizabeth "Lizzie" Lane, a singer from New York who finds deadly espionage and unexpected romance in the neutral city of Lisbon, Portugal: a haven and departure point for refugees from many countries during World War II.

"Last Day in Lisbon," though it shares some stylistic and structural elements with her early murder-mysteries, was unlike anything else in Margaret Millar's oeuvre. What prompted her to write it (apparently in 1940 or '41)? Was this the story she did at the behest of *The American*? (Interestingly, "Lisbon," like "Mind Over Murder," includes a male character named Ross.)

Set in a city its author never saw, "Lisbon" (published early in 1943 in Dell's *Five-Novels Monthly*) suffers in spots from guidebook-style descriptions. But the text is enlivened by Margaret Millar's wit ("I tried to make my voice crisp, but it wilted around the edges") and pithy thumbnail-sketches: "She was so pale her face had a faint greenish lustre. I guessed she was about thirty and she looked every hour of it. She wore no makeup, her hair was black and untidily pinned into a bun at the back of her head, and her clothes were good but unflattering."

And might the character of Duarte be a caricature of W. H. Auden, whom the Millars knew in Michigan and whom both would "use" in novels? "Lisbon" 's ambiguous cop bears a certain unkind likeness to the young English poet: "a thin, shrivelled little man with a lazy, insolent smile. He looked like a street urchin, and it was a shock to hear his voice. It was pure Oxford."

Another British author, John Buchan, seems to have influenced the writing of "Last Day in Lisbon," which echoes events and devices from that writer's classic spy-thriller *The Thirty-Nine*

Steps. A month or two after "Lisbon" was published, Kenneth Millar (already engaged in his lifelong "friendly and healthful competition" with his writer wife) would also draw on *Steps* for some of the feel and structure of his first, quickly-written novel, *The Dark Tunnel*—after which Ken Millar would join the US Navy and see actual service in the global conflict about which he and his wife had both just written fiction.

LAST DAY IN LISBON

From my seat in the brass and marble lobby of the Avenida Palace I had a view of two doors. The first, and the most important at that moment since it was after one o'clock, was the one which led into the dining room. Through it passed a steady stream of people, representing every country of Europe—a Serbian family who had checked in the day before and still looked weary and train-dusty; a group of French diplomats; a fat Jewess from Rumania who, during the two weeks I had seen her, had lost twenty pounds; a thin young, aristocratic looking Englishwoman, badly dressed in black crepe.

She came towards my chair, glaring impartially around the lobby, and sat down near me. Though we had seen each other frequently for two weeks she made no gesture of recognition but sat with her eyes fixed on the door which led in from the street.

Lisbon has a reputation for noise. Even the revolving door squeaked and groaned on its hinges, and over that you could hear the trains rumble into Central Station directly behind the hotel, and rumble out again having deposited the latest cargo of refugees. A little later the refugees would stream through the door, carrying their own baggage, looking faintly relieved but still uneasy, realizing that the end wasn't yet in sight.

Their eyes said, "Well, here we are. We've gotten this far—"

Another rumble. The twelve-thirty overnight train from France, nearly an hour late as usual.

The Englishwoman lit a cigarette without taking her eyes from the door. I wondered idly if she was waiting for someone. It was the first time I had wondered about anyone or anything for two weeks, except myself. But now I could afford to wonder. Pinned to the inside of my dress was my Clipper ticket, my escape, my passage to home. It was there, pinned to my dress, and all I had to do was take a taxi to the airport in Cintra and get on the plane. A plane to New York.

The dining room was gradually emptying, but still I waited in my chair. I wanted to see the new arrivals from France. Perhaps there would be an American among them, someone I could talk to. I was tired of Portuguese.

They began to arrive, pouring through the door, jostling each other on the way to the desk, talking in French and some language I didn't recognize: a prosperous looking couple with three children and a dog, the inevitable contingent of minor diplomats; a young man with bright red hair and wearing a grey shapeless suit was talking to an older man, incredibly thin and sick looking.

"Not bad," the young man said, and his voice came straight from New York!

I watched them and so did the Englishwoman, though she was more nonchalant now, almost contemptuous.

They stopped at the desk. The older man did the talking while the young one stared around the lobby in pleased surprise. His eyes flicked over me and the Englishwoman, coming to rest at last on a tall, dark, beautiful girl a few feet to his right.

The girl was standing beside the desk as if she were waiting for someone. She had been there for some time, looking cool despite the silver foxes she was carrying over one brown arm. It was July and the silver foxes had me puzzled until I heard her speak to the clerk in Portuguese. She was a native, I decided, and she had seen too many cinemas.

As I watched I saw her move her arm suddenly and her handbag flew out of her hand and landed about a foot away from the young man with the red hair. She bent over, blushing, and began to ram the stuff back into the bag.

I got up and moved slowly towards the dining room, passing the desk just as the red-haired young man was leaping to the rescue of the handbag.

The girl was giggling inanely and talking in Portuguese with many pretty gestures of apology.

I brushed past and handed my doorkey to the clerk. As I turned to leave I thought I heard the girl say, "George Tobacco."

"Quite all right," the young man said pleasantly. "Sorry I don't understand Portuguese."

And then again, "George tobacco," all mixed up with gestures and Portuguese and smiles.

I moved away without looking back and went into the dining room. I usually lunched late in order to avoid the crowds and have a table to myself by the windows.

From the window I could see the beginning of the Avenida da Liberdade, a vast boulevard with three roadways flanked by palm and judas trees and a small stream gurgling along the side. The Avenida is Lisbon's Fifth Avenue, and even in the heat it was crowded with strolling couples dressed in the kind of clothes that had been fashionable in New York before I'd left for England two years previously. The fashions in Portugal move as slowly as everything else.

I ordered an omelette and sat back in my chair to while away the inevitable half-hour required by Lisbon cooks to make an omelette. I saw the dark beautiful girl come in, dangling the silver foxes over her arm. She had a man with her, a small fat Portuguese whom she called Pedro. They sat a couple of tables away with the girl facing me.

The young man with the red hair came in, too. He was alone and he carried a newspaper under his arm. He sat at the opposite end of the dining room and opened up his paper. I watched him as he read. It was pleasant to see an American again, especially a young one, and more especially since I had the Clipper ticket pinned inside my dress.

He scowled as he read, and then folded the paper and walked out without having ordered his lunch. I looked out the window again at the bronze statue of a man riding a horse.

A voice behind me said, "Miss Lane?"

I turned and saw the thin English-woman standing beside my table, smiling down at me. I didn't like the smile. It was bright and false and half-coy, the smile of a woman who is going to ask a favor and knows she doesn't deserve one.

"Yes," I said as politely as possible. "Won't you sit down? I'm afraid I don't know your name."

She seemed surprised. "I'm Violet Featherstone. My father is the Honorable *Cecil* Featherstone."

I had never heard of the Honorable Cecil Featherstone, but I managed to look impressed and at the same time signal the waiter to hurry up the omelette. The waiter nodded, smiled, and remained stationary.

"Lazy dogs," said the Honorable Violet.

She sat back in her chair and the sun from the windows caught her face. She was so pale her skin had a faint greenish lustre. I guessed she was about thirty and she looked every hour of it. She wore no makeup, her hair was black and untidily pinned into a bun at the back of her head, and her clothes were good but unflattering. I had never seen her in anything but black.

She had a queer voice, not loud but penetrating, like a shouted whisper:

"Are you an *American* citizen?"

I said, yes. She waited for me to go on, so I added that I was a singer, that I'd been touring the music halls in England for nearly two years, that I'd dodged several bombs and wanted to go home.

She leaned across the table. "By Clipper? You're expecting a seat on the Clipper?"

Again that urgent whisper. Looking back now I think the whisper was the first sign of danger that I recognized. There were other signs before that, I know now, but the urgency in the Honorable Violet's voice was unmistakable. She was afraid.

"Aren't you?" she repeated.

I nodded, trying to keep my hand from straying to the front of my dress to make sure the ticket was still there.

"You're—anxious to *get away?*"

I smiled dryly. "You wouldn't be knowing how anxious. Look out that window."

Passing a few feet in front of the window was a swarthy man in civilian clothes. He carried a huge sign under his arm, and by twisting my neck a little I could read the top line of printing: "500,000 *prisioneiros sovieticos.*" I couldn't understand or speak Portuguese, but my college Spanish served its purpose, then and later. I read the rest of the sign aloud:

"Half a million Russian prisoners captured in four weeks of war; 10,000 tanks demolished."

The swarthy gentleman passed on.

To my surprise the Honorable Violet was smiling. "Waste of

paper," she said. "Most Portuguese can't read and those who can
are too lazy to read."

"Maybe," I said. "In any case I want to get out before the Nazis
get in."

"There's no danger." She fumbled with the clasp of her purse
for a moment. "I want your *seat on the Clipper*, the one you got
this morning at nine o'clock, the one you have pinned to your
dress. I'll pay *ten thousand dollars*."

I sat there, unable to move or speak.

"Life or death," she said hoarsely. "It's a matter of life or death.
I've got to *get out of here*."

I didn't know what to do so I signalled to the waiter again to
fill in time. He responded with a friendly wave of his hand. There
was no use in shouting to him because he spoke no English—
very few in Lisbon do—so I took a couple of escudos from my
bag and waved them at him. It was like tossing a dime to a news-
boy.

"Is that your answer?" Violet Featherstone whispered.

"I'm sorry," I said. "I've waited some time for this ticket. I'm
not high on the priorities list. Besides I wouldn't know what to
do with ten thousand dollars."

She put her finger to her lips as the waiter approached. "What
do you want, Miss Lane? I'll tell him."

"Food," I said. "Just food."

She snorted out a word, he snorted one back and it was arranged.
At least he walked away very slowly and thoughtfully.

"Fifteen thousand," she said. "And a promise that if anything
happens to this country, *you'll be all right*."

"Being as how you're a friend of Hitler?" I said.

"No, no, that's not it. But I promise you. *I have friends*."

"Hitler," I said, "will be the one who counts."

"Don't give me your answer *now*. I'll come to your room *tonight*."

"You have my answer. No."

She got up quickly and walked towards the door without looking around. I could tell by the way she walked she didn't think I
would hold out, and when she went out I caught a glimpse of
her profile. The set of her face was grim but satisfied, as if she
had done a good job under difficult circumstances and was con-
gratulating herself.

I said, "Nuts to you, Honorable Violet," secure in the knowledge that no one would understand me.

The dining room was almost deserted now and the only people near my table were the Portuguese couple, the dark girl who had dropped her purse, and her small fat friend, Pedro.

I found a certain pleasure in talking aloud so I looked straight at the girl and said, "I bet you go to the movies."

She smiled very faintly and replied in a crisp English voice. "Frequently. I adore Clark Gable and George—"

Pedro turned around and gave me a black scowl. Then he spoke roughly in Portuguese first to the girl, then to the waiter. The waiter came at a trot and made out a check. With a final frown in my direction Pedro got up and walked out keeping his hand on the girl's arm.

My omelette arrived, slightly jaundiced and watery in the middle. The waiter, stimulated by the tip I gave him, stood near the window and watched me with friendly interest. He had dark, intelligent eyes, and he looked as if he might lean over at any moment and quote Emily Post at me in clear, accurate English. I stood it as long as I could.

"Can you speak English?" I asked.

"Manuel," he said with a broad smile.

"No English at all, Manuel?"

"Manuel Henriques."

"Mine is Elizabeth Lane," I said. "Now beat it."

I made a gesture which he interpreted as meaning that I wanted my check. I didn't argue. I was glad to get away from the omelette. I went out and collected my key and went upstairs.

Since I had expected to be in Lisbon no longer than two days I had taken the best room I could get. It was on the second floor and the front window boasted a view of the Largo de Camões, the small square connecting the Avenida da Liberdade with the Rocio. I had a private bathroom, an easy chair, a radio and a telephone. To offset these advantages, the water in both hot and cold taps was lukewarm, the radio didn't work, the telephone was useless because I couldn't speak the language, and the towels never looked quite clean. I strongly suspected the chambermaid removed the towels each day, ran an iron over them, and brought them back.

She was there when I walked in, padding around in felt slippers, taking an occasional swipe at the furniture with her duster.

She was fat, slow and ugly, and every time she went in to clean the bathroom she made small noises in the back of her throat which evidently indicated she disapproved of bathing.

That day she seemed a little more cheerful than usual. She kept pointing towards the locked door which led into the adjoining room, and giggling.

"Maria," I said, "you've been hitting the bottle again."

She chose to construe this as meaning she was to leave and not bother finishing my room. I tried to explain but Maria was an opportunist and was already steaming down the hall.

I looked at the door which connected my room and the next and wondered what was so funny. The other room had been empty for several days. I decided that Maria was giggling because it was still empty and therefore didn't require cleaning. It was the sort of joke which would appeal to a Portuguese servant.

I walked over to the door and put my ear to the keyhole. Someone was in the next room. There was a sound of breathing, quick, heavy breathing like a series of snorts. I moved my ear to make room for my eye. The lock was the old-fashioned kind with a good sized opening.

What I saw was the end of a bed and one foot dangling over the edge. It was a girl's foot clad in a black suede shoe. As I watched, the foot moved a little and the snorting noises ceased.

I stood up, feeling uneasy and puzzled. That foot looked familiar and that room had been empty.

I picked up the telephone and poured my whole vocabulary into it. "Senhor! Senhor!"

"Senhor Mendez speaks," came the smooth voice of the manager. "Is it that anything ails you?"

Mendez was a Portuguese who had learned English in France. The result was often confusing. But I welcomed him now, he was the only member of the hotel staff who spoke adequate English.

I opened my mouth to ask him if anyone had taken the room adjoining mine. At the same instant I heard footsteps through the door. I felt like a fool. Of course the room was booked, and the girl who had booked it had simply lain down for a rest. Now she was awake, walking around in her room.

I stalled off the concierge by saying, "There's no hot water, Senhor."

The footsteps stopped and began again. They were coming towards my door. Well, that was all right. Perhaps the girl was simply investigating my room through the keyhole as I had investigated hers.

"The water is dangerously hot," said Senhor Mendez, "in some rooms. Perhaps not in your room, Miss Lane, but certainly in some rooms it is assuredly dangerously hot."

I hung on to Mendez and kept my eye on the door. The knob began to turn slowly.

"Only this morning," Mendez went on, "I said to Maria, 'Maria, with the water as dangerously hot as it is, you must exercise caution.' "

"Put that phone down!"

The door had opened quickly and noiselessly. I was looking into the barrel of an automatic. That was all I saw at first, just the automatic pointing at me very steadily. I let out a gasp.

"You may well be transfixed with astonishment," Senhor Mendez said warmly. "But that is what I said, 'Of a certainty, Maria, the pipes will collapse—' "

"Put it down," the man repeated. He moved the automatic to emphasize his command. "Now!"

I dragged my eyes away from the gun and put the telephone receiver back on the hook. The click it made was a horribly final sound.

I forced myself to look up again. The man was watching me warily. He looked young and desperate. His face had a shiny pallor and his eyes, almost hidden by the brim of a battered felt hat, were frightened, almost bewildered. He moved his head slightly, and I had a glimpse of red hair under the hat. That was how I recognized him, by his hair—his face seemed different from that of the young man who had picked up a purse and said "That's quite all right. Sorry I don't speak Portuguese."

"Who are you?" he asked hoarsely.

I took a deep breath and practised voice control. The result was good. I sounded almost bored.

"Elizabeth Lane. Sorry, I didn't quite catch your—"

His face didn't change. "This your room?"

I said, "Yes."

"American?"

I nodded. "New York. Same as you."

His eyes narrowed. "How do you know?" But he didn't wait for an answer. He pointed with his free hand towards the door that he'd come through. "This supposed to be locked?"

"Of course." My voice control was no longer working so well and I had to clench my hands together to keep them from shaking. "It's always locked."

"Not today." He looked at me and again I had the impression he was trying desperately to fit me into some puzzle. "How long have you been here?"

"Two weeks," I said. "I'm leaving tomorrow morning."

"Leaving?" He tasted the word and liked it. "Yeah? By Clipper?"

I nodded. I didn't like the way he was watching me, speculatively.

"The room next door is mine," he said.

"Indeed?"

"Yeah, indeed," he said. "Want to see it?"

"No."

"I must insist."

His way of insisting was hard to resist. He took a step forward and gestured with the automatic.

I said, "Oh well, if you insist," and got up. My knees folded but I stiffened them again and walked slowly towards the door. The automatic followed me.

"Like it?" he said.

"Very cozy—" My mouth closed with a snap.

There was a girl lying on the bed. She was naked except for a pair of stockings and black suede shoes. She was looking towards me, her eyes open in surprise, but she made no move to pull the sheet over her.

The young man was looking over my shoulder. He said, "Know the lady?"

My knees really folded this time. I sat down on the floor.

"I asked you if you knew the lady," he repeated. "Don't be afraid of hurting her feelings. She's stone deaf and stone blind, and damn near stone cold."

His voice was cruel and bitter.

My tongue lolled around my mouth fumbling for words. But I could only nod at him.

"Who is she?"

"I don't know," I whispered.

He bent over and put his free hand roughly on my shoulder. "Get up. Go and sit in that chair."

I didn't move.

"Get over to that chair!"

I whispered, "You wouldn't—dare—shoot."

"That's right, I wouldn't," he said. "But I might crack your skull. Move."

I moved, half-crawling, half-walking. When I reached the chair I began to cry. Without a word the young man wheeled round and went into the bathroom. When he came out he was carrying a glass of water.

"Cry into this," he said nastily.

I drank the water and blew my nose. The diversion calmed me and my voice came back in a rush.

"I don't know her. I saw her at the desk before lunch."

"I picked up her purse," he said.

"Yes. And—"

"And what?"

"I heard her say something to you, something in English."

The sweat was beading on his forehead.

"What was it?"

"It sounded like 'George Tobacco.' "

"That's what I thought," he said. "But she couldn't have said it because I'd never seen her before in my life. I've never been in Lisbon before and I've never seen this girl before. Do you understand what this means?"

"Sure," I said. "It means you're scared silly."

His face relaxed. For a minute I thought he was going to smile. "Scared silly. That's right. I've got a corpse in my bed. And last night—"

"Not another one last night?" I said dryly, "Who knows? Maybe I'm on tonight's program."

"Last night," he went on, paying no attention to my tone, "I was standing on the platform between two cars of the train, getting a breath of air. The door at the side was open and the train was travelling at full speed."

"And somebody pushed you."

"That's right. Somebody pushed me."

He said it without emphasis, almost without interest, as if he'd given up hope of convincing me and didn't care whether I believed him or not.

But I did believe him. I believed him so much that I lost my voice, it stuck in my throat like a cold lump of fear.

"I got hold of the railing," he said, still in that flat voice, "and here I am."

"Who—who was it?"

"The pusher?" He shrugged. "I don't know. I'm not even worried about that. What I want to know first is, why?" He glanced towards the bed, his eyes angry. "And why this girl? Why this girl?"

I turned my head away. "Because she spoke to you," I said.

"Again why?" He looked at me, almost hesitantly. "You didn't—"

"I didn't," I said as calmly as possible. "I don't even know how she was—was killed."

"Opium in some form. Probably morphine. Look at her eyes."

"No, I won't," I said unsteadily. "No."

"Pinpoint pupils."

"Please. I don't want to hear about it. Let me go back to my room."

"Let you!" He gave a hard laugh and replaced the automatic in his pocket. "Stage prop. No cartridges. Go on back to your room."

"Don't order me around," I said feebly. "What—what are you going to do with—that?"

"Do?" His eyes narrowed. "What in hell can I do? Any suggestions?"

"The broom closet."

"Go on."

"It's at the end of the corridor. It's big enough—for a body."

There was a long silence after that. I sat looking down at my hands, feeling guilty and angry and frightened at the same time. The broom closet. That was no place for this girl with her dark beautiful hair and her eyes, gentle and surprised in death. Naked and dead in a broom closet—

I put my hands over my eyes.

"Yeah, I know," the young man said. "You feel like hell for suggesting that. But it might save my life, if that means anything to you."

"It doesn't!"

"Well, all right, it doesn't. How far is this closet?"

"A couple of yards beyond my room. Would she—be heavy?"

He didn't answer that. He said crisply, "Will you help?"

"Me! No, please."

"Okay. Go on back and relax. And thanks for the tip."

I got up and moved towards the door. I didn't look around but I heard him walk to the bed and I heard the squeak of springs as he bent over the girl.

"Wait," I said. "Sometimes people—I mean, this is a busy corridor sometimes."

"That's what I meant by helping," he said coldly. "I don't need any two by four blonde to help me carry—Oh well, skip it."

"I'll let you know if the corridor's clear," I said and went back into my own room.

I stopped in front of the bureau for a minute to remove the traces of tears. Anger and humiliation had stung the color into my cheeks. The reaction had set in—I called myself a fool and a dupe—but I went out into the corridor anyway.

It was empty and I began to whistle "You're Okay." The door of the young man's room opened slightly. At the same instant another door opened further down the hall and a small fat man emerged carrying a straw hat. An American diplomat, now gone from the hotel, had introduced the fat man to me as Mr. Henhoeffer, an ex-German ex-banker.

"Oh, Mr. Henhoeffer," I said shrilly.

The fat man turned and peered suspiciously in my direction. When he recognized me his face splintered into smiles.

"Isn't this a lovely day for a walk?" I cried, walking towards him. He waited for me. Even his smile didn't hide his surprise—I had had to shake him off a number of times during the past two weeks.

He spoke English of a sort. He said, "Luffly. Almost as luffly as a certain young lady."

"Oh, you old flatterer," I yelled.

I was right up to him now, close enough to see his eyes, pig-small and stone-dead behind his smile.

I lowered my voice. "I was just going for a walk around the Rocio."

"I, too," Mr. Henhoeffer said warmly. "Perhaps we could go together?"

He held out his arm gallantly. I took it and nearly dragged him towards the steps. Mr. Henhoeffer, still surprised but willing, palpitated along beside me while I babbled inanities about the broadening effects of travel.

At the bottom of the steps I dropped his arm, murmured an excuse about forgetting my purse, and went back to the second floor, leaving a patiently puzzled Mr. Henhoeffer at the desk.

I walked down the hall, past Mr. Henhoeffer's room and the room that I knew belonged to the Honorable Violet, and stopped in front of the young man's door. I hissed gently through the crack.

He opened the door. He had wrapped the Portuguese girl in a sheet and flung her over his shoulder. He looked pale and grim and hot. It was only a few yards to the broom closet. I stayed in the corridor keeping my eyes glued to the top of the steps.

It was all over pretty fast. The man came back wiping his forehead with his handkerchief.

"Okay," he said. "Thanks."

When I hesitated he swung round sharply. "Okay. Now pretend you've never seen me."

"That suits me fine," I said.

"For your own good."

He put his handkerchief back in his pocket beside the gun. I noticed then he was still carrying his newspaper jammed into his other pocket. He saw me looking at it and ripped it out savagely and thrust it in front of my face.

On the front page was a picture of a middle-aged man in uniform and the caption in French: "Admiral Diamant a Suicide."

"My last interview," the young man said harshly. "I seem to be hard to take. Typhoid Tom Ross of the New York Examiner."

"You are hard to take, Mr. Ross," I said and walked away. I collected my purse and key from my room and went downstairs.

At the desk Senhor Mendez was telling Mr. Henhoeffer that Americanos were very, very reckless, they demanded the water hot to the point of pipe collapse.

"Baths," he said. "Baths. Always baths."

"I'm not reckless," I said, handing him my key. "I'm going out for a walk to give the pipes a chance to collapse in my absence."

The walk itself was enjoyable, the air windless and warm and scented with roses and camellias. Mr. Henhoeffer was not so enjoyable. He was, it developed shortly, addicted to pinching and heavy-handed compliments. He said he was crazy about Yankee girls (he pronounced it Yonky) they were as tortuous and intriguing as Lisbon itself.

We walked around Rocio Square which, Mr. Henhoeffer informed me, was also called Roly Poly Square because of the pavement. It was paved with black and white pebbles in an undulating snake-like design that made me a little seasick. The traffic was very heavy and Mr. Henhoeffer found it necessary to take my arm to thrust me out of the way of the innumerable taxis and trams, and to guide me past the hawkers, the shoeshiners, the cameramen and the vendors of lottery tickets who approached us in swarms.

From the Rocio we went into the Praca de Figueira where the market thronged with bare-footed peasants carrying huge baskets on their heads. The smell here was not so pleasant—fish, sweat and rotting food. The food made Mr. Henhoeffer very sad.

"So much vitamins," he said. "So much calories going to waste with poor hungry France a few hundred miles away."

"It's not your fault, Mr. Henhoeffer," I said kindly. "Cheer up."

"Never again will I cheer up," Mr. Henhoeffer said, pinching my arm.

I didn't argue. I just started to walk back to the hotel as fast as I could with Mr. Henhoeffer wheezing along beside me.

I said, "You were in the dining room for lunch?"

He looked at me sharply. "No. I was indisposed. I was in my room. Why do you ask?"

"I didn't see you there," I said. "I just wondered."

"After the concentration camp my stomach is weak." He patted his stomach tenderly.

I said, "Let's go back and see if the hotel has blown up."

He grabbed my arm. We both stopped. I saw that his face was very pale. "Blown up? You fear the war will come to this country?"

"The pipes," I said.

"The pipes." He let out his breath. "Ah, yes, the pipes."

He walked on without speaking for some time. Then he began to tell me how Herr Hitler was ruining the women of Germany, how they had all lost their figures by working in the fields and factories, and how they were all enceinte.

We were back at the Largo de Camôens by this time and the hotel was almost directly across the road. But Mr. Henhoeffer stopped in front of a small shop which bore the sign: "American and English Magazines and Cigarettes." The windows were grimy and the magazines were piled haphazardly on top of each other. At the front of the window were some photographs of American motion picture stars. It was to these that Mr. Henhoeffer directed his full attention. For the moment I was the forgotten woman, so I amused myself by strolling into the store and buying a package of cigarettes.

Standing in front of the counter with his back to me was Tom Ross. He was leafing through a copy of Punch.

Behind the counter stood a tall, cadaverous, middle-aged Englishman carrying on a one-sided conversation with Tom Ross in cockney.

" 'E wasn't any too pleased—Yes, miss?"

I told him what I wanted and waited for Tom Ross to turn around and speak. He didn't. He merely raised his head, gave me a blank disinterested stare, and went back to his Punch.

I started to speak, but the Cockney didn't give me a chance. He explained the tax on cigarettes and magazines, letting his h's drop where they would.

Outside, Mr. Henhoeffer came to and looked around and missed me. Then he waddled into the store. He and the Cockney greeted each other effusively.

"I gort a beaut," the Cockney announced with a broad wink. Mr. Henhoeffer leaned over the counter. "What is it?"

"Greta Garbo," said the Cockney.

Mr. Henhoeffer's face fell. "Not Myrna Loy?"

"Oo's Myrna Loy?" the Cockney said contemptuously. "Now Greta Garbo—"

Greta Garbo was duly wrapped and paid for. I took Mr. Henhoeffer's arm and we went out followed by the Cockney's injunctions to "come again soon."

At the desk of the hotel I ditched Mr. Henhoeffer and wandered into the main reading room. It was comfortably fitted with small desks and imitation leather chairs. In one of the chairs, almost hidden by a potted palm tree, was the Honorable Violet. She was writing a letter. When I walked over to her she put her hand over the letter, not very subtly.

"I won't peek," I said. "I just came over to tell you that my answer is still no and will continue to be no."

She stood up, staring at me, and said in her honorable voice: "My dear young lady! What *are* you talking about?"

"The ticket."

"What ticket?" she demanded. "I'm sure I haven't the faintest idea what you're talking about!"

I looked around the room. There was no one else within hearing distance.

"I must ask you to stop bothering me," the Honorable Violet said haughtily. "I know you are having a difficult time obtaining a berth on the Clipper, but there is absolutely nothing I can do for you."

She sat down and resumed her letter. I walked away very fast. I got my key from Mendez and went up to my room. I was trembling with anger.

Keeping my eyes turned away from the broom closet, I unlocked my door and went inside. The afternoon sun was pouring in both windows giving the room an appearance of artificial gaiety. I sat down on the edge of the bed.

I thought of home and the naked dead girl in the broom closet and the shiny pallor of Tom Ross' face. I thought of Violet Featherstone as I'd seen her before lunch steadily watching the door, of the fat Portuguese Pedro.

I was back at the girl again. I remembered her smile, her soft voice, the twitch of her foot as she died.

I felt the tears pressing hard on my eyes, tears of anger and fear and bewilderment and self-pity. And homesickness. Tomorrow seemed far away. I wanted to leave then, to get away from them all. Then I heard the noise in Tom Ross' room and the whisper through the keyhole:

"Miss Lane?"

I jumped up and opened the door.

He came in, this time without his hat and gun. He looked excited and more hopeful, and even managed a grin.

"Sorry," he said.

"What for? Sit down."

He sat down warily on the small chair beside the telephone table. I could tell from the way he watched me that something important had happened to him, and he didn't know whether to trust me or not.

"Who's your friend?" he asked with elaborate casualness.

"What friend?" I said coldly. "If you mean the man I went out with to save your skin, his name is Henhoeffer. He used to be a banker in Germany and he collects pictures of American actresses."

"What did you talk about?"

I stared at him. "We talked about me, and Lisbon and the great army of pregnant women in Germany. Now tell me all about yourself."

He ignored the irony. He said gravely. "I left Vichy last night. I have orders to return home. I wanted one really good interview to take back with me, and I got one yesterday. With Admiral Diamant."

He paused and took out the copy of the newspaper containing the story of Diamant's suicide.

"We talked impersonally- -about Petain and the possibility of the Nazis demanding the French fleet, the ordinary things a correspondent wants to know. Then he told me he was going on leave soon and we began talking about holidays. He had been in Central America, he said. He owned a small island near Martinique. He had friends in New York and gave me a couple of telephone numbers."

He was quiet for so long that I thought he'd forgotten me. I took out a cigarette and lit it.

"I wrote down the telephone numbers along with the rest of the interview and went back to my hotel to pack. Diamant was killing himself while I was packing. The paper says he had been despondent for some time. He left no suicide note."

I looked at the picture of Diamant. He was a fat, cheerful looking man with shrewd little eyes.

"He wasn't despondent," Tom Ross said. "He was excited and talkative, not a suicidal type, and certainly not the type to kill himself without explaining at length why he was doing it."

"So?" I said.

"So he was killed," Tom said. "The rest of it you know. Someone tried to push me off the train. When that didn't work, someone killed the girl and put her in my room."

"Why?" I asked.

"The police," Tom replied. "If I were arrested for murder I'd be in Portugal for some time, maybe forever. And somebody wants me here very badly."

My voice came out thin and high. "They'll try again."

"That's right."

"Are you—being careful?"

He really grinned that time. "Yeah, I'm being careful as hell. The automatic is no longer a stage prop. It contains bullets. The problem is, what do I shoot at?"

"Where did you get the bullets?"

He took a long time to answer. It was as if he had closed the shutters over his face and only his eyes peered out, wary, and suspicious.

"So you're a singer?" he said at last.

"Of a sort," I said. "Who told you?"

"A friend."

"Then you have friends?" I almost added, "Besides me."

He said carefully, "I had two friends. One of them is dead."

"The girl?"

"Yes."

"But you'd never seen her before."

"No."

I got up and walked impatiently towards the window. "All right. Don't tell me. I didn't want to get mixed up in your own personal little mess. I don't care if the whole French fleet scuttles itself. You'd better go back to your room. I want to pack."

I looked out the window. There were no sounds of departure behind me. I turned around and found Tom Ross watching me.

"Well?" I said.

"I located Mr. George," he said at last.

"Mr. George?"

"George Tobacco."

I could feel my face stiffening, the suspicion pouring through my body like liquid air. "Well," I said. "Quick work."

"You didn't do so badly yourself," he said.

"Me?"

"Or did your friend Henhoeffer do it for you?"

I managed a cold laugh. "We can't seem to trust each other. Why try?" When he didn't answer I added, "I don't know any George Tobacco, take it or leave it."

" 'I gort a beaut,' " Tom quoted.

"The Cockney?" I said.

"Yes."

He paused to let it sink in. I remembered the grimy windows, the piles of dusty magazines, the photographs. I remembered the tall, thin Englishman giving me my change out of a cash register, and over the cash register the small sign: E. George, Tobacco.

I kept my voice casual. "Well, it's a small world. What did George Tobacco have to say?"

"He said," Tom replied, "that I'm to lock my door, keep my windows closed, carry a gun and stay away from strangers until I get to Cintra in the morning and board the Clipper."

"Sound advice. Hadn't you better take it and stop pouring your story into my unwilling ears?"

"Yeah, but I may not get to Cintra."

I raised one brow. "So?"

"You will, though."

"So?"

He said nastily, "Stop the bored-and-beautiful act, Lizzie Lane. We're playing bombs, not marbles."

"Bombs?" I whispered. I sounded scared and I didn't like that, so I added, "So you're Tom Ross, the famous international spy."

"I'd forgotten how wise you wise girls are. Now that you've reminded me you can skip it. And listen. The chances of me getting away are small. Your chances are better if you're careful, if you don't recognize me in front of anyone, if you can keep your mouth buttoned."

"All right," I said. "What do I do?"

"You phone down to the desk and tell the desk clerk you've discovered this door is unlocked. Make a fuss about it—it's a natural thing to do and it may help to detract suspicion from you."

"Suspicion?"

"That you've had anything to do with me."

"But how will anyone else find out about the fuss I am about to make?" I demanded.

Tom said, "There's hardly a desk clerk in Europe who isn't being paid by the Nazis or the French or the British or all three. You tell the clerk and leave the rest to him."

I was impressed but didn't admit it. "And where is my Secret Message?"

"Better phone down now," he said. "And one more thing."

"Yes?"

"Try having dinner tonight with your fat friend Henhoeffer."

"Why?"

"So I'll know where he is," Tom said, and walked back into his own room, shutting the door firmly behind him.

I picked up the telephone and called Senhor Mendez. I didn't have to do any faking to sound angry.

I bellowed, "I have just made an appalling discovery. Come up here at once and bring your keys." Then I hung up.

Mendez arrived in three minutes and heaved himself into my room. I pointed to the door which connected my room with Tom's.

"That," I said haughtily, "is unlocked, and there is someone in the room. It sounds like a man."

Mendez flourished his keys, flung himself at the door, locked it, bowed three times in my direction and said he was transfixed, horrified, and struck by thunder. He knew exactly, precisely how I felt. How could it have happened! What great grossness had been committed! Could I forgive him?

It was a question of forgiving him or listening to another speech, so I said, "Yes."

Still he was not satisfied. There *was* a man in the adjoining room, but certainly. But such a man! An Americano, a fine young man, of unimpeachable character. Now would I forgive him?

"I forgive everybody," I said weakly.

"And you have enough hot water?"

"Plenty," I said. "Gallons of it." I looked pointedly towards the door but still he lingered, his sad brown eyes regarding me woefully. He was smaller than I'd thought, no higher than my ear. His skin was very dark with the deep red-brown flush on his cheeks that I'd seen on peasant women at the market.

"Miss Lane is happy here?" he said.

"Happy isn't quite the word."

"We are too crowded, too busy to do our best for you at present. We are the bottleneck of Europe," he added proudly. "Perhaps Miss Lane will return later when we are no longer the bottleneck?"

I said I'd do my best and put my hand on the doorknob. This time he took the hint and bowed himself out. I stood in the doorway and watched him waddle down the hall to the main staircase.

I was about to close my door again when I heard someone shouting in Portuguese in one of the rooms across the hall. A few seconds later the Honorable Violet's door opened abruptly and Maria sailed into the corridor, her face twisting into grimaces like the India rubber man at Coney Island. The Honorable Violet came out, too, saw me standing there, and instantly became a lady again.

"Filthy dogs," she said to me, with a contemptuous nod at Maria. "I told her she'd have to do my room properly or I'll report her to the concierge."

"Did you," I said politely.

Maria giggled and shuffled off towards the broom closet.

"I hate dirt," said the Honorable Violet.

Words stuck in my throat. I wanted to yell at Maria to stop her, but she kept on shuffling towards the closet.

"I hate dirt, too," I shouted at the Honorable Violet. She looked a little surprised and annoyed, as if I were stealing her lines.

Maria had her hand on the doorknob of the closet. She gave it a leisurely turn. The door opened. The next instant Maria had fallen forward on her knees and was raising her hands to heaven and shouting at the top of her lungs.

The Honorable Violet emerged into the corridor.

"Wh-what's she saying?" I managed to gasp.

"She's praying," Violet said curtly. "Maria!" She shouted at Maria in Portuguese, but Maria only redoubled her cries. Extremely annoyed, Violet walked towards her and gave her a stinging blow across the cheek. Then she looked inside the closet and saw the girl standing propped up in the corner shrouded in the sheet.

She staggered back and fell against Maria.

Maria was wailing, *"Em pe! Em pe!"*

Violet picked herself up and began brushing off her skirt quite calmly.

Mr. Henhoeffer now joined us. He was in his shirtsleeves and looked as if he had just awakened. Then the door of the room beside Violet's opened abruptly and a man came out. He was quite young but he looked terribly ill. His face was grey and his suit hung loosely over his bones. I recognized him as the man who had come into the hotel with Tom Ross before lunch.

"What's the matter here?" he asked in French. His voice was sick, too. He looked across the hall at me and repeated his question.

Tom completed the group. He came out of his room, yawning and stretching in a convincing manner.

"There's a dead woman in there," said the Honorable Violet in English. "Maria is praying because she thinks it's Don Francisco Tregian. You know, the standing corpse of the Englishman buried here?" Violet was enjoying herself putting on an exhibition of the well-known British aplomb.

Tom and the Frenchman were at the closet door taking the girl out and laying her on the floor of the hall. Maria had simply vanished. Mr. Henhoeffer was absently pinching my arm and saying, "Tut, tut, tut." None of us paid any attention to the

Honorable Violet's account of the Englishman who'd been buried standing up.

She caught on finally and changed her tune. "I shall inform Senhor Mendez," she announced. "I expect this is a matter for the police. In any case we must all keep cool."

She tripped down the step. For all her self-assurance, her face was the color of putty and her knees wobbled as she walked.

Tom got to his feet and wiped his forehead. "I could stand a drink. Anyone care to join me?"

Mr. Henhoeffer practically dropped me on the floor in his rush for a free drink.

The Frenchman hesitated. He looked as if he was going to faint. "Rochat?" Tom said.

"Thank you," Rochat said. "Yes, I don't think a drink would matter now."

We all went into Tom's room. I was terrified that Tom might have left some evidence of the girl in his room. But the bed was neatly made and the pillows shaken out.

"Sit down, Miss—" Tom said.

"Lane," I said. Tom introduced the Frenchman as Pierre Rochat, a French refugee he'd met on the train. Mr. Henhoeffer, drink in hand, introduced himself.

Rochat drank slowly, coughing a great deal between sips. I suspected he had T.B.

"Are you waiting for the Clipper?" I asked him.

He said no, and pointed to his chest. "They do not want people like me in your country."

There was a long and uncomfortable silence broken finally by Rochat himself. "I don't blame them. I don't blame anyone for anything. We are all victims of an inexorable fate even as the young woman lying in the corridor."

There was another silence. Even Mr. Henhoeffer, with his third free drink, was lost in gloom. I was glad when I heard the sound of footsteps in the corridor outside the door and the babble of voices all talking at once. Tom went over and opened the door.

Rochat made a hopeless gesture with his hands. "The police," he said to me. "Possibly we shall be put in jail." Rochat was not a cheerful man.

"Why should they put us in jail? We haven't done anything," I said.

"Fate," Rochat said tersely. "Dead women do not walk into broom closets."

"I haf been in many jails," Mr. Henhoeffer mused. "Some I like, some I do not like. Have you effer been in jail, Miss Lane?"

I said no, the police weren't smart enough to catch me.

"You joke," Mr. Henhoeffer said glumly. "Ha, ha, ha."

Tom came in again, followed by two men in uniform. One seemed to be an ordinary traffic cop, the kind I'd seen standing at street corners directing traffic with their clubs. He was quite tall for a Portuguese and had a small, black Chaplin mustache perched under his nose. His name was De Castro.

The smaller one, Duarte, was a thin, shrivelled little man with a lazy, insolent smile. He looked like a street urchin, and it was a shock to hear his voice. It was pure Oxford. "I am the official interpreter for the police department," he announced, smiling around the room at each of us. "Mr. De Castro cannot speak English. Mr. De Castro is the investigator in authority."

De Castro stared at us woodenly, then broke into a torrent of Portuguese. Duarte listened to him, never losing his smile.

He translated. "Mr. De Castro would like to know if any one of you recognize the unfortunate woman?" He pronounced it unfawtunit.

We were all silent. At last I said, "I don't know her but I saw her in the dining room at lunch. She was lunching with a man, a Portuguese. She called him—"

"Ah?" Duarte said. He hurled the words at De Castro. Both of them stood looking down at me as I huddled in my chair.

"Who discovered the body?"

"The chambermaid," I said unsteadily. "Her name is Maria. Miss Featherstone and I were in the hall and—"

Again he interrupted. "Where is Maria?"

"I don't know," I said. "She just—vanished."

"Ah?" Duarte said. "It is an unfortunate business all around. Mr. De Castro does not like to have foreigners murdered in Lisbon."

"Foreigners?" I echoed. I could see Tom's jaws tightening and Rochat leaning forward in his chair.

"The girl was not Portuguese?" Rochat said.

"Hardly," Duarte smiled.

At this point Violet came in with Mendez and Manuel, the waiter. Apparently Manuel had seen the girl's body. He was shaking all over and his skin had a peculiar, purplish-brown tinge. Mendez, trying to emulate Violet's calmness, stood stiff and dignified beside Manuel.

He said apologetically to us all, "Manuel has a tenderness of heart. You will forgive him."

Violet had sailed over to the two policemen and was giving them what sounded like a large piece of her mind. When she had finished the policeman nodded gravely and Violet turned to the rest of us and said:

"I have just informed these two louts that it is preposterous to suspect any of us of this—this murder—"

"Murder," Mendez repeated weakly. The starch had gone out of him and he was sagging almost as badly as Manuel.

"—simply because we live in this particular corridor," Violet continued. "None of us would be so foolish as to leave evidences of the crime in a place which would connect us with it immediately. I, for one, have never even seen this girl before."

I handed it to Violet. She was one of the best liars I've ever heard.

"That's funny," I said coldly. "She was in the dining room at lunch, and so were you."

Violet regarded me stonily. "Miss Lane apparently knows the girl. Go on, Miss Lane."

"Ask the waiter," I said.

Violet did. She shouted at Manuel in Portuguese. Duarte watched her lazily.

"Manuel says," Violet translated, "that the girl had lunch in the dining room with some man. That makes everything quite simple, I think. The man gave her the poison and escaped."

"Poison?" Tom said. "What kind of poison?"

Violet's face had turned a lustrous light green. I thought she was going to faint, but she put out her hand and grasped the back of Rochat's chair to steady herself.

Duarte said, "Mr. De Castro is of the opinion that morphine was administered to the girl."

Tom was leaning against the wall, looking bored. "Yeah? Why

not find the man then, as Miss Featherstone suggests? Perhaps Manuel could identify him."

Manuel couldn't have identified his own mother. He was standing with his face to the wall crying loudly and without shame. The rest of us sat frozen with embarrassment. Mr. Rochat studied the ceiling and kept repeating, "*Lacrimae rerum, Lacrimae rerum.*"

So it went on. We were in the room for another hour listening to Violet's haughty protests and Manuel's crying, and Mendez's attempts to explain the girl's death as a suicide. The policemen did not interrupt. At five o'clock De Castro yawned and walked to the door.

"Mr. De Castro is fatigued," Duarte said, and started to follow De Castro to the door.

"But nothing has been settled!" Violet cried. "What is our position? Are we free to leave?"

Duarte turned around and smiled at her. "You'll stay, of course." He included me in the order.

"You incompetent ape," I said. "You won't even let me tell my story. You keep interrupting. You didn't even ask the proper questions. You couldn't solve a murder if you had ten eye-witnesses."

I felt Rochat's hand pressing my arm. I shook him off.

"I've got a seat on the Clipper and I'm leaving tomorrow! I've been waiting for two weeks."

"You're young," Duarte said easily.

I opened my mouth to say more, but Rochat's fingers pressed tight around my wrist.

"Please control yourself," he said. "The Portuguese cannot be hurried."

Duarte grinned and went out, and that was that. We all straggled back to our rooms. The girl's body had been taken away but the sheet in which it had been wrapped lay beside the door of the broom closet in a crumpled heap. When I saw it my anger at the incompetence of the police boiled up in my throat. Incompetence—or worse, indifference.

And then I remembered something which had been nagging at me for the past two hours: Duarte hadn't even asked us our names! Yet he had called both Violet and me by name.

I remembered Tom's statement, "There isn't a desk clerk in Europe who isn't being paid by the Nazis or the French or the British. Or all three."

But not Mendez, I thought, pleasant ineffectual little Mendez.

"—bull fight," Mr. Henhoeffer was saying.

He was lingering beside my door, sad and not quite sober. I said "Pardon?"

"Would you go to the bullfight tonight?" he repeated.

I said I would if he could persuade Duarte to act as the bull, otherwise no.

Mr. Henhoeffer looked wistful. "A movie, perhaps? Or dinner?"

"Maybe," I said, and backed into my room and closed the door. I took off my shoes and lay down on the bed.

The afternoon was hot and moist by that time, and the air was filled with the rumble of trains, the incessant blare of taxi horns and the shouting of hawkers.

I shut my eyes and thought of the dead girl. She was English, Duarte had said. What was she doing in Lisbon? How had she known Tom Ross well enough to warn him? Why was she lunching with the fat Portuguese, Pedro?

Had he poisoned her then? Or had he poisoned her at all? I thought of Violet's remark, "The man gave her the poison and escaped." How had Violet known the girl was poisoned?

I was turning dozens of questions in my mind when I became aware, suddenly and horribly, that there was someone in the room with me.

Someone was breathing deeply and heavily. I couldn't tell where it was coming from, it was just there, the sound of breathing.

My eyes were still closed, and in my effort to keep them closed my eyelids fluttered madly. Other people might be able to get away with feigning sleep, but not I.

I opened my eyes expecting to see anything at all, a ghost, an animal, Duarte. I didn't expect what I did see—nothing, exactly nothing. But the breathing went on, evenly and heavily as before. The room was filled with sunshine and I could see into every corner, even into the clothes closet. There was no place where anyone could hide, except—

I leaped off the bed as if I'd been shot out of a cannon.

I said in a trembling but belligerent voice: "All right, you under the bed! What's the idea?"

There was a small snort and the sound of someone rolling over. I leaned over and looked under the bed. Maria was staring up at me, eyes rolling.

I was so weak with relief that I began to giggle. After a time Maria began to giggle, too. Her fat body shook with laughter, and the bed shook, too, because she was still under it. I don't know how long we laughed, me on my knees beside the bed and Maria lying under it. When I finally got myself reorganized I told her with gestures to come out and sit down. She came, slowly, still giggling and shaking and blinking the tears out of her eyes.

I sank into the chair beside the telephone table and my eyes fell on the telephone pad and pencil. Suddenly I had an idea which I have since regretted. I could speak neither Portuguese nor Spanish, but I could still write Spanish. And written Spanish is like written Portuguese. Now if Maria could read and write—

I picked up the pad and pencil and wrote in Spanish: "My name is Elizabeth Lane. What is your name?"

Maria nodded eagerly, took the pad, and reached for the pencil. She wrote slowly and laboriously, "Maria Henriques," and handed the pad back to me. Both of us were trembling with excitement, I because I was sure Maria could provide some useful information, Maria because she considered it a wonderful new game.

"Did you see the dead girl before?" I wrote.

Maria pointed to the door which led into Tom Ross' room and made motions of taking off her clothes. Then she wrote, "Love," and giggled some more. I let that pass and grabbed the pencil again.

"Do you know what the girl's name is?"

She shook her head.

"Was there anyone in the room with her?"

She shook her head again, not so vigorously this time.

"Anyone in the hall?"

She grinned, then drew down the corners of her mouth and threw up her head very haughtily. It was a perfect wordless description of the Honorable Violet.

"What was she doing?" I wrote.

Maria tossed her head around and made scolding sounds in her throat, then moved her hands as if she were sweeping. I was disappointed but I kept on.

"Did you see the girl go into Mr. Ross' room?"

She shook her head. Then she wrote, "I saw a tall man. He was coming out."

"Out of where?"

She imitated Violet again.

"Who was he?"

She didn't know.

"Is Manuel Henriques your husband?"

She nodded.

"Did he know the girl?" She shook her head. "Did Mendez know her?"

She made a dive for the pencil. "Mendez knows. The girl has been here before. She comes to eat. Manuel says so. Manuel tells me about her before. He says, a dark beautiful English lady. Under the bed I remember this. I know it is the same lady. English ladies are not dark and beautiful much."

She was exhausted with this effort and had to wipe the sweat off her forehead with her apron. She was beginning to look anxious too, as if she wanted to get away. She seemed frightened somehow by the mention of Mendez.

I wrote, "Will you tell me if Manuel tells you any more about the dead girl?"

She nodded and edged towards the door. I opened my purse and gave her all the Portuguese currency I had in my bag, a handful of escudos. Then I wrote, "Please don't tell the police about seeing the girl in Mr. Ross' room."

She took the money and nodded cautiously. I went to the door and peered into the hall. There was no one in sight, so I motioned to her to go out quickly. She lumbered out and went towards the stairs.

Back in my room I gathered up the sheets of the telephone pad and rapped very softly on Tom's door. I could hear him whistling Old Black Joe—"I'm coming. I'm coming, though my head is bending low"—and pretty soon the door opened and he came in, holding a penknife in his hand. I must have looked impressed, for he said:

"Practically the first thing you learn at prep school is how to pick locks with a knife. What do you want?"

I handed him the sheets. He scowled at them. "Well, what am I supposed to do? Eat them?"

"I'll translate if you like," I said smugly.

He sat in silence while I read off my conversation with Maria. Then he said, "Well, well," in a voice that sounded like Rochat's. It was hopeless, resigned.

"Too many people," he said, "know too many things."

I tried to make my voice crisp, but it wilted around the edges. "What of it? We're learning." He didn't answer, so I said, "Tom."

He raised his eyes. "Yeah?"

"I don't like that policeman. Or Violet Featherstone."

I told him about my conversation with her in the dining room.

"Write it down," he barked.

"What?"

"Everything she said."

"Why?" I asked, but he only frowned and handed me the pencil and an envelope. When I had finished I had something like this:

"I'm Violet Featherstone. My father is the Honorable Cecil Featherstone. Are you an American citizen? Are you expecting a seat on the Clipper? Are you anxious to get away? Most Portuguese can't read or are too lazy to read. There's no danger. I'll pay you ten thousand dollars for your seat on the Clipper. It's a matter of life or death. If anything happens to this country you'll be all right. I have friends. I'll come to your room tonight."

Tom read it. I could see the excitement leap into his eyes.

"What was her voice like?" he said sharply.

"Hoarse," I said. "Husky."

"Loud or soft?"

"Both. It seemed to be out of control. As if she had stage fright."

He seemed extremely pleased. "Loud and soft," he repeated softly.

He gathered up the envelope and the sheets of paper, put them in the ashtray and lit a match. When they had burned he ground the ashes up very fine. Then he broke one of my cigarettes in two, smoked both ends and left the butts in the ashtray.

"Neat little lad," I said.

He smiled wryly at me. "I'm learning," he said, "to be careful. But I might not learn in time."

"What do you mean?"

He adjusted his face to a careful blankness. "I mean that my interview with Admiral Diamant is gone."

"Gone?"

"Vanished. Taken out of my brief case. Except"—he smiled grimly—"the last page. The last page is in my head. I burned it after I found the girl."

"Why?" I whispered.

"Diamant's telephone numbers," he said.

There was a silence. I could hear my own breath rasping through my throat.

"The island?" I said at last. "Diamant's island."

Tom nodded. "He said he owned an island in the Caribbean near Martinique. I believed him. But I think the island has passed into Nazi hands."

"Martinique," I repeated.

"I believe Diamant was a patriot who decided that collaboration was the only possible course for France. Collaboration up to a point. But when the Germans bought, or swindled him out of, his island by their pseudo-legal methods, he balked—and died. When they took away his island he knew what it meant, America is next."

I made a feeble gesture of protest. He paid no attention.

"When I came in this afternoon I looked up Martinique in the gazetteer in the reading room. Latitude, 14° 46′ North, longitude 60° 53′ West. And the telephone numbers Diamant gave me were 1535 N and 6127 W. Repeat them."

I repeated them in a whisper.

"Again," he commanded.

I said them again and once again, 1535, 6127.

"Diamant's island is within bombing range of the Panama Canal. A Nazi submarine base in the Caribbean could play havoc with our shipping. Those numbers go to the Navy Department in Washington. Via me, if possible. If not, via you."

I swallowed hard and said, "What if they don't believe me? The Navy Department, I mean."

"I don't think," Tom said slowly, "that it will be a terrific surprise to them." He came over to me. "Take care of yourself," he said and kissed me on the mouth and was gone before I could say a word.

I sat there with my hand to my mouth and felt like crying. I heard the lock slipping into place behind Tom. I didn't move for a long time and then only because I heard a clock strike six.

I dragged myself out of the chair and began to dress for dinner. I was afraid even to go into the bathroom and take a bath. It was half-past six by the time I'd dressed and rubbed on rouge to cover my pallor. I think now the only thing that got me through that night was not patriotism, or courage, or my feeling for Tom or pity for the dead girl—it was my new white silk jersey dinner dress with the red cummerbund.

I locked my door and walked down the hall, the new dress swishing elegantly around my legs. Violet's door was partly open and I saw her standing in front of the mirror smoothing her hair. She turned around and scowled at me. I scowled back and went on walking.

At the desk I handed my key to Senhor Mendez. He was busy registering several new arrivals, three men and two women who talked in a language I didn't know, and who looked incredibly weary and dusty.

All the foreigners who came to the hotel looked tired, I thought.

Senhor Mendez took my key and told me how appalled, horrified, and so on, he was at the tragedy. He said it would ruin his business.

I said I didn't think so and looked pointedly at the hotel register crammed with names and addresses.

Senhor Mendez blushed slightly. "Now, of course, we are very busy. That is natural."

I was still glancing at the register. Every country in Europe was represented. The five who had just arrived were from Athens.

"Senhor," I said.

Mendez looked uneasy, as if he wanted me to go away. "Miss Lane, I am extremely occupied," he said.

"Senhor, I saw the girl who was murdered having her lunch here. You were at the desk. She went right past—"

He touched his forehead. "I have a memory the most execrable. I tell you from my heart—"

"I don't like what's happening around here," I said. "First that door was unlocked. Then the murder. What next?"

"Nothing next," he said weakly. "Most assuredly, Miss Lane, there will be nothing next."

He bustled away as Mr. Henhoeffer came up and handed in his key. Mr. Henhoeffer had squeezed himself into a dinner jacket that he must have bought before his stomach became bloated with hunger. He came at me in a series of little bounces.

"What a most delightful surprise, Miss Lane!" he cried.

I told him it was a small world.

"Let us not be serious," Mr. Henhoeffer said cheerfully. "Let us forget the world. I am most happy. First I see you, then I see Myrna Loy."

"Oh?" I said. "When did she blow in?"

Mr. Henhoeffer gave his three polite little laughs, ha ha ha, and said Myrna Loy was at the cinema. We went into the dining room.

Without waiting for the headwaiter I led Mr. Henhoeffer past the platform where a five-piece string orchestra was strumming out a garbled version of "Trees." We sat at the other end of the dining room, as far from the windows as I could get. I didn't want to have to look at the table where the dead girl had sat with Pedro at lunch time.

Mr. Henhoeffer calf-eyed me across the table. "Such a luffly dress, Miss Lane."

"Glad you like it," I said. "I dressed specially for you." I didn't add, as I wanted to, "So that Tom will know exactly where you are tonight, because he doesn't trust you."

"And I for you," Mr. Henhoeffer said with a sigh, looking down at his dinner coat stretched taut across his middle.

Mr. Henhoeffer had, happily, a one-track mind. When he was working on me he really worked. But as soon as the food arrived he forgot my existence and began to work his way methodically through the courses with the energy of a beaver cutting down trees.

The Honorable Violet came in late and alone. Her moments

before the mirror had been in vain—her hair still straggled at the back, her slip was showing and her lipstick was smeared. She ignored Mr. Henhoeffer and me and sat down, surveying the room and its occupants like a nasty tempered queen.

Mr. Henhoeffer was in no need of being entertained, having just ploughed into his second charlotte russe, so I had lots of time on my hands. I used it staring at Violet until she had to look up and acknowledge me. I smiled sweetly, and we called it quits.

I asked Mr. Henhoeffer if he was enjoying himself. He looked at me as if he'd never seen me before and said, "I beg your pardon?"

"That's all right," I said.

I spent the rest of the meal thinking how simple it would be to be married to Mr. Henhoeffer if you could keep him at the table most of the time. It wouldn't be at all simple to be married to Tom Ross, I thought grimly, it might even be hell.

But hell or not, I kept thinking about him and wondering whether he danced and how much time he spent dashing around foreign countries.

I felt a pinch on the back of my hand. Mr. Henhoeffer had returned to consciousness.

"You will need a coat," he said dreamily, thinking of the charlotte russe. "The night will be cool. Perhaps it will rain."

"I'll get one," I said.

Mr. Henhoeffer waited at the desk while I went upstairs. I heard Mr. Rochat in his room, coughing and repeating sonorous rhythmical sentences in French. I listened a minute, then rapped on his door. I heard the squeak of bedsprings as he got up. He opened the door, coughing and holding a handkerchief over his mouth.

"Is there anything I could—could get you?" I said feebly. "I heard you coughing."

"Nothing, thank you," he said in his sick voice. "You are very kind, Miss Lane."

I blushed and felt foolish and wished I had the brains to mind my own business.

He must have sensed my embarrassment, for he said kindly, "I think all Americans are kind. Perhaps it is because you are a young race, a naïve race. When you see someone who is—is dying like me—"

"Please," I said.

"—you think you can stave off fate. You do not believe in fate, in the inevitable. You all believe that if you are very good little boys and girls, St. Nicholas will fill your stockings." He made a funny little noise which might have been a laugh or a cough.

I was getting mad. I could listen quite comfortably to my father haranguing me on American complacency, but to hear this man who was dying—

I took a deep breath. "Fate is one thing," I said. "The ersatz stuff put up in cans by Mr. Hitler is another."

"Do not take it personally," Mr. Rochat said gently. "You will learn what I say is right."

I said "Bosh!" and slammed my door behind me. I strode over to the closet and grabbed a coat from the rack. As I did so a dress fell off its hanger onto the floor.

It was the beige dress I'd worn that afternoon, the one that I'd been too tired to put away, that I'd left *lying on top of the suitcase.*

Nothing else in the closet looked different. I went carefully through my suitcase then through the drawers of my bureau. The lid on a jar of cleansing cream had been screwed on crookedly, and when I took off the lid I found the cream smooth and even. Not the way I'd left it.

I tried the door leading into Tom's room and found it locked. Then I looked under the bed just to make sure. I would have felt better, or at least no worse, if I'd found someone in the room.

I sat down at the telephone table and tried to think. My room had been searched and the searcher hadn't been any too skillful. Perhaps he'd been in a hurry. Or perhaps I had been intended to find evidences of the search, as a warning to me.

My eyes were fixed on the telephone pad, blankly at first, and then with growing horror. Because it was perfectly smooth, the thin onionskin paper was smooth, and it shouldn't have been smooth! Maria and I had written on that pad. I dimly remembered removing the sheets we had written on and seeing the pencil indentations on the blank sheet below.

The blank sheet was gone now.

"We don't stand a chance against them," I heard my own voice whispering. "We're amateurs. Tom won't be coming back."

I tried to think of what Maria and I had written last, what marks would be clearest on the blank sheet. When I remembered I wished I hadn't. It was: "Please don't tell the police about seeing the girl in Mr. Ross' room."

It couldn't have been any worse. And that thought, strangely enough, made me feel less scared and like shouting "Do your damnedest!" at everyone.

I flung my red coat over my arm, went out into the hall and relocked my door. Downstairs I found Mr. Henhoeffer and Senhor Mendez discussing the German campaign in Russia. They broke off sharply when they saw me and Senhor Mendez arranged his face for my benefit into an arch smile.

"You attend the cinema and not the bull fight?" he said winningly.

I told him I didn't like bull fights.

"But the *espadas* are gentle with the bulls, very gentle," Mendez insisted. "We are not like the Spaniards. They are a viciously cruel race. Me, I do not like the Spaniards."

"Obviously not," I said. "Are you ready, Mr. Henhoeffer?"

Mr. Henhoeffer took my arm and we went off. I saw the Honorable Violet watching us from behind a palm tree in the lobby. As we passed her I said, "Boo!" very pleasantly and was rewarded by a haughty glare. I glared back.

Mr. Henhoeffer seemed puzzled by this exchange. "You do not like the English lady?" he asked.

"Of course I do," I said. "I just like to play games."

"Her father is what you Yonkies would call a big shot. He is in jail."

I stopped walking. "In jail?"

"Oh, yes. He is concentrated, interned, as you say, in England. He talked too much," Mr. Henhoeffer added sadly. "Senhor Mendez told me."

"What did he talk about?"

"Democracy," Mr. Henhoeffer said. "He didn't like it."

"Oh," I paused. "I think I remember reading about it. What is his name?"

"Herbert, I think it is. I recall it because it is like my own name, Herman. Herbert, Herman. Very alike, yes?"

I said "Yes," thinking of Violet's words at lunch: "My father is the Honorable Cecil Featherstone."

So what, I wondered. So the Honorable Violet was a congenital liar, or Mr. Henhoeffer's memory was bad.

The cinema was only a few blocks down the Avenida so we walked there. The air was heavy with the scent of roses. All I could think of was Tom and funerals and more funerals and Tom. Where had he gone? Why hadn't he locked himself in his room as Mr. George had advised?

The streets were filled with people on their way to movies or the bull fight, or just strolling. They all seemed friendly and happy and careless. Occasionally one of them called out at us seeing Mr. Henhoeffer's dinner jacket and my long dress and red coat.

At the door of the theatre we could hear a vast clamor from inside, whistles, shouts, boos and the stamping of feet.

We sat down near the back of the house. The newsreel was on, showing King George and Queen Elizabeth reviewing troops at Aldershot. The audience seemed to be nicely divided, half of them for and half of them against. Mr. Henhoeffer got into the spirit of the thing immediately and began to clap and shout, "Bravo!" After that we had a view of Hitler on the Russian front and Mr. Henhoeffer went into reverse and shouted some insulting sounding words in German. It was one of the noisiest evenings I ever spent.

We came out about ten-thirty and Mr. Henhoeffer invited me to have coffee at a sidewalk cafe. I agreed, chiefly because I was afraid to go back to the hotel, afraid Tom wouldn't be there and the police would.

Mr. Henhoeffer pulled out my chair with a little flourish. He ordered coffee and cognac and told me I was as pale and beautiful as a camellia. A couple of men sitting at the next table looked up when they heard us talking in English.

I said, "We mustn't speak so loudly. You never know who is listening."

"This is not Germany," Mr. Henhoeffer protested. "There is no Gestapo in Portugal, and I am only telling you how you are beautiful."

I changed the subject by asking him how he had gotten out of Germany.

"I left before the war," he said. "I had friends. And"—he looked at me pointedly—"I had money."

"Aren't you afraid?" I asked.

He thumped the table with his fist. "Never have I been afraid! The Nazis do not want me and I do not want them. We are agreed."

It sounded reasonable enough, from both viewpoints. It also sounded too easy, much too easy.

"Didn't they come after you?" I asked.

"Oh, poof!" Mr. Henhoeffer said petulantly. "Are all Yonky girls serious like you? I talk of your beauty and you talk of the Nazis."

I attached a smile to my face and looked around at the people near us. The first person I saw was Duarte. He was at a table a few yards away, watching me and smiling. I nodded distantly and turned aside.

A few seconds later I heard his voice in my ear. "You like our wine?"

"Are you following me?" I demanded.

Mr. Henhoeffer gave me a sickly grin, and told me I mustn't forget my manners. He had a real respect for the police, even Portuguese.

"I come here every night," Duarte said pleasantly. "To drink, to watch."

"Watch what?" I said, gulping.

"Oh, people. Like Mr. Henhoeffer here. Mr. Henhoeffer and I are old friends."

Mr. Henhoeffer smiled biliously and said nothing.

"You leave tomorrow," Duarte said to me. It didn't sound like a question or an order. It was a statement—with reservations: You leave tomorrow if you can, if you're alive.

I said, "I think we'd better go back now, Mr. Henhoeffer. It's late."

Duarte stood and watched us leave. I could feel his eyes boring into my back as I walked away.

Mr. Henhoeffer and I walked in silence for some time. I looked back once or twice to see if we were being followed.

Mr. Henhoeffer was rather annoyed. "You fear the policeman, Duarte?"

"He looks sly," I said.

"Oh, sly." He shrugged, dismissing slyness as one of the lesser evils of policemen.

"I don't believe he's the interpreter," I said. "I think he's the big shot himself, using De Castro as a screen, thinking he'll get more out of us."

Mr. Henhoeffer gave me a sharp glance. "That is very shrewd, Miss Lane. I, too, have considered it. But you have nothing to fear. Duarte has only to look at you to know you are as innocent as a flower."

I thought of the telephone pad, the sentence in Spanish in my handwriting: "Please don't tell the police about seeing the girl in Mr. Ross' room."

Innocent as a flower. I said, "You reassure me."

We had nearly reached the hotel now. Mr. Henhoeffer had recovered his amiability and was telling me about the bull fights he had seen in Porto. He said, "And to entice the bull out of the ring they surround him with beautiful beribboned cows."

I thought that was a lovely piece of whimsy. "Just like a bull," I said. "You men are all alike."

The hotel lobby was nearly deserted when we arrived. Violet was still propped against her palm tree. I wondered whether she'd been sitting there all evening, but Violet was not the type of person of whom you asked inane personal questions.

Mendez was not at the desk. His place had been taken by a young man who spoke beautiful French, but no English. I got my key from him and went up to my room alone. Mr. Henhoeffer had discovered he was out of cigarettes and had gone out again.

When I unlocked my door I found that the lights which I had left on were now turned off. A gust of warm air blew out into the corridor. It had a queer sweetish odor that I didn't recognize.

I stood there for a full minute, not daring to go inside. Then I closed my door quietly and went downstairs again, clinging to the bannister to steady myself. It was the sight of Violet Featherstone sitting beside the palm tree which calmed me somewhat. She was so aloof and contemptuous of her surroundings.

I swallowed my pride and walked straight over to her. "I know you don't like me and I'm not crazy about you either, but I want to talk to s-s-somebody," I said.

I was getting accustomed to surprises, but the Honorable Violet's next words nearly knocked me out. Without moving her head or her mouth a fraction of an inch, she hissed:

"Go back to your room, you damn dumb little blonde."

I stepped back, directly into the path of Mr. Henhoeffer. He didn't even notice me. His eyes were glazed and his voice was a feeble bleat. Violet just stood there as though everything were as usual.

"Fire! Fire!" he croaked. "Fire!"

He staggered towards the desk. I ran after him, shouting, "Where? Where is it?"

He began to jabber in German, pointing and rolling his eyes. Senhor Mendez materialized behind the desk. The lobby seemed to come alive suddenly, the doors vomited out people.

Mendez reached across the desk and grabbed Mr. Henhoeffer's arm. He spat out a word in German. Mr. Henhoeffer calmed down somewhat.

"A bomb," he whispered. "A bomb. I heard it. I was nearly killed."

"Where?" I shrieked.

"That shop. That English shop—"

I didn't wait to hear more. I was running toward the door, dimly aware there were people following me. From the steps I could see the flames and smoke and the crowds pressing in close.

I ran along the street, and cried as I ran. My body felt light, almost weightless, as if the laws of gravity had been suspended to hurry me on my way to the shop with its grimy windows. I knew there'd be a body or parts of one. The long thin body of the Cockney. E. George, Tobacco.

I stopped running because I was bumping into people, and because in all that mass of humanity the only person I was aware of was Duarte. It was as if he'd been waiting for me there, for he turned instantly and caught my eye and shouldered his way through the crowd towards me. I backed away. I felt the heat of the flames on my face, I heard the shriek of sirens, the smash of glass, but I was conscious chiefly of Duarte coming toward me with that strange challenging smile.

He was near enough to touch me. I heard his voice faintly in my ears. "Bad fire. Go back. Go back. A man was killed."

"Who was it?" I whispered.

He couldn't hear me over the roar of fire, the shriek of sirens, but he sensed what the question was. He said, "Mr. George."

I swung round and started back to the hotel. People swept past me toward the fire. They all looked the same to me, they were all thin and pale and English—hundreds of Georges. One of them grasped my hand and turned out to be Senhor Mendez. I shook him off.

At the door of the hotel I stopped and leaned against a pillar gasping for breath. I had been running for sanctuary, for safety—and the only sanctuary I had was my room with its two frail locks and the queer, sickening odor I couldn't name. Tom was gone. Mr. George was gone. I was the only one left now.

In the street nearby I heard someone cough, and I thought of Mr. Rochat pointing to his chest and holding the handkerchief to his mouth. I thought of the French refugees machine-gunned on the roads, the shattered buildings I'd seen in London, the children playing beside bomb craters. I thought of the swarthy little man carrying his poster: "500,000 *prisioneiros sovieticos.*"

I opened the door and sailed into the hotel, blind mad. I kicked someone's ankle as I strode up to the desk. The ankle belonged to the Honorable Violet and that made me feel better.

She said, "Really!" in her great-lady voice.

"Out of my way, duchess," I said. "I'm in a hurry."

"What a pity," Violet drawled. "Everyone's gone to see the fire and you'll have to wait for your key."

I held up my key. "Why aren't you at the fire? You should be. An Englishman was killed, with a bomb. Bombs are quicker than morphine, aren't they?"

Not a muscle in her face quivered.

I tried again. "I'm so interested in the English aristocracy. I've been looking up your family tree. I found lots of monkeys but not one Cecil Featherstone."

Violet Featherstone was the most surprising person I've ever met. The only reaction I got from her was an annoyed frown and, "You pronounce Cecil as in trestle, not Cecil as in weasel."

Then she turned her head away and began tapping her foot impatiently on the marble floor. I was too stunned to move.

Mendez came in then and scurried behind the desk. When

Violet left I said casually. "You knew the owner of the shop that was burned, Senhor?"

He tugged at his collar and looked cautiously around the lobby. Then he leaned closer to me. "Not to say, *know* him. I have seen him. I have on one or two occasions talked to him."

"But you didn't know him?" I said dryly.

Mendez shrugged. "That is so. In Lisbon people come and go and go and come. So difficult—"

I walked away, knowing I wouldn't get anything out of the slippery little Mendez. As I walked up the stairs Maria's words came back to me: "Mendez knows the girl." Mendez apparently had a habit of disowning his acquaintances as soon as they died. I had a most unpleasant vision of him viewing my battered body and saying, "I don't actually *know* her."

When I opened my door the funny smell floated out to me again, but I didn't allow myself time to think about it. I was inside with my hand on the light switch before I could change my mind.

The light went on. Maria was lying on my bed with her throat slit.

She had one arm flung out and the blood was still flowing sluggishly down it and dripping on to the floor, playing a little tune, drip—plunk—plunk—drip, like a leaking tap.

I sat down and closed my eyes and put my hands over my ears, but I could still see her, lying there with her throat open, I could still hear the little tune, plunk—drip. Then other images joined Maria's—Duarte smiling, the English girl wrapped in the sheet, Mr. Rochat, Duarte again. My ears were alive with voices:

"You leave tomorrow."

"Cecil as in trestle—"

"Drip—plunk—plunk."

"As innocent as a flower."

"You will learn. You will learn."

Drip—

I let my hands fall and opened my eyes. There was a new sound now, the creak of a board in the floor. It came from Tom's room. I got up, hanging onto the back of my chair, and began to giggle.

I couldn't stop. "Tom, Tom, the piper's son," I said, giggling, "Stole a pig, and away he run. Tom, Tom—"

And then he came through the door and I tried to go to him and found I was floating. Mr. Henhoeffer and I were floating together to New York—Mr. Henhoeffer had smuggled a pair of wings out of Germany—he had friends and money and so we were floating. He didn't pinch me, he slapped my face, very hard.

"Wake up," Tom was saying. "Please, darling!"

He slapped me again.

"Don't," I whispered. "Tom."

He held me very quietly for a long time, stroking my hair, not talking. I pressed my face against his coat and floated again. This time I was with Tom and we were dancing and I was saying, "I love your coat. Your coat is different from all other coats—"

I opened my eyes and saw Tom looking down at me. He was grinning broadly and stroking my cheek.

I disentangled myself and said coldly, "I must have been raving. They turn out coats like yours by the million. I don't even think it's a nice color."

"Liar." He kissed me again, hard. Then he thrust me into a chair and went over to Maria. He mumbled something that sounded like "Sorry," then he turned back to me.

"You'll have to get out of here tonight, now. I can't move her like the girl. We couldn't get rid of the bloodstains."

"They won't let me go," I whispered. "The police. Duarte." I told him about the pages from the telephone pad, about meeting Duarte twice that night. I said I thought Duarte had taken the pages.

"Have you a dark dress? Get into it. Put your papers and money in your purse and grab a coat. A dark one."

"No—" I protested.

"Hurry up," he said grimly. "I'll be back."

He slipped back into his room. I got into a black wool dress and coat, and stuffed my purse with everything I could get into it. I was trying to close the zipper when I heard a soft knock on my door, the door that led into the corridor.

I couldn't pretend to be asleep because my light was on and I knew it could be seen under the door. I called out, "Who's there? I'm just undressing."

"Pierre Rochat. I won't bother you." His voice was feeble and sad. "I wanted to apologize."

He coughed for a minute. When he stopped I said, "That's all right," making my voice sound sleepy. "Goodnight, Mr. Rochat."

He said, "Goodnight," and moved across the hall. I heard his door close with a little click.

Tom came back wearing his hat and a topcoat with its pockets bulging. I began to pour out questions: "How are we going? Where are we going? There's no place—"

He didn't answer but went over to the side window, opened it wide, and looked out.

"You're—you're coming too?" I said.

He nodded.

"Won't it look suspicious, both of us vanishing together?"

He turned around. "Six hours to go. If we get out now and stay out we'll be all right. As for suspicions—" He glanced over to the bed where Maria lay. "That shows that they know, everything."

"The police won't let us go. When they find Maria they'll arrest me."

"*If* they find you," Tom said. He had taken a coil of thin rope from his pocket and was tying it to the bedstead, talking half to himself, half to me. "The fire was a break. There won't be anyone on this street and it's only one floor down. Think you can make it?"

"Think I can?" I said bitterly. "I damn well have to."

"Fine." Tom smiled. "Turn out the light."

I turned off the light, jammed my purse in my coat pocket and went to the window. Tom gave me his gloves of heavy pigskin. I put them on and flung one leg over the window sill.

Tom kissed me. "Don't look down. See you later."

Of course I looked down immediately. The street below was dimly lit, the lamps obscured by the thick foliage on the trees. As I looked I saw something move behind a tree and the light gleamed for an instant on a face turned up to my window.

I flung myself back into the room. "Someone down there," I whispered hoarsely. "Someone—"

Tom grabbed my hand and pulled me through the door into his room. He peered out into the corridor and motioned me to come out.

I walked out toward the stairs. Tom was right behind me, moving swiftly and silently. He spoke one word, "Kitchen," and then walked ahead of me. For all his speed he managed to appear quite casual as he made for the dining room. The clerk who was taking Mendez' place behind the desk didn't even look up as he passed, and the only other people in the lobby were the people who arrived from Athens. They were near the main door talking and gesticulating, probably about the fire.

The dining room was dark and I kept stumbling into chairs, but I knew the place well enough to reach the kitchen.

The light was off here, too, and I heard sounds of scuffling feet and whispered curses and deep, painful breathing. I could see nothing at all but I moved toward the sounds, raising my purse over my head ready to strike. My purse at its fullest is practically a lethal weapon, and I was prepared to use it when I heard a soft thud a few feet in front of me and Tom's voice coming out of the darkness.

"Over here. Hurry."

I stepped over something soft and squishy and followed the sound of Tom's voice. He had opened the back door and a thin ribbon of yellow light streamed into the kitchen from a lamp outside the door.

Then we were in a narrow alley enclosed on each side by a high stone wall, and leading, I guessed, into Central Station. Tom stood a moment in the shadow of the wall, looking back at the door, holding one hand against his side. He had his automatic pointed toward the doorway.

"Are you hurt?" I whispered.

He moved to get between me and the door. The next instant I saw why.

The Honorable Violet was standing in the doorway. Her clothes were torn and the dim yellow light had jaundiced her face. She had a large, queer shaped piece of metal in her hand, and I didn't know until I heard a "pop" that it was a pistol with a silencer attached.

Tom's automatic clattered to the alley. Another "pop" and I felt something whiz past my ear, and then I was running, running as I'd never run before, down the alley with Tom behind me. We reached a curve and Tom pulled me up behind it and looked back. There was a third "pop," very faint this time.

"Okay," Tom said. "She's not following."

Right in front of us we heard a vast rumble and knew we must be somewhere in the station.

The next half-hour was confused. I was aware of swarms of people milling around us and the whistle and rumble of trains; I remember getting into a noisy taxi, and getting out, and getting into another noisy taxi. I remember going up and down hills at a crazy speed, and Tom holding his side and saying, "That damn little so-and-so got me in the ribs with her elbow."

I didn't ask where we were going. I sat with my head on Tom's shoulder, and I could think of nothing but that we were safe, we were leaving Lisbon. I closed my eyes and the taxi rattled on.

When I woke up we were in the country and Tom and the taxi driver were conversing in very halting French. I sat up straight. To the left were huge hills massed with foliage. On the top of one distant hill in the pale light of the quarter moon gleamed a stone castle, overlooking a ravine.

Tom said Cintra was in the ravine. Beyond the next bend in the road Cintra itself came into view, clinging to the side of the hill, with a few lights glittering here and there.

Tom and the driver talked again, and instead of turning off into the city the driver kept on the main road, and we left Cintra behind. About five miles further on I began to smell the ocean and hear the roar of the surf. I opened the back window of the taxi and the moist air poured over my face, tangy and fresh.

In the dim moonlight the beach was silver and white against the black water. The taxi stopped and we got out. Tom paid the driver and he drove off. I remember watching the tail-light grow smaller and fainter and vanish altogether, and the feeling of panic came back to me. The beach was lonely, the water black.

"Tom—"

He turned toward me, but there was no comfort for me in his face. It too looked strange and grim and as pallid as the sand.

I whispered again, "Tom—"

"Now what?" he said crossly and the sound of his voice made everything all right again. It had just that blend of impatience and condescension men use the world over when their women develop nerves. I laughed with relief, and Tom laughed, too, and grabbed my arm. We began to walk.

"Where are we?" I asked.

"Praia das Macas," he said.

"But why?"

"That's why." He pointed across the sand to a small white stone cottage between us and the sea. I could see the dim outline of what seemed to be a fishing boat moored behind it. The cottage was dark. Tom approached it first, and as he was mounting the steps a light was turned on in one of the front rooms, and a minute later the door opened.

A man's voice said, "Ross?"

Tom said, "Yeah," and then to me, "Come on!"

I followed him up the steps and into the cottage, blinking my eyes in the sudden light. The door closed behind me. I looked around at the man who had closed it and my knees began to shake.

Because, unless I was stark staring mad, I was looking at the ghost of Mr. George.

I was absorbing my shocks better now. I said dully but politely, "How do you do? I thought you were dead."

Mr. George's ghost held up the lamp so I could see him better. Then he smiled and said, "You may pinch me or you may pinch yourself. Either will serve the purpose."

"S-someone is dead," I whispered.

Mr. George sobered. "A great many people are dead. In my profession you expect it."

He turned and led the way into a small parlor which looked to me like the sitting room of a tiny English country pub, except for the orange tree growing in a tub near the window. Mr. George put the lamp on a table and brought me a glass of some sweet deep red wine.

"But the fire?" I asked. "And the bomb?"

Tom said, "Mr. George made the bomb."

Mr. George smiled modestly. "It is a kind of little hobby of mine," he said with magnificent understatement. "That particular bomb had been prepared for some time, waiting."

"Waiting?" I repeated.

"Waiting for the time for Pedro or one of the many Pedros to come and get me. No bomb ever served a better purpose—it got the man who killed Alice and provided me with a painless entré to the obit columns. It was better for me to die. It does away with a number of small technicalities." He turned to Tom and his voice was crisper. "Tell me what happened."

Tom told him. When he had finished, Mr. George sat back in his chair and smiled.

"Violet's a crack shot," he mused.

"You know her?" I gasped.

"Very well indeed," he replied. "Agents frequently know each other—in Prague I was well acquainted with a German agent—especially in capital cities like this where foreign agents are tripping over each other and over themselves."

He filled my glass again. Despite the questions that were bubbling on my lips I was getting sleepy and my eyes kept closing except when I held my lids open rigidly. Finally I gave it up entirely and just listened to Tom and Mr. George discussing the events of the night. Their voices were a drowsy drone in my ears, but I managed to piece together some things that had been bothering me.

Tom had apparently gone to Mr. George's shop early in the evening and Mr. George had given him the location of the cottage in case he needed sanctuary. He had even specified the taxi we were to take—the driver was an old friend of Mr. George's. I learned also that Mendez, for a consideration, supplied Mr. George with a list of his new guests, their phone calls, mail, friends and behaviour. He did the same for anyone else who cared to meet his price.

I dimly remember Mr. George talking about the girl, Alice. "—a double spy, ostensibly for the Nazis, actually one of the best agents I've ever worked with, cool, intelligent, resourceful. Her husband was killed in Norway and the Intelligence Department sent her here because she had lived in Portugal when she was a child."

I went to sleep thinking of Alice's smile when she spoke to me across the table. And then I was standing on the desk in the hotel, wearing Tom's pigskin gloves and singing, "Do you remember sweet Alice, Ben Bolt?" until I was hoarse. The lobby was filled with people shouting at me, and in front of me was Violet, holding her pistol; and every time I stopped singing she shot at me and I had to start all over again. When I couldn't sing any longer she shot me through the shoulder.

When I woke someone was grasping my shoulder and saying urgently, "Wake up, Lane!" The voice was unpleasantly familiar. It sounded like Violet's voice in my dream, saying, "Sing it again!"

I propped my eyelids open and then let them fall again as quickly as possible. I began to sing in a quavering falsetto, "Oh, do you remember sweet Alice—"

The unpleasantly familiar voice said, "She's tight as a tick. Lane, wake up."

I knew then that I wasn't asleep, that I wasn't even crazy, that the Honorable Violet herself was sitting beside me and wanted me to wake up before she shot me. She wanted the numbers, of course. She'd already killed Tom and Mr. George.

Then the voice again. "What's she been drinking? Vodka?"

My eyelids began to flutter and I kept swallowing hard. I couldn't pretend any longer, so I sat up straight and opened my eyes.

I was still in the chair in Mr. George's sitting room. Violet was standing beside the table pouring some water into a glass. Mr. George was there, too, watching Violet and smiling. There was no sign of Tom.

"Wh-what have you done with him?" I shouted at Mr. George. "You traitor!"

The Honorable Violet turned to me with an air of polite interest and handed me the glass of water. "Drink this and wake up. We have work to do."

I didn't move.

Violet said to Mr. George, "Haven't you told her?"

"She went to sleep," Mr. George replied. "Anyway, I thought she'd know by this time."

"Everyone else may know," Violet said nastily, "but not Lane." She turned to me. "So you think I couldn't have shot you at that distance with a Luger? In a better light I could have removed your eyelashes, one by one."

Mr. George said, "Don't boast, Violet. If you didn't hammer it home to everyone that you were a crack shot, we wouldn't be in this mess."

She looked at him steadily. "Cecil was suspicious before I let these two get away. I wouldn't have lasted another week once Cecil had arrived."

"Who is Cecil?" I said in a high thin squeak. "Who are you? Who's anyone?"

"Violet Featherstone," Violet said, looking slightly surprised as she had the first time I asked her her name.

"But your father?"

Violet smiled. "My father is Herbert Featherstone, now in the care of His Majesty's Government."

"He is really interned?"

"Of course. Marvelous bait for the Nazis, as you can imagine. I was contacted less than a week after Herbert was arrested. I thought I'd take the job and see a bit of the world. Rome, Bucharest, and then here."

"And now?" Mr. George said softly. "Now that you're spotted?"

"Now," Violet said carefully, "I disappear for a time and then turn up—where, George?"

Mr. George smiled at her. "Wherever the fishing schooner will take us."

They were a wonderful pair, Mr. George with his little hobby, and Violet seeing a bit of the world. I must have been gaping with admiration because Violet blushed and abruptly changed the subject.

"Better relieve Ross, George."

Mr. George went out.

"Relieve Tom?" I said. "What do you mean?"

"We're expecting company," Violet said tersely. She picked up her Luger from the table and balanced it in her hand. "Someone I want a crack at very badly—the man who got Alice. Not the man who poisoned her, Pedro was just a hired killer. I want Cecil, the man who ordered her to be killed, the man who saw her warn Tom Ross when she dropped her purse."

"But why did she do it if Cecil was there?"

"She didn't know him," Violet said grimly. "But she knew Tom Ross from his description."

"Description?"

"We were all warned by telephone last night that Ross was coming to Lisbon, all the Nazi agents, real and otherwise, including Alice and me. The foreign correspondents in unoccupied France are well watched. So, I may add, are French naval officers like Diamant. The Nazis know that the French navy, more than the army, is against them. So Diamant was watched, and Diamant talked—and the Nazi agents here were ordered to see that Diamant's talking did no harm. We were told to get Ross."

I sat shivering and silent.

"So I parked in the lobby and waited for him to come. Alice was there, too. She warned Tom Ross the best way she could. But Cecil saw her and I had to tell her that Cecil saw her. That's where you came in." She paused and drew in her breath.

"I wasn't talking to you at lunch. I was talking to Alice. Pedro couldn't speak English and I knew you wouldn't catch on."

I said in a small voice, "No, I didn't. But I think Tom figured it out later when I told him what you said and how your voice sounded."

"He's a bright boy. Alice and I have used that method of communication for months and haven't been spotted. Alice was the go-between for George and me. She'd come to lunch or dinner at the hotel, and I'd attach myself to someone at a nearby table and talk. It was simple and it worked."

"You did it very well," I said.

"Practice," Violet said dryly. "And I always was a good liar. Alice, of course, could always get me to feed her. She didn't stay at the hotel." She paused again. "Well, I told her Cecil had come and that she was to get out right away, but it was too late."

There was a silence, and then Tom came in. He gave me a sweet and decidedly sheepish smile. I stared at him coldly.

"Why didn't you tell me about Violet?" I demanded.

Violet, said dryly, "Oh, come now, Lane. You wouldn't begrudge a man his chance to be a hero in front of the girl he loves. Listen."

She held up her hand and we were both quiet. Over the roar of the breakers we could hear a new sound, the sound of a motor, then the shriek of brakes. I looked at Violet. She was listening and smiling.

Mr. George came into the room carrying a gun.

"He's come," he said.

"Good," Violet said calmly. "Is he alone?"

"Can't tell. It's too dark."

Violet turned to Tom. "Take Lane into the kitchen and be quiet. You have a gun?"

"Tom nodded and gave me a push out the door. I heard Violet say to Mr. George, "I knew he couldn't resist coming."

"It's dangerous," Mr. George said quietly. "For the two kids in there especially. You and I, well—"

"Dangerous," Violet said. "But he doesn't know they're here. I told him I was going to track you down, that I had information about this cottage. I didn't know the Americans would be here. How could Cecil know?"

The door closed then, and I was crouched in the dark kitchen with Tom beside me. The luminous dial on my watch said 4:45. I could hear Violet moving around in the hall beyond the door, then a soft knock at the front door and the creak of a hinge, Violet's calm voice saying, "Hello, Cecil."

I strained closer to the kitchen door. A voice I knew well, a gloomy, sick voice was saying, "Hello Violet. Put down your gun, please."

"Are you alone, Cecil?" Violet asked.

They sounded like two old friends who understood each other very well.

"No, not alone." The man I knew as Rochat stopped to cough, and I knew from the sound he was holding his handkerchief to his mouth. "Not alone. I brought two friends with me. One of them is at the back door, well armed I may add, and the other is in the car at the front. And they have orders to let no one but me out of this house, alive."

"So?" Violet's voice didn't have a tremor. "Well, whatever happens, you're through, Cecil. Your friends don't like incompetence and failure. They're suspicious of their French agents anyway, aren't they? Yes, whatever happens you're going to pay for killing Alice. That was a mistake."

Rochat said, "You think so?"

"And Maria? You did that yourself, perhaps?"

"Yes," Rochat said. "I'd paid her not to tell anyone that she saw me coming out of Ross' room. Then Miss Lane paid her a little more than I did, and the upshot was that she had to die. However, that's beside the point, Violet. You understand that certain deaths are inevitable."

"Yours," Violet said, calm and hard.

"Mine certainly. Yours, too. Perhaps the two Americans—"

"They're gone."

"It's too late to lie."

"But I have a friend with me. I imagine he's got a gun pointing right at your head. That's the worst of our business. We can't trust each other."

"Your friend, the Englishman?" Rochat laughed softly. "I've never seen him but I've heard things, here and there. A pity about his shop. I imagine the corpse was Pedro. Pedro seems to be missing."

"It was Pedro," Violet said grimly.

"I liked your method of communicating with Alice. Quite new to me. Too bad you'll never use it again."

"You've got delusions of grandeur," Violet said contemptuously.

There was a silence, then a soft laugh. "Did you think I'd let you live when I have to die, Violet? Do you think I could bear to die knowing you were alive? I'd like to crush every flower, uproot every tree and blade of grass, because I don't want anything to be alive after my time—"

"You're mad, Cecil," Violet said coolly. "I've always thought you were mad, even in Bucharest when I first met you."

"Where are the Americans?"

"Gone."

"I have only to call out, Violet, and have two men with submachine guns at my side. I believe you're already acquainted with Duarte and De Castro. And more are coming. Where are the Americans?"

I felt the pressure of Tom's fingers on my arm. Duarte here, with a submachine gun, Duarte—

"More are coming, Violet. I'm giving you your chance. Not one of you will get away, Violet, not one. We're strong, we're organized, and we can fight. Even when we're dying we can fight your poor little race of shopkeepers—"

There was a "pop," a sound like a cork being pulled out of a bottle of champagne, then a cough and a thud and a deep silence.

Tom opened the door. Rochat was lying on the floor of the hall and Violet was standing looking down at him. The air smelled of cordite.

We waited tensely, expecting the sharp staccato of a machine gun. But there was no noise from outside the house except the surf.

Mr. George came into the hall. Violet looked up and said, "Sorry."

"They didn't hear it," Mr. George whispered. "The ocean covered the shot."

"Then he did bring Duarte and De Castro?" Violet said.

Mr. George nodded. "They're out there all right. I have suspected before now that Duarte was in their pay. And more coming."

"Sorry," Violet said again. "I guess I couldn't stand that damned Fascist standing there telling me how well they can fight. Have I—wrecked our chances?"

Mr. George said, "No. No, wait." He bent over Rochat and began tugging at the sleeves of his coat, talking as he worked. "We're both tall, both thin."

"You couldn't fool Duarte like that. There's not a chance." Violet put her hand on his shoulder, but Mr. George thrust her away, none too gently. He had Rochat's topcoat off now. There was blood on it.

"You must be mad!" Violet cried.

"No, wait." He was buttoning the coat and picking up Rochat's hat from the floor.

"You couldn't fool a baby," Violet said savagely.

"The darkness will cover me until I get to the car. One man is in the car, the other is at the back of the house. What I'm going to do is this: I'm going to walk halfway to the car. I'll be safe until then. Violet, you'll be at the window of the front bedroom upstairs. Ross, you'll be at the kitchen window. When I'm halfway to the car, I'll light a cigarette."

"And then?" Violet said, calmly now.

"Then the man in the car will see that I'm not Cecil. He'll be able to see my face, and anyway he'll know that Cecil doesn't smoke."

"So?" Violet said.

"So he'll shoot at me. And you, Violet—you'll shoot him by the flash of his own gun."

"Can't be done," Violet said flatly. "Can't."

"It has been done," Mr. George said. "In the last war a German sniper got one of my men when he lit a match."

"I'm not a sniper. I couldn't risk—Oh, damn you, George."

Mr. George knew he had won. He grinned and said, "Bless you, Violet. Get upstairs."

Tom shoved me into a chair in the sitting room and turned down the wick of the lamp. And there I sat, like a bump on a log, while a man casually walked toward death and a woman stood at a window with her gun raised, her eyes straining into the darkness.

I heard the front door creak as it opened, footsteps descending the veranda steps, and then nothing—nothing but the sound of the ocean and the blood pounding against my ears.

I crept to the window, moved the blind a little, and looked out. I could see the dim outline of a car, I could see a man walking, stopping for a second, and then the sudden flare of a match.

From the car came a flash and a volley of quick sharp shots, a pause and another volley. A shadow was crawling towards the car like some wounded beast of the night.

From the kitchen I heard the crash of glass and a new kind of shot, deafeningly loud, and Tom's voice cursing. He told me afterwards he shot Duarte when he moved out of the shadow of the house to run to the car. There was one more shot, the kind I'd come to know, the cork-out-of-a-bottle sound of Violet's gun.

I don't know how long I clung there to the window sill, frozen with fear, peering out into the darkness. I heard Violet come crashing down the stairs and out the front door, and I knew by the buoyant sound of her steps that she hadn't missed.

I have heard Americans speak of the "decadent English upper classes," but I'm sure they could never have met Violet Featherstone. It was Violet who sterilized Tom's pen-knife and dug the bullet out of George's arm and bandaged him with strips of a tablecloth.

"Will you two be able to handle the fishing smack, with George's arm wounded?" Tom said.

Mr. George smiled impassively and touched his arm. "It's my left arm, and it's only a flesh wound. The weather's good, and I can handle the tiller. Violet's been sailing boats since she was a baby."

Violet spoke softly. "We shall be all right." It was hard not to believe her.

"But where are you going?" I said.

"You can't reach England in a fishing smack."

Violet smiled, almost for the first time since I had seen her. Her smile seemed to me to be a recognition of all peril and an answer to all fear. "We shall be all right," she repeated. "The Atlantic is still a British ocean. I think we'll sail due west into the shipping lanes. Ever since I was a girl I've wanted to sail due west into the Atlantic." Her voice broke off, and she turned to Tom. "It's nearly dawn. You've less than an hour to get to Cintra and board the Clipper. You must leave now."

"Take my car," said Mr. George. "I won't be needing it. And Duarte's car might be recognized."

We said our goodbyes on the wharf behind the cottage. Violet had put on a pair of Mr. George's trousers and a sweater, and was shaking out the great brown triangular sail of the fishing smack. The faint light from the east was turning the black water to the greyness of lead. I felt chilled and frightened for a moment. Our two friends were alive, and our enemies were dead. But the grey water sucking at the wharf seemed menacing and sullen, and the dark continent of Europe seemed menacing behind us.

Violet's smile when she said goodbye reassured me. I shall never forget that warm, proud, invincible smile. She waved her hand as gaily as if she were going for a sail on the Thames, and turned back to her work. Tom and I shook hands with Mr. George. Neither of us said anything. We climbed up the bank to the car, and turned towards Cintra and the Clipper and the dawn . . . .

The stewardess adjusted my safety belt and gave me a paper bag. I settled back in the seat and prepared to ask Tom the questions I hadn't had time to ask before.

I said, "Tom."

Tom opened his eyes very slightly.

"What about Mr. Henhoeffer?"

"He's all right," Tom said drowsily.

"Really a refugee?"

"Mmm."

"Now that I've thought it all over, of course I know it couldn't have been anyone else but Rochat who was responsible for Maria's death. Remember when we were in my room and he knocked on my door and said he wanted to apologize?"

"Mmm."

"That's how he knew we were going to try to get away. He knew Maria was in my room dead, you see; so when I pretended I was just going to bed he knew I was lying, that I was going to get away if I could. He went out and waited to watch my window. Are you listening, Tom?"

No answer.

"Tom, are we—are we going to get married?"

Tom opened his eyes and said, "Sure," and was asleep five seconds later.

McGOWNEY'S MIRACLE

McGowney's Miracle
Preface by Tom Nolan

Mystery expert Dilys Winn stated that Margaret Millar wrote "the greatest opening lines since 'In the beginning ...'"

Millar, said Winn, "hooks you in the first paragraph. You might just as well begin reading her with someone else, or you're going to spend all your time chasing after friends saying, 'Listen to this,' and then reading out great chunks of books."

"Mrs. Millar," contended Ms. Winn (herself rather quotable), "doesn't attract fans; she creates addicts."

The first sentence of this shocker that follows seems a fine example of what Dilys Winn meant: "When I finally found him, it was by accident." The next line tells us we're in San Francisco, and every sentence that follows has the visual precision and dramatic inevitability that mark the work of a master.

Notes

" 'the greatest opening lines' ": *Murderess Ink: The Better Half of the Mystery*, perpetrated by Dilys Winn (Workman, 1979).

" 'hooks you in the first paragraph' ": *Murder Ink: Revived, revised, still unrepentant*, perpetrated by Dilys Winn (Workman, 1984)

" 'she creates addicts' ": *Murderess Ink*, ibid.

McGowney's Miracle

When I finally found him, it was by accident. He was waiting for a cable car on Powell Street, a dignified little man about sixty, in a black topcoat and a grey fedora. He stood apart from the crowd, aloof but friendly, his hands clasped just below his chest, like a minister about to bless a batch of heathen. I knew he wasn't a minister.

A sheet of fog hung over San Francisco, blurring the lights and muffling the clang of the cable cars.

I stepped up behind McGowney and said, "Good evening." There was no recognition in his eyes, no hesitation in his voice. "Why, good evening, sir." He turned with a little smile. "It is kind of you to greet a stranger so pleasantly."

For a moment, I was almost ready to believe I'd made a mistake. There are on record many cases of perfect doubles, and what's more, I hadn't seen McGowney since the beginning of July. But there was one important thing McGowney couldn't conceal: his voice still carried the throaty accents of the funeral parlour.

He tipped his hat and began walking briskly up Powell Street toward the hill, his topcoat flapping around his skinny legs like broken wings.

In the middle of the block, he turned to see if I was following him. I was. He walked on, shaking his head from side to side as if genuinely puzzled by my interest in him. At the next corner, he stopped in front of a department store and waited for me, leaning against the window, his hands in his pockets.

When I approached, he looked up at me frowning. "I don't know why you're following me, young man, but—"

"Why don't you ask me, McGowney?"

But he didn't ask. He just repeated his own name, "McGowney," in a surprised voice, as if he hadn't heard it for a long time.

I said, "I'm Eric Meecham, Mrs. Keating's lawyer. We've met before."

"I've met a great many people. Some I recall, some I do not."

"I'm sure you recall Mrs. Keating. You conducted her funeral last July."

"Of course, of course. A great lady, a very great lady. Her demise saddened the hearts of all who had the privilege of her acquaintance, all who tasted the sweetness of her smile—"

"Come off it, McGowney. Mrs. Keating was a sharp-tongued virago without a friend in this world."

He turned away from me, but I could see the reflection of his face in the window, strained and anxious.

"You're a long way from home, McGowney."

"This is my home now."

"You left Arbana very suddenly."

"To me it was not sudden. I had been planning to leave for twenty years, and when the time came, I left. It was summer then, but all I could think of was the winter coming on and everything dying. I had had enough of death."

"Mrs. Keating was your last—client?"

"She was."

"Her coffin was exhumed last week."

A cable car charged up the hill like a drunken rocking horse, its sides bulging with passengers. Without warning, McGowney darted out into the street and sprinted up the hill after the car. In spite of his age, he could have made it, but the car was so crowded there wasn't a single space for him to get a handhold. He stopped running and stood motionless in the centre of the street, staring after the car as it plunged and reared up the hill. Oblivious to the honks and shouts of motorists, he walked slowly back to the curb where I was waiting.

"You can't run away, McGowney."

He glanced at me wearily, without speaking. Then he took out a half-soiled handkerchief and wiped the moisture from his forehead.

"The exhumation can't be much of a surprise to you," I said. "You wrote me the anonymous letter suggesting it. It was postmarked Berkeley. That's why I'm here in this area."

"I wrote you no letter," he said.

"The information it contained could have come only from you."

"No. Somebody else knew as much about it as I did."

"Who?"

"My—wife."

"Your wife." It was the most unexpected answer he could have given me. Mrs. McGowney had died, along with her only daughter, in the flu epidemic after World War I. The story is the kind that still goes the rounds in a town like Arbana, even after thirty-five years: McGowney, unemployed after his discharge from the Army, had had no funds to pay for the double funeral, and when the undertaker offered him an apprenticeship to work off the debt, McGowney accepted. It was common knowledge that after his wife's death he never so much as looked at another woman, except, of course, in line of duty.

I said, "So you've married again."

"Yes."

"When?"

"Six months ago."

"Right after you left Arbana."

"Yes."

"You didn't lose much time starting a new life for yourself."

"I couldn't afford to. I'm not young."

"Did you marry a local woman?"

"Yes."

I didn't realize until later that he had taken "local" to mean Arbana, not San Francisco as I had intended.

I said, "You think your wife wrote me that anonymous letter?"

"Yes."

The street lights went on, and I realized it was getting late and cold. McGowney pulled up his coat collar and put on a pair of ill-fitting white cotton gloves. I had seen him wearing gloves like that before; they were as much a part of his professional equipment as his throaty voice and his vast store of sentimental aphorisms.

He caught me staring at the gloves and said, with a trace of apology, "Money is a little tight these days. My wife is knitting me a pair of woollen gloves for my birthday."

"You're not working?"

"No."

"It shouldn't be hard for a man of your experience to find a job in your particular field." I was pretty sure he hadn't even applied for one. During the past few days, I had contacted nearly every mortician within the Bay area; McGowney had not been to any of them.

"I don't want a job in my particular field," McGowney said.

"It's the only thing you're trained for."

"Yes. But I no longer believe in death."

He spoke with simple earnestness, as if he had said, I no longer play blackjack, or I no longer eat salted peanuts.

Death, blackjack, or salted peanuts—I was not prepared to argue with McGowney about any of them, so I said, "My car's in the garage at the Canterbury Hotel. We'll walk over and get it, and I'll drive you home."

We started toward Sutter Street. The stream of shoppers had been augmented by a flow of white-collar workers, but all the people and the noise and the confusion left McGowney untouched. He moved sedately along beside me, smiling a little to himself, like a man who has developed the faculty of walking out on the world from time to time and going to live on some remote and happy island of his own. I wondered where McGowney's island was and who lived there with him.

I knew only one thing for sure: on McGowney's island there was no death.

He said suddenly, "It must have been very difficult."

"What was?"

"The exhumation. The ground gets so hard back East in the wintertime. I presume you didn't attend, Mr. Meecham?"

"You presume wrong."

"My, that's no place for an amateur."

For my money, it was no place for anyone. The cemetery had been white with snow that had fallen during the night. Dawn had been breaking, if you could call that meagre, grudging light a dawn. The simple granite headstone had read, ELEANOR REGINA KEATING, OCTOBER 3, 1899—JUNE 30, 1953. A BLESSED ONE FROM US IS GONE, A VOICE WE LOVED IS STILL.

The blessed one had been gone, all right. Two hours later, when the coffin was pulled up and opened, the smell that rose from it was not the smell of death, but the smell of newspapers rotted with dampness and stones grey-greened with mildew.

I said, "You know what we found, don't you, McGowney?"

"Naturally. I directed the funeral."

"You accept sole responsibility for burying an empty coffin?"

"Not sole responsibility, no."

"Who was in with you? And why?"

He merely shook his head.

As we waited for a traffic light, I studied McGowney's face, trying to estimate the degree of his sanity. There seemed to be no logic behind his actions. Mrs. Keating had died quite unmysteriously of a heart attack and had been buried, according to her instructions to me, in a closed coffin. The doctor who had signed the death certificate was indisputably honest. He had happened to be in Mrs. Keating's house at the time, attending to her older daughter, Mary, who had had a cold. He had examined Mrs. Keating, pronounced her dead, and sent for McGowney. Two days later I had escorted Mary, still sniffling (whether from grief or the same cold, I don't know), to the funeral. McGowney, as usual, said and did all the correct things.

Except one. He neglected to put Mrs. Keating's body in the coffin.

Time had passed. No one had particularly mourned Mrs. Keating. She had been an unhappy woman, mentally and morally superior to her husband, who had been killed during a drinking spree in New Orleans, and to her two daughters, who resembled their father. I had been Mrs. Keating's lawyer for three years. I had enjoyed talking to her; she had had a quick mind and a sharp sense of humour. But as in the case of many wealthy people who have been cheated of the privilege of work and the satisfactions it brings, she had been a bored and lonely woman who carried despair on her shoulder like a pet parakeet and fed it from time to time on scraps from her bitter memories.

Right after Mrs. Keating's funeral, McGowney had sold his business and left town. No one in Arbana had connected the two events until the anonymous letter arrived from Berkeley shortly before Mrs. Keating's will was awaiting admission into probate. The letter, addressed to me, had suggested the exhumation and stated the will must be declared invalid since there was no proof of death. I could think of no reason why McGowney's new wife wrote the letter, unless she had tired of him and had chosen a roundabout method of getting rid of him.

The traffic light changed and McGowney and I crossed the
street and waited under the hotel marquee while the doorman
sent for my car.

I didn't look at McGowney, but I could feel him watching me
intently.

"You think I'm mad, eh, Meecham?"

It wasn't a question I was prepared to answer. I tried to look
noncommittal.

"I don't pretend to be entirely normal, Meecham. Do you?"

"I try."

McGowney's hand, in its ill-fitting glove, reached over and
touched my arm, and I forced myself not to slap it away. It
perched on my coat sleeve like a wounded pigeon. "But suppose
you had an abnormal experience." *Dialogue only advances story*

"Like you?"

"Like me. It was a shock, a great shock, even though I had
always had the feeling that someday it would happen. I was on
the watch for it every time I had a new case. It was always in
my mind. You might even say I *willed* it."

Two trickles of sweat oozed down behind my ears into my
collar. "What did you will, McGowney?"

"I willed her to live again."

I became aware the doorman was signalling to me. My car
was at the curb with the engine running.

I climbed in behind the wheel, and McGowney followed me
into the car with obvious reluctance, as if he was already
regretting what he'd told me.

"You don't believe me," he said, as we pulled away from the
curb.

"I'm a lawyer. I deal in facts."

"A fact is what happens, isn't it?"

"Close enough."

"Well, this happened."

"She came back to life?"

"Yes."

"By the power of your will alone?"

He stirred restlessly in the seat beside me. "I gave her oxygen
and adrenalin." *WTF*

"Have you done this with other clients of yours?"

"Many times, yes."

"Is this procedure usual among members of your profession?"

"For me it was usual," McGowney said earnestly. "I've always wanted to be a doctor. I was in the Medical Corps during the war, and I picked up a little knowledge here and there."

"Enough to perform miracles?"

"It was not my knowledge that brought her back to life. It was my will. She had lost the will to live, but I had enough for both of us."

If it is true only a thin line separates sanity and madness, McGowney crossed and recrossed that line a dozen times within an hour, jumping over it and back again, like a child skipping rope.

"You understand now, Meecham? She had lost all desire. I saw it happening to her. We never spoke—I doubt she even knew my name—but for years I watched her pass my office on her morning walk. I saw the change come over her, the dullness of her eyes and the way she walked. I knew she was going to die. One day when she was passing by, I went out to tell her, to warn her. But when she saw me, she ran. I think she realized what I was going to say."

He was telling the truth, according to his lights. Mrs. Keating had mentioned the incident to me last spring. I recalled her words: "A funny thing occurred this morning, Meecham. As I was walking past the undertaking parlour, that odd little man rushed out and almost scared the life out of me. . ."

In view of what subsequently happened, this was a giant among ironies. As we drove toward the Bay Bridge and Berkeley, McGowney told me his story.

It was midday at the end of June, and the little backroom McGowney used as a lab was hot and humid after a morning rain.

Mrs. Keating woke up as if from a long and troubled sleep. Her hands twitched, her mouth moved in distress, a pulse began to beat in her temple. Tears squeezed out from between her closed lids and slithered past the tips of her ears into the folds of her hair.

McGowney bent over her, quivering with excitement. "Mrs. Keating! Mrs. Keating, you are alive!"

"Oh—God."

"A miracle has just happened!"

"Leave me alone. I'm tired."

"You are alive, you are *alive!*"

Slowly she opened her eyes and looked up at him. "You officious little wretch, what have you done?"

McGowney stepped back, stunned and shaken. "But—but you are alive. It's happened. My miracle has happened."

"Alive. Miracle." She mouthed the words as if they were lumps of alum. "You meddling idiot."

"I—But I—"

"Pour me a glass of water. My throat is parched."

He was trembling so violently he could hardly get the water out of the cooler. This was his miracle. He had hoped and waited for it all his life, and now it had exploded in his face like an April-fool cigar.

He gave her the water and sat down heavily in a chair, watching her while she drank very slowly, as if in her short recess from life her muscles had already begun to forget their function.

"Why did you do it?" Mrs. Keating crushed the paper cup in her fist as if it were McGowney himself. "Who asked you for a miracle, anyway?"

"But I—Well, the fact is—"

"The fact is, you're a blooming meddler, that's what the fact is, McGowney."

"Yes, ma'am."

"Now what are you going to do?"

"Well, I—I hadn't thought."

"Then you'd better start right now."

"Yes, ma'am." He stared down at the floor, his head hot with misery, his limbs cold with disappointment. "First, I had better call the doctor."

"You'll call no one, McGowney."

"But your family—they'll want to know right away that—"

"They are not going to know."

"But—"

"No one is going to know, McGowney. No one at all. Is that clear?"

"Yes."

"Now sit down and be quiet and let me think."

He sat down and was quiet. He had no desire to move or to speak. Never had he felt so futile and depressed.

"I suppose," Mrs. Keating said grimly, "you expect me to be grateful to you."

McGowney shook his head.

"If you do, you must be crazy." She paused and looked at him thoughtfully. "You *are* a little crazy, aren't you, McGowney?"

"There are those who think so," he said, with some truth. "I don't agree."

"You wouldn't."

"Can't afford to, ma'am."

The windows of the room were closed and no street sounds penetrated the heavy frosted glass, but from the corridor outside the door came the sudden tap of footsteps on tile.

McGowney bolted across the room and locked the door and stood against it.

"Mr. McGowney? You in there?"

McGowney looked at Mrs. Keating. Her face had turned chalky, and she had one hand clasped to her throat.

"Mr. McGowney?"

"Yes, Jim."

"You're wanted on the telephone."

"I—can't come right now, Jim. Take a message."

"She wants to talk to you personally. It's the Keating girl, about the time and cost of the funeral arrangements."

"Tell her I'll call her back later."

"All right." There was a pause. "You feeling okay, Mr. McGowney?"

"Yes."

"You sound kind of funny."

"I'm fine, Jim. Absolutely first-rate."

"Okay. Just thought I'd ask."

The footsteps tapped back down the tile corridor.

"Mary loses no time." Mrs. Keating spoke through dry, stiff lips. "She wants me safely underground so she can marry her electrician. Well, your duty is clear, McGowney."

"What is it?"

"Put me there."

McGowney stood propped against the door like a wooden soldier. "You mean, b-b-bury you?"

"Me, or a reasonable facsimile."

"That I couldn't do, Mrs. Keating. It wouldn't be ethical."

"It's every bit as ethical as performing unsolicited miracles."

"You don't understand the problems."

"Such as?"

"For one thing, your family and friends. They'll want to see you lying in—What I mean is, it's customary to put the body on view."

"I can handle that part of it all right."

"How?"

"Get me a pen and some paper."

McGowney didn't argue, because he knew he was at fault. It was his miracle; he'd have to take the consequences.

Mrs. Keating predated the letter by three weeks, and wrote the following:

> To whom it may concern, not that it should concern anybody except myself:
>
> I am giving these instructions to Mr. McGowney concerning my funeral arrangements. Inasmuch as I have valued privacy during my life, I want no intrusion on it after my death. I am instructing Mr. McGowney to close my coffin immediately and to see it stays closed, in spite of any mawkish pleas from my survivors.
>
> Eleanor Regina Keating

She folded the paper twice and handed it to McGowney. "You are to show this to Mary and Joan and to Mr. Meecham, my lawyer." She paused, looking very pleased with herself. "Well. This is getting to be quite exciting, eh, McGowney?"

"Quite," McGowney said listlessly.

"As a matter of fact, it's given me an appetite. I don't suppose there's a kitchen connected with this place?"

"No."

"Then you'd better get me something from the corner drugstore. A couple of tuna-salad sandwiches, on wheat, with plenty of coffee. Lunch," she added with a satiric little smile, "will have to be on you. I forgot my handbag."

"Money," McGowney said. *"Money."*

"What about it?"

"What will happen to your money?"

"I made a will some time ago."

"But *you*, what will you live on?"

"Perhaps," Mrs. Keating said dryly, "you'd better perform another miracle."

When he returned from the drugstore with her lunch, Mrs. Keating ate and drank with obvious enjoyment. She offered McGowney a part of the second sandwich, but he was too disheartened to eat. His miracle, which had started out as a great golden bubble, had turned into an iron ball chained to his leg.

Somehow he got through the day. Leaving Mrs. Keating in the lab with some old magazines and a bag of apples, McGowney went about his business. He talked to Mary and Joan Keating in person and to Meecham on the telephone. He gave his assistant, Jim Wagner, the rest of the afternoon off, and when Jim had gone, he filled Mrs. Keating's coffin (the de luxe white-and-bronze model Mary had chosen out of the catalogue) with rocks packed in newspapers, until it was precisely the right weight.

McGowney was a small man, unaccustomed to physical exertion, and by the time he had finished, his body was throbbing with weariness.

It was at this point Mary Keating telephoned to say she and Joan had been thinking the matter over, and since Mrs. Keating had always inclined toward thrift, it was decided she would never rest at ease in such an ostentatious affair as the white and bronze. The plain grey would be far more appropriate, as well as cheaper.

"You should," McGowney said coldly, "have let me know sooner."

"We just decided a second ago."

"It's too late to change now."

"I don't see why."

"There are—certain technicalities."

"Well, really, Mr. McGowney. If you're not willing to put yourself out a little, maybe we should take our business somewhere else."

"No! You can't do that—I mean, it wouldn't be proper, Miss
Keating."

"It's a free country."

"Wait a minute. Suppose I give you a special price on the white
and bronze."

"How special?"

"Say, twenty-five per cent off?"

There was a whispered conference at the other end of the line,
and then Mary said, "It's still a lot of money."

"Thirty-five?"

"Well, that seems more *like*," Mary said, and hung up.

The door of McGowney's office opened, and Mrs. Keating
crossed the room, wearing a grim little smile.

McGowney looked at her helplessly. "You shouldn't be out here,
ma'am. You'd better go back and—"

"I heard the telephone ring, and I thought it might be Mary."

"It wasn't."

"Yes, it was, McGowney. I heard every word."

"Well," McGowney cleared his throat. "Well. You shouldn't
have listened."

"Oh, I'm not surprised. Or hurt. You needn't be sorry for me. I
haven't felt so good in years. You know why?"

"No, ma'am."

"Because I don't have to go home. I'm free. Free as a bird." She
reached over and touched his coat sleeve. "I don't have to go
home, do I?"

"I guess not."

"You'll never tell anyone."

"No."

"You're a very good man, McGowney."

"I have never thought I wasn't," McGowney said simply.

When darkness fell, McGowney got his car out of the garage and
brought it around to the ambulance entrance behind his office.

"You'd better hide in the back seat," he said, "until we get out
of town."

"Where are we going?"

"I thought I'd drive you into Detroit, and from there you can
catch a bus or a train."

"To where?"

"To anywhere. You're free as a bird."

She got into the back seat, shivering in spite of the mildness of the night, and McGowney covered her with a blanket.

"McGowney."

"Yes, ma'am?"

"I felt freer when I was locked in your little lab."

"You're a bit frightened now, that's all. Freedom is a mighty big thing."

He turned the car toward the highway. Half an hour later, when the city's lights had disappeared, he stopped the car and Mrs. Keating got into the front seat with the blanket wrapped around her shoulders, Indian style. In the gleam of oncoming headlights, her face looked a little troubled. McGowney felt duty-bound to cheer her up, since he was responsible for her being there in the first place.

"There are," he said firmly, "wonderful places to be seen."

"Are there?"

"California, that's the spot I'd pick. Flowers all year round, never an end to them." He hesitated. "I've saved a bit throughout the years. I always thought someday I'd sell the business and retire to California."

"What's to prevent you?"

"I couldn't face the idea of, well, of being alone out there without friends or a family of some kind. Have you ever been to California?"

"I spent a couple of summers in San Francisco."

"Did you like it?"

"Very much."

"I'd like it, too, I'm sure of that." He cleared his throat. "Being alone, though, that I wouldn't like. Are you warm enough?"

"Yes, thanks."

"Birds—well, birds don't have such a happy time of it that I can see."

"No?"

"All that freedom and not knowing what to do with it except fly around. A life like that wouldn't suit a mature woman like yourself, Mrs. Keating."

"Perhaps not."

"What I mean is—"

"I know what you mean, McGowney."

"You—you do?"

"Of course."

McGowney flushed. "It's—well, it's very unexpected, isn't it?"

"Not to me."

"But I never even thought of it until half an hour ago."

"I did. Women are more foresighted in these matters."

McGowney was silent a moment. "This hasn't been a very romantic proposal. I ought to say something a bit on the sentimental side."

"Go ahead."

He gripped the steering wheel hard. "I think I love you, ma'am."

"You didn't have to say that," she replied sharply. "I'm not a foolish young girl to be taken in by words. At my age, I don't expect love. I don't want to—"

"But you are loved," McGowney declared.

"I don't believe it."

"Eventually you will."

"Is this another of your miracles, McGowney?"

"This is the important one."

It was the first time in Mrs. Keating's life she had been told she was loved. She sat beside McGowney in awed silence, her hands folded on her lap, like a little girl in Sunday school.

McGowney left her at a hotel in Detroit and went home to hold her funeral.

Two weeks later they were married by a justice of the peace in a little town outside Chicago. On the long and leisurely trip West in McGowney's car, neither of them talked much about the past or worried about the future. McGowney had sold his business, but he'd been in too much of a hurry to wait for a decent price, and so his funds were limited. But he never mentioned this to his bride.

By the time they reached San Francisco, they had gone through quite a lot of McGowney's capital. A large portion of the remainder went toward the purchase of the little house in Berkeley.

By late fall, they were almost broke, and McGowney got a job as a shoe clerk in a department store. A week later along with his first pay cheque, he received his notice of dismissal.

That night at dinner, he told Eleanor about it, pretending it was all a joke, and inventing a couple of anecdotes to make her laugh.

She listened, grave and unamused. "So that's what you've been doing all week. Selling shoes."

"Yes."

"You didn't tell me we needed money that badly."

"We'll be all right, I can easily get another job."

"Doing what?"

"What I've always done."

She reached across the table and touched his hand. "You don't want to be a mortician again."

"I don't mind."

"You always hated it."

"I *don't mind*, I tell you."

She rose decisively.

"Eleanor, what are you going to do?"

"Write a letter," she said with a sigh.

"Eleanor, don't do anything drastic."

"We have had a lot of happiness. It couldn't last forever. Don't be greedy."

The meaning of her words pierced McGowney's brain. "You're going to let someone know you're alive?"

"No. I couldn't face that, not just yet. I'm merely going to show them I'm not dead so they can't divide up my estate."

"But why?"

"As my husband, you're entitled to a share of it if anything happens to me."

"Nothing will ever happen to you. We agreed about that, didn't we?"

"Yes, McGowney. We agreed."

"We no longer believe in death."

"I will address the letter to Meecham," she said.

"So she wrote the letter." McGowney's voice was weary. "For my sake. You know the rest, Meecham."

"Not quite," I said.

"What else do you want to know?"

"The ending."

"The ending." McGowney stirred in the seat beside me and let out his breath in a sigh. "I don't believe in endings."

I turned right at the next traffic light, as McGowney directed. A sign on the lamppost said, LINDEN AVENUE.

Three blocks south was a small green-and-white house, its eaves dripping with fog.

I parked my car in front of it and got out, pleasantly excited at the idea of seeing Mrs. Keating again. McGowney sat motionless, staring straight ahead of him, until I opened the car door.

"Come on, McGowney."

"Eh? Oh. All right. All right."

He stepped out on the sidewalk so awkwardly he almost fell.

I took his arm. "Is anything wrong?"

"No."

We went up the porch steps.

"There are no lights on," McGowney said. "Eleanor must be at the store. Or over at the neighbours'. We have some very nice neighbours."

The front door was not locked. We went inside, and McGowney turned on the lights in the hall and the sitting room to the right.

The woman I had known as Mrs. Keating was sitting in a wing chair in front of the fireplace, her head bent forward as if she was in deep thought. Her knitting had fallen on the floor, and I saw it was a half-finished glove in bright colours. McGowney's birthday present.

In silence, McGowney reached down and picked up the glove and put it on a table. Then he touched his wife gently on the forehead. I knew from the way his hand flinched that her skin was as cold as the ashes in the grate.

I said, "I'll get a doctor."

"No."

"She's dead?"

He didn't bother to answer. He was looking down at his wife with a coaxing expression. "Eleanor dear, you must wake up. We have a visitor."

"McGowney, for God's sake—"

"I think you'd better leave now, Mr. Meecham," he said in a firm, clear voice. "I have work to do."

He took off his coat and rolled up his sleeves.

THE COUPLE NEXT DOOR

THE COUPLE NEXT DOOR
Preface by Tom Nolan

People were passing, children were playing on the sidewalk, the sun shone, the palm trees rustled with wind—everything outside seemed normal and human and real. By contrast, the shape of the idea that was forming in the back of his mind was so grotesque and ugly that he wanted to run out of the office, to join the normal people passing on the street below. But he knew he could not escape by running. The idea would follow him, pursue him until he turned around and faced it.

Characters are often forced to confront unpleasant truths in the fiction of Margaret Millar, a writer who, as author Dean James has pointed out, "had the gift of taking the seemingly ordinary routines of daily life and finding the sinister undercurrents just beneath the surface."

In this story, Mr. Sands—an Inspector no more—discovers sinister and ugly things flourish just as well in the California sunshine as they did in the chill of his native Toronto.

Note

" 'had the gift of taking the seemingly ordinary routines of daily life' ": Dean James commentary on *A Stranger in My Grave*, from *100 Favorite Mysteries of the Century: Selected by the Independent Mystery Booksellers Association*, edited by Jim Huang (Crum Creek Press, 2000).

THE COUPLE NEXT DOOR

It was by accident that they lived next door to each other, but by design that they became neighbors—Mr. Sands, who had retired to California after a life of crime investigation, and the Rackhams, Charles and Alma. Rackham was a big, innocent-looking man in his fifties. Except for the accumulation of a great deal of money, nothing much had ever happened to Rackham, and he liked to listen to Sands talk, while Alma sat with her knitting, plump and contented, unimpressed by any tale that had no direct bearing on her own life. She was half Rackham's age, but the fullness of her figure, and her air of having withdrawn from life quietly and without fuss, gave her the stamp of middle-age.

Two or three times a week Sands crossed the concrete driveway, skirted the eugenia hedge, and pressed the Rackhams' door chime. He stayed for tea or for dinner, to play gin or scrabble, or just to talk. "That reminds me of a case I had in Toronto," Sands would say, and Rackham would produce martinis and an expression of intense interest, and Alma would smile tolerantly, as if she didn't really believe a single thing Sands, or anyone else, ever said.

They made good neighbors: the Rackhams, Charles younger than his years, and Alma older than hers, and Sands who could be any age at all ...

It was the last evening of August and through the open window of Sands' study came the scent of jasmine and the sound of a woman's harsh, wild weeping.

He thought at first that the Rackhams had a guest, a woman on a crying jag, perhaps, after a quarrel with her husband.

He went out into the front yard to listen, and Rackham came around the hedge, dressed in a bathrobe.

He said, sounding very surprised, "Alma's crying."

"I heard."

"I asked her to stop. I begged her. She won't tell me what's the matter."

"Women have cried before."

"Not Alma." Rackham stood on the damp grass, shivering, his forehead streaked with sweat. "What do you think we should do about it?"

The *I* had become *we*, because they were good neighbors, and along with the games and the dinners and the scent of jasmine, they shared the sound of a woman's grief.

"Perhaps you could talk to her," Rackham said.

"I'll try."

"I don't think there is anything physically the matter with her. We both had a check-up at the Tracy clinic last week. George Tracy is a good friend of mine—he'd have told me if there was anything wrong."

"I'm sure he would."

"If anything ever happened to Alma I'd kill myself."

Alma was crouched in a corner of the davenport in the living room, weeping rhythmically, methodically, as if she had accumulated a hoard of tears and must now spend them all in one night. Her fair skin was blotched with patches of red, like strawberry birthmarks, and her eyelids were blistered from the heat of her tears. She looked like a stranger to Sands, who had never seen her display any emotion stronger than ladylike distress over a broken teacup.

Rackham went over and stroked her hair. "Alma, dear. What is the matter?"

"Nothing ... nothing ..."

"Mr. Sands is here, Alma. I thought he might be able—we might be able—"

But no one was able. With a long shuddering sob, Alma got up and lurched across the room, hiding her blotched face with her hands. They heard her stumble up the stairs.

Sands said, "I'd better be going."

"No, please don't. I—the fact is, I'm scared stiff. Alma's always been so quiet."

"I know that."

"You don't suppose—there's no chance she's losing her mind?"

If they had not been good neighbors Sands might have remarked that Alma had little mind to lose. As it was, he said cautiously, "She might have had bad news, family trouble of some kind."

"She has no family except me."

"If you're worried, perhaps you'd better call your doctor."

"I think I will."

George Tracy arrived within half an hour, a slight, fair-haired man in his early thirties, with a smooth unhurried manner that imparted confidence. He talked slowly, moved slowly, as if there was all the time in the world to minister to desperate women.

Rackham chafed with impatience while Tracy removed his coat, placed it carefully across the back of the chair, and discussed the weather with Sands.

"It's a beautiful evening," Tracy said, and Alma's moans sliding down the stairs distorted his words, altered their meaning: *a terrible evening, an awful evening.* "There's a touch of fall in the air. You live in these parts, Mr. Sands?"

"Next door."

"For heaven's sake, George," Rackham said, "will you hurry up? For all you know, Alma might be dying."

"That I doubt. People don't die as easily as you might imagine. She's in her room?"

"Yes. Now will you *please—*"

"Take it easy, old man."

Tracy picked up his medical bag and went towards the stairs, leisurely, benign.

"He's always like that." Rackham turned to Sands, scowling. "Exasperating son-of-a-gun. You can bet that if he had a wife in Alma's condition he'd be taking those steps three at a time."

"Who knows?—perhaps he has."

"I know," Rackham said crisply. "He's not even married. Never had time for it, he told me. He doesn't look it but he's very ambitious."

"Most doctors are."

"Tracy is, anyway."

Rackham mixed a pitcher of martinis, and the two men sat in front of the unlit fire, waiting and listening. The noises from upstairs gradually ceased, and pretty soon the doctor came down again.

Rackham rushed across the room to meet him. "How is she?"

"Sleeping. I gave her a hypo."

"Did you talk to her? Did you ask her what was the matter?"

"She was in no condition to answer questions."

"Did you find anything wrong with her?"

"Not physically. She's a healthy young woman."

"Not *physically*. Does that mean—?"

"Take it easy, old man."

Rackham was too concerned with Alma to notice Tracy's choice of words, but Sands noticed, and wondered if it had been conscious or unconscious: Alma's a healthy young woman ... Take it easy, old man.

"If she's still depressed in the morning," Tracy said, "bring her down to the clinic with you when you come in for your X-rays. We have a good neurologist on our staff." He reached for his coat and hat. "By the way, I hope you followed the instructions?"

Rackham looked at him stupidly. "What instructions?"

"Before we can take specific X-rays, certain medication is necessary."

"I don't know what you're talking about."

"I made it very clear to Alma," Tracy said, sounding annoyed. "You were to take one ounce of sodium phosphate after dinner tonight, and report to the X-ray department at 8 o'clock tomorrow morning without breakfast."

"She didn't tell me."

"Oh."

"It must have slipped her mind."

"Yes. Obviously. Well, it's too late now." He put on his coat, moving quickly for the first time, as if he were in a rush to get away. The change made Sands curious. He wondered why Tracy was suddenly so anxious to leave, and whether there was any connection between Alma's hysteria and her lapse of memory about Rackham's X-rays. He looked at Rackham and guessed, from his pallor and his worried eyes, that Rackham had already made a connection in his mind.

"I understood," Rackham said carefully, "that I was all through at the clinic. My heart, lungs, metabolism—everything fit as a fiddle."

"People," Tracy said, "are not fiddles. Their tone doesn't improve with age. I will make another appointment for you and send you specific instructions by mail. Is that all right with you?"

"I guess it will have to be."

"Well, good night, Mr. Sands, pleasant meeting you." And to Rackham, "Good night, old man."

When he had gone, Rackham leaned against the wall, breathing hard. Sweat crawled down the sides of his face like worms and hid in the collar of his bathrobe. "You'll have to forgive me, Sands. I feel—I'm not feeling very well."

"Is there anything I can do?"

"Yes," Rackham said. "Turn back the clock."

"Beyond my powers, I'm afraid."

"Yes ... Yes, I'm afraid."

"Good night, Rackham." *Good night, old man.*

"Good night, Sands." *Good night old man to you, too.*

From his study Sands could see the lighted windows of Rackham's bedroom. Rackham's shadow moved back and forth behind the blinds as if seeking escape from the very light that gave it existence. Back and forth, in search of nirvana.

Sands read until far into the night. It was one of the solaces of growing old—if the hours were numbered, at least fewer of them need be wasted in sleep. When he went to bed, Rackham's bedroom light was still on.

They had become good neighbors by design; now, also by design, they became strangers. Whose design it was, Alma's or Rackham's, Sands didn't know.

There was no definite break, no unpleasantness. But the eugenia hedge seemed to have grown taller and thicker, and the concrete driveway a mile away. He saw the Rackhams occasionally; they waved or smiled or said, "Lovely weather," over the backyard fence. But Rackham's smile was thin and painful, Alma waved with a leaden arm, and neither of them cared about the weather. They stayed indoors most of the time, and when they did come out they were always together, arm in arm, walking slowly and in step. It was impossible to tell whose step led, and whose followed.

At the end of the first week in September, Sands met Alma by accident in a drug store downtown. It was the first time since the night of the doctor's visit that he'd seen either of the Rackhams alone.

She was waiting at the prescription counter wearing a flowery print dress that emphasized the fullness of her figure and the bovine expression of her face. A drug-store length away, she looked like a rather dull, badly dressed young woman with a passion for starchy foods, and it was hard to understand what Rackham had seen in her. But then Rackham had never stood a drug-store length away from Alma; he saw her only in close-up, the surprising, intense blue of her eyes, and the color and texture of her skin, like whipped cream. Sands wondered whether it was her skin and eyes, or her quality of serenity which had appealed most to Rackham, who was quick and nervous and excitable.

She said, placidly, "Why, hello there."

"Hello, Alma."

"Lovely weather, isn't it?"

"Yes ... How is Charles?"

"You must come over for dinner one of these nights."

"I'd like to."

"Next week, perhaps. I'll give you a call—I must run now. Charles is waiting for me. See you next week."

But she did not run, she walked; and Charles was not waiting for her, he was waiting for Sands. He had let himself into Sands' house and was pacing the floor of the study, smoking a cigarette. His color was bad, and he had lost weight, but he seemed to have acquired an inner calm. Sands could not tell whether it was the calm of a man who had come to an important decision, or that of a man who had reached the end of his rope and had stopped struggling.

They shook hands, firmly, pressing the past week back into shape.

Rackham said, "Nice to see you again, old man."

"I've been here all along."

"Yes. Yes, I know. ... I had things to do, a lot of thinking to do."

"Sit down. I'll make you a drink."

"No, thanks. Alma will be home shortly, I must be there."

Like a Siamese twin, Sands thought, *separated by a miracle, but returning voluntarily to the fusion—because the fusion was in a vital organ.*

"I understand," Sands said.

Rackham shook his head. "No one can understand, really, but you come very close sometimes, Sands. Very close." His cheeks flushed, like a boy's. "I'm not good at words or expressing my emotions, but I wanted to thank you before we leave, and tell you how much Alma and I have enjoyed your companionship."

"You're taking a trip?"

"Yes. Quite a long one."

"When are you leaving?"

"Today."

"You must let me see you off at the station."

"No, no," Rackham said quickly. "I couldn't think of it. I hate last-minute depot farewells. That's why I came over this afternoon to say good-bye."

"Tell me something of your plans."

"I would if I had any. Everything is rather indefinite. I'm not sure where we'll end up."

"I'd like to hear from you now and then."

"Oh, you'll hear from me, of course." Rackham turned away with an impatient twitch of his shoulders as if he was anxious to leave, anxious to start the trip right now before anything happened to prevent it.

"I'll miss you both," Sands said. "We've had a lot of laughs together."

Rackham scowled out of the window. "Please, no farewell speeches. They might shake my decision. My mind is already made up. I want no second thoughts."

"Very well."

"I must go now. Alma will be wondering—"

"I saw Alma earlier this afternoon," Sands said.

"Oh?"

"She invited me for dinner next week."

Outside the open window two hummingbirds fought and fussed, darting with crazy accuracy in and out of the bougainvillea vine.

"Alma," Rackham said carefully, "can be very forgetful sometimes."

"Not that forgetful. She doesn't know about this trip you've planned, does she? ... Does she, Rackham?"

"I wanted it to be a surprise. She's always had a desire to see the world. She's still young enough to believe that one place is different from any other place ... You and I know better."

"Do we?"

"Good-bye, Sands."

At the front door they shook hands again, and Rackham again promised to write, and Sands promised to answer his letters. Then Rackham crossed the lawn and the concrete driveway, head bent, shoulders hunched. He didn't look back as he turned the corner of the eugenia hedge.

Sands went over to his desk, looked up a number in the telephone directory, and dialed.

A girl's voice answered, "Tracy clinic, X-ray department."

"This is Charles Rackham," Sands said.

"Yes, Mr. Rackham."

"I'm leaving town unexpectedly. If you'll tell me the amount of my bill I'll send you a check before I go."

"The bill hasn't gone through, but the standard price for a lower gastro-intestinal is twenty-five dollars."

"Let's see. I had that done on the—"

"The fifth. Yesterday."

"But my original appointment was for the first, wasn't it?"

The girl gave a does-it-really-matter sigh. "Just a minute, sir, and I'll check." Half a minute later she was back on the line. "We have no record of an appointment for you on the first, sir."

"You're sure of that?"

"Even without the record book, I'd be sure. The first was a Monday. We do only gall bladders on Monday."

"Oh. Thank you."

Sands went out and got into his car. Before he pulled away from the curb he looked over at Rackham's house and saw Rackham pacing up and down the veranda, waiting for Alma.

The Tracy clinic was less impressive than Sands had expected, a converted two-story stucco house with a red tile roof. Some of the tiles were broken and the whole building needed paint, but the furnishings inside were smart and expensive.

At the reception desk a nurse wearing a crew cut and a professional smile told Sands that Dr. Tracy was booked solid for the entire afternoon. The only chance of seeing him was to sit in the second-floor waiting room and catch him between patients.

Sands went upstairs and took a chair in a little alcove at the end of the hall, near Tracy's door. He sat with his face half hidden behind an open magazine. After a while the door of Tracy's office opened and over the top of his magazine Sands saw a woman silhouetted in the door frame—a plump, fair-haired young woman in a flowery print dress.

Tracy followed her into the hall and the two of them stood looking at each other in silence. Then Alma turned and walked away, passing Sands without seeing him because her eyes were blind with tears.

Sands stood up. "Dr. Tracy?"

Tracy turned sharply, surprise and annoyance pinching the corners of his mouth. "Well? Oh, it's Mr. Sands."

"May I see you a moment?"

"I have quite a full schedule this afternoon."

"This is an emergency."

"Very well. Come in."

They sat facing each other across Tracy's desk.

"You look pretty fit," Tracy said with a wry smile, "for an emergency case."

"The emergency is not mine. It may be yours."

"If it's mine, I'll handle it alone, without the help of a poli—I'll handle it myself."

Sands leaned forward. "Alma has told you, then, that I used to be a policeman."

"She mentioned it in passing."

"I saw Alma leave a few minutes ago. ... She'd be quite a nice-looking woman if she learned to dress properly."

"Clothes are not important in a woman," Tracy said, with a slight flush. "Besides, I don't care to discuss my patients."

"Alma is a patient of yours?"

"Yes."

"Since the night Rackham called you when she was having hysterics?"

"Before then."

Sands got up, went to the window, and looked down at the street.

People were passing, children were playing on the sidewalk, the sun shone, the palm trees rustled with wind—everything outside seemed normal and human and real. By contrast, the shape of the idea that was forming in the back of his mind was

so grotesque and ugly that he wanted to run out of the office, to
join the normal people passing on the street below. But he knew
he could not escape by running. The idea would follow him, pursue him until he turned around and faced it.

It moved inside his brain like a vast wheel, and in the middle
of the wheel, impassive, immobile, was Alma.

Tracy's harsh voice interrupted the turning of the wheel. "Did
you come here to inspect my view, Mr. Sands?"

"Let's say, instead, your viewpoint."

"I'm a busy man. You're wasting my time."

"No. I'm giving you time."

"To do what?"

"Think things over."

"If you don't leave my office immediately, I'll have you thrown
out." Tracy glanced at the telephone but he didn't reach for it,
and there was no conviction in his voice.

"Perhaps you shouldn't have let me in. Why did you?"

"I thought you might make a fuss if I didn't."

"Fusses aren't in my line." Sands turned from the window.
"Liars are, though."

"What are you implying?"

"I've thought a great deal about that night you came to the
Rackhams' house. In retrospect, the whole thing appeared too
pat; too contrived: Alma had hysterics and you were called to
treat her. Natural enough, so far."

Tracy stirred but didn't speak.

"The interesting part came later. You mentioned casually to
Rackham that he had an appointment for some X-rays to be
taken the following day, September the first. It was assumed
that Alma had forgotten to tell him. Only Alma *hadn't* forgotten.
There was nothing to forget. I checked with your X-ray
department half an hour ago. They have no record of any
appointment for Rackham on September the first."

"Records get lost."

"This record wasn't lost. It never existed. You lied to Rackham.
The lie itself wasn't important, it was the *kind* of lie. I could
have understood a lie of vanity, or one to avoid punishment or
to gain profit. But this seemed such a silly, senseless, little lie. It
worried me. I began to wonder about Alma's part in the scene

that night. Her crying was most unusual for a woman of Alma's inert nature. What if her crying was also a lie? And what was to be gained by it?"

"Nothing," Tracy said wearily. "Nothing was gained."

"But something was *intended*—and I think I know what it was. The scene was played to worry Rackham, to set him up for an even bigger scene. If that next scene has already been played, I am wasting my time here. Has it?"

"You have a vivid imagination."

"No. The plan was yours—I only figured it out."

"Very poor figuring, Mr. Sands." But Tracy's face was gray, as if mold had grown over his skin.

"I wish it were. I had become quite fond of the Rackhams."

He looked down at the street again, seeing nothing but the wheel turning inside his head. Alma was no longer in the middle of the wheel, passive and immobile; she was revolving with the others—Alma and Tracy and Rackham, turning as the wheel turned, clinging to its perimeter.

Alma, devoted wife, a little on the dull side ... What sudden passion of hate or love had made her capable of such consummate deceit? Sands imagined the scene the morning after Tracy's visit to the house. Rackham, worried and exhausted after a sleepless night: "*Are you feeling better now, Alma?*"

"*Yes.*"

"*What made you cry like that?*"

"*I was worried.*"

"*About me?*"

"*Yes.*"

"*Why didn't you tell me about my X-ray appointment?*"

"*I couldn't. I was frightened. I was afraid they would discover something serious the matter with you.*"

"*Did Tracy give you any reason to think that?*"

"*He mentioned something about a blockage. Oh, Charles, I'm scared! If anything ever happened to you, I'd die. I couldn't live without you!*"

For an emotional and sensitive man like Rackham, it was a perfect set-up: his devoted wife was frightened to the point of hysterics, his good friend and physician had given her reason to be frightened. Rackham was ready for the next step ...

"According to the records in your X-ray department," Sands said, "Rackham had a lower gastrointestinal X-ray yesterday morning. What was the result?"

"Medical ethics forbid me to—"

"You can't hide behind a wall of medical ethics that's already full of holes. What was the result?"

There was a long silence before Tracy spoke. "Nothing."

"You found nothing the matter with him?"

"That's right."

"Have you told Rackham that?"

"He came in earlier this afternoon, alone."

"Why alone?"

"I didn't want Alma to hear what I had to say."

"Very considerate of you."

"No, it was not considerate," Tracy said dully. "I had decided to back out of our—our agreement—and I didn't want her to know just yet."

"The agreement was to lie to Rackham, convince him that he had a fatal disease?"

"Yes."

"Did you?"

"No. I showed him the X-rays, I made it clear that there was nothing wrong with him … I tried. I tried my best. It was no use."

"What do you mean?"

"He wouldn't believe me! He thought I was trying to keep the real truth from him." Tracy drew in his breath sharply. "It's funny, isn't it?—after days of indecision and torment I made up my mind to do the right thing. But it was too late. Alma had played her role too well. She's the only one Rackham will believe."

The telephone on Tracy's desk began to ring but he made no move to answer it, and pretty soon the ringing stopped and the room was quiet again.

Sands said, "Have you asked Alma to tell him the truth?"

"Yes, just before you came in."

"She refused?"

Tracy didn't answer.

"She wants him to think he is fatally ill?"

"I—yes."

"In the hope that he'll kill himself, perhaps?"

Once again Tracy was silent. But no reply was necessary.

"I think Alma miscalculated," Sands said quietly. "Instead of planning suicide, Rackham is planning a trip. But before he leaves, he's going to hear the truth—from you and from Alma." Sands went towards the door. "Come on, Tracy. You have a house call to make."

"No, I can't." Tracy grasped the desk with both hands, like a child resisting the physical force of removal by a parent. "I won't go."

"You have to."

"No! Rackham will ruin me if he finds out. That's how this whole thing started. We were afraid, Alma and I, afraid of what Rackham would do if she asked him for a divorce. He's crazy in love with her, he's obsessed!"

"And so are you?"

"Not the way he is. Alma and I both want the same things—a little peace, a little quiet together. We are alike in many ways."

"That I can believe," Sands said grimly. "You want the same things, a little peace, a little quiet—and a little of Rackham's money?"

"The money was secondary."

"A very close second. How did you plan on getting it?"

Tracy shook his head from side to side, like an animal in pain. "You keep referring to plans, ideas, schemes. We didn't start out with plans or schemes. We just fell in love. We've been in love for nearly a year, not daring to do anything about it because I knew how Rackham would react if we told him. I have worked hard to build up this clinic; Rackham could destroy it, and me, within a month."

"That's a chance you'll have to take. Come on, Tracy."

Sands opened the door and the two men walked down the hall, slowly and in step, as if they were handcuffed together.

A nurse in uniform met them at the top of the stairs. "Dr. Tracy, are you ready for your next—?"

"Cancel all my appointments, Miss Leroy."

"But that's imposs—"

"I have a very important house call to make."

"Will it take long?"

"I don't know."

The two men went down the stairs, past the reception desk, and out into the summer afternoon. Before he got into Sands' car, Tracy looked back at the clinic, as if he never expected to see it again.

Sands turned on the ignition and the car sprang forward.

After a time Tracy said, "Of all the people in the world who could have been at the Rackhams' that night, it had to be an ex-policeman."

"It's lucky for you that I was."

"Lucky." Tracy let out a harsh little laugh. "What's lucky about financial ruin?"

"It's better than some other kinds of ruin. If your plan had gone through, you could never have felt like a decent man again."

"You think I will anyway?"

"Perhaps, as the years go by."

"The years." Tracy turned, with a sigh. "What are you going to tell Rackham?"

"Nothing. You will tell him yourself."

"I can't. You don't understand. I'm quite fond of Rackham, and so is Alma. We—it's hard to explain."

"Even harder to understand." Sands thought back to all the times he had seen the Rackhams together and envied their companionship, their mutual devotion. Never, by the slightest glance or gesture of impatience or slip of the tongue, had Alma indicated that she was passionately in love with another man. He recalled the games of scrabble, the dinners, the endless conversations with Rackham, while Alma sat with her knitting, her face reposeful, content. Rackham would ask, "Don't you want to play, too, Alma?" And she would reply, "No, thank you, dear, I'm quite happy with my thoughts."

Alma, happy with her thoughts of violent delights and violent ends.

Sands said, "Alma is equally in love with you?"

"Yes." He sounded absolutely convinced. "No matter what Rackham says or does, we intend to have each other."

"I see."

The blinds of the Rackham house were closed against the sun.

Sands led the way up the veranda steps and pressed the door chime, while Tracy stood, stony-faced and erect, like a bill collector or a process server.

Sands could hear the chimes pealing inside the house and feel their vibrations beating under his feet.

He said, "They may have gone already."

"Gone where?"

"Rackham wouldn't tell me. He just said he was planning the trip as a surprise for Alma."

"He can't take her away! He can't force her to leave if she doesn't want to go!"

Sands pressed the door chime again, and called out, "Rackham? Alma?" But there was no response.

He wiped the sudden moisture off his forehead with his coat sleeve. "I'm going in."

"I'm coming with you."

"No."

The door was unlocked. He stepped into the empty hall and shouted up the staircase, "Alma? Rackham? Are you there?"

The echo of his voice teased him from the dim corners.

Tracy had come into the hall. "They've left, then?"

"Perhaps not. They might have just gone out for a drive. It's a nice day for a drive."

"Is it?"

"Go around to the back and see if their car's in the garage."

When Tracy had gone, Sands closed the door behind him and shot the bolt. He stood for a moment listening to Tracy's nervous footsteps on the concrete driveway. Then he turned and walked slowly into the living room, knowing the car would be in the garage, no matter how nice a day it was for a drive.

The drapes were pulled tight across the windows and the room was cool and dark, but alive with images and noisy with the past:

"I wanted to thank you before we leave, Sands."

"You're taking a trip?"

"Yes, quite a long one."

"When are you leaving?"

"Today."

"You must let me see you off at the station. . . ."

But no station had been necessary for Rackham's trip. He lay in front of the fireplace in a pool of blood, and beside him was his companion on the journey, her left arm curving around his waist.

Rackham had kept his promise to write. The note was on the mantel, addressed not to Sands, but to Tracy.

> Dear George:
> You did your best to fool me but I got the truth from Alma. She could never hide anything from me, we are too close to each other. This is the easiest way out. I am sorry that I must take Alma along, but she has told me so often that she could not live without me. I cannot leave her behind to grieve.
> Think of us now and then, and try not to judge me too harshly.
>
> *Charles Rackham*

Sands put the note back on the mantel. He stood quietly, his heart pierced by the final splinter of irony: before Rackham had used the gun on himself, he had lain down on the floor beside Alma and placed her dead arm lovingly around his waist.

From outside came the sound of Tracy's footsteps and then the pounding of his fists on the front door.

"Sands, I'm locked out. Open the door. Let me in! Sands, do you hear me? Open this door!"

Sands went and opened the door.

THE PEOPLE ACROSS THE CANYON

THE PEOPLE ACROSS THE CANYON
Preface by Tom Nolan

Readers and writers enamored of craft (or simply of well-turned phrases) will savor examples all through "The People Across the Canyon" of Margaret Millar's elegant way with words.

For instance: "… she had something on her mind which she wanted to transfer to his. The transference, intended to halve the problem, often merely doubled it."

Or the yellow school-bus "like a circus cage full of wild captive children screaming for release."

Biographers of Margaret and Kenneth Millar may be forgiven for hearing, in "the mocking muted roar" of this 1961 story's cream-colored Austin-Healy, a symbolic echo of the white Simca sports car that drove Linda Millar away from her UC Davis campus and into a ten-day disappearance in the spring of 1959 …

THE PEOPLE ACROSS THE CANYON

The first time the Bortons realized that someone had moved into the new house across the canyon was one night in May when they saw the rectangular light of a television set shining in the picture window. Marion Borton knew it had to happen eventually, but that didn't make it any easier to accept the idea of neighbors in a part of the country she and Paul had come to consider exclusively their own.

They had discovered the site, had bought six acres, and built the house over the objections of the bank, which didn't like to lend money on unimproved property, and of their friends who thought the Bortons were foolish to move so far out of town. Now other people were discovering the spot, and here and there through the eucalyptus trees and the live oaks, Marion could see half-finished houses.

But it was the house directly across the canyon that bothered her most; she had been dreading this moment ever since the site had been bulldozed the previous summer.

"There goes our privacy." Marion went over and snapped off the television set, a sign to Paul that she had something on her mind which she wanted to transfer to his. The transference, intended to halve the problem, often merely doubled it.

"Well, let's have it," Paul said, trying to conceal his annoyance.

"Have what?"

"Stop kidding around. You don't usually cut off Perry Mason in the middle of a sentence."

"All I said was, there goes our privacy."

"We have plenty left," Paul said.

"You know how sounds carry across the canyon."

"I don't hear any sounds."

"You will. They probably have ten or twelve children and a howling dog and a sports car."

"A couple of children wouldn't be so bad—at least, Cathy would have someone to play with."

Cathy was eight, in bed now, and ostensibly asleep, with the night light on and her bedroom door open just a crack.

"She has plenty of playmates at school," Marion said, pulling the drapes across the window so that she wouldn't have to look at the exasperating rectangle of light across the canyon. "Her teacher tells me Cathy gets along with everyone and never causes any trouble. You talk as if she's deprived or something."

"It would be nice if she had more interests, more children of her own age around."

"A lot of things would be nice *if*. I've done my best."

Paul knew it was true. He'd heard her issue dozens of weekend invitations to Cathy's schoolmates. Few of them came to anything. The mothers offered various excuses: poison oak, snakes, mosquitoes in the creek at the bottom of the canyon, the distance of the house from town in case something happened and a doctor was needed in a hurry ... These excuses, sincere and valid as they were, embittered Marion. *"For heaven's sake, you'd think we lived on the moon or in the middle of a jungle."*

"I guess a couple of children would be all right," Marion said. "But please, no sports car."

"I'm afraid that's out of our hands."

"Actually, they might even be quite *nice* people."

"Why not? Most people are."

Both Marion and Paul had the comfortable feeling that something had been settled, though neither was quite sure what. Paul went over and turned the television set back on. As he had suspected, it was the doorman who'd killed the nightclub owner with a baseball bat, not the blonde dancer or her young husband or the jealous singer.

It was the following Monday that Cathy started to run away.

Marion, ironing in the kitchen and watching a quiz program on the portable set Paul had given her for Christmas, heard the school bus groan to a stop at the top of the driveway. She waited for the front door to open and Cathy to announce in her high thin voice, "I'm home, Mommy."

The door didn't open.

From the kitchen window Marion saw the yellow bus round the sharp curve of the hill like a circus cage full of wild captive children screaming for release.

Marion waited until the end of the program, trying to convince herself that another bus had been added to the route and would come along shortly, or that Cathy had decided to stop off at a friend's house and would telephone any minute. But no other bus appeared, and the telephone remained silent.

Marion changed into her hiking boots and started off down the canyon, avoiding the scratchy clumps of chapparal and the creepers of poison oak that looked like loganberry vines.

She found Cathy sitting in the middle of the little bridge that Paul had made across the creek out of two fallen eucalyptus trees. Cathy's short plump legs hung over the logs until they almost touched the water. She was absolutely motionless, her face hidden by a straw curtain of hair. Then a single frog croaked a warning of Marion's presence and Cathy responded to the sound as if she was more intimate with nature than adults were, and more alert to its subtle communications of danger.

She stood up quickly, brushing off the back of her dress and drawing aside the curtain of hair to reveal eyes as blue as the periwinkles that hugged the banks of the creek.

"Cathy."

"I was only counting waterbugs while I was waiting. Forty-one."

"Waiting for what?"

"The ten or twelve children, and the dog."

"What ten or twelve chil—" Marion stopped. "I see. You were listening the other night when we thought you were asleep."

"I wasn't listening," Cathy said righteously. "My ears were hearing."

Marion restrained a smile. "Then I wish you'd tell those ears of yours to hear properly. I didn't say the new neighbors have ten or twelve children, I said they *might* have. Actually, it's very unlikely. Not many families are that big these days."

"Do you have to be old to have a big family?"

"Well, you certainly can't be very young."

"I bet people with big families have station wagons so they have room for all the children."

"The lucky ones do."

Cathy stared down at the thin flow of water carrying fat little minnows down to the sea. Finally she said, "They're too young, and their car is too small."

In spite of her aversion to having new neighbors, Marion felt a quickening of interest. "Have you seen them?"

But the little girl seemed deaf, lost in a water world of minnows and dragonflies and tadpoles.

"I asked you a question, Cathy. Did you see the people who just moved in?"

"Yes."

"When?"

"Before you came. Their name is Smith."

"How do you know that?"

"I went up to the house to look at things and they said, hello, little girl, what's your name? And I said, Cathy, what's yours? And they said Smith. Then they drove off in the little car."

"You're not supposed to go poking around other people's houses," Marion said brusquely. "And while we're at it, you're not supposed to go anywhere after school without first telling me where you're going and when you'll be back. You know that perfectly well. Now why didn't you come in and report to me after you got off the school bus?"

"I didn't want to."

"That's not a satisfactory answer."

Satisfactory or not, it was the only answer Cathy had. She looked at her mother in silence, then she turned and darted back up the hill to her own house.

After a time Marion followed her, exasperated and a little confused. She hated to punish the child, but she knew she couldn't ignore the matter entirely—it was much too serious. While she gave Cathy her graham crackers and orange juice, she told her, reasonably and kindly, that she would have to stay in her room the following day after school by way of learning a lesson.

That night, after Cathy had been tucked in bed, Marion related the incident to Paul. He seemed to take a less serious view of it than Marion, a fact of which the listening child became well aware.

"I'm glad she's getting acquainted with the new people," Paul said. "It shows a certain degree of poise I didn't think she had. She's always been so shy."

"You're surely not condoning her running off without telling me?"

"She didn't run far. All kids do things like that once in a while."

"We don't want to spoil her."

"Cathy's always been so obedient I think she has *us* spoiled. Who knows, she might even teach us a thing or two about going out and making new friends." He realized, from past experience, that this was a very touchy subject. Marion had her house, her garden, her television sets; she didn't seem to want any more of the world than these, and she resented any implication that they were not enough. To ward off an argument he added, "You've done a good job with Cathy. Stop worrying ... Smith, their name is?"

"Yes."

"Actually, I think it's an excellent sign that Cathy's getting acquainted."

At three the next afternoon the yellow circus cage arrived, released one captive, and rumbled on its way.

"I'm home, Mommy."

"Good girl."

Marion felt guilty at the sight of her: the child had been cooped up in school all day, the weather was so warm and lovely, and besides Paul hadn't thought the incident of the previous afternoon too important.

"I know what," Marion suggested, "let's you and I go down to the creek and count waterbugs."

The offer was a sacrifice for Marion because her favorite quiz program was on and she liked to answer the questions along with the contestants. "How about that?"

Cathy knew all about the quiz program; she'd seen it a hundred times, had watched the moving mouths claim her mother's eyes and ears and mind. "I counted the waterbugs yesterday."

"Well, minnows, then."

"You'll scare them away."

"Oh, will I?" Marion laughed self-consciously, rather relieved that Cathy had refused her offer and was clearly and definitely a little guilty about the relief. "Don't you scare them?"

"No. They think I'm another minnow because they're used to me."

"Maybe they could get used to me, too."

"I don't think so."

When Cathy went off down the canyon by herself Marion realized, in a vaguely disturbing way, that the child had politely

but firmly rejected her mother's company. It wasn't until dinner
time that she found out the reason why.

"The Smiths," Cathy said, "have an Austin-Healey."

Cathy, like most girls, had never shown any interest in cars,
and her glib use of the name moved her parents to laughter.

The laughter encouraged Cathy to elaborate. "An Austin-
Healey makes a lot of noise—like Daddy's lawn mower."

"I don't think the company would appreciate a commercial from
you, young lady," Paul said. "Are the Smiths all moved in?"

"Oh, yes. I helped them."

"Is that a fact? And how did you help them?"

"I sang two songs. And then we danced and danced."

Paul looked half pleased, half puzzled. It wasn't like Cathy to
perform willingly in front of people. During the last Christmas
concert at the school she'd left the stage in tears and hidden in
the cloak room … Well, maybe her shyness was only a phase
and she was finally getting over it.

"They must be very nice people," he said, "to take time out
from getting settled in a new house to play games with a little
girl."

Cathy shook her head. "It wasn't games. It was real dancing—
like on Ed Sullivan."

"As good as that, eh?" Paul said, smiling. "Tell me about it."

"Mrs. Smith is a night-club dancer."

Paul's smile faded, and a pulse began to beat in his left temple
like a small misplaced heart. "Oh? You're sure about that,
Cathy?"

"Yes."

"And what does Mr. Smith do?"

"He's a baseball player."

"You mean that's what he does for a living?" Marion asked.
"He doesn't work in an office like Daddy?"

"No, he just plays baseball. He always wears a baseball cap."

"I see. What position does he play on the team?" Paul's voice
was low.

Cathy looked blank.

"Everybody on a ball team has a special thing to do. What
does Mr. Smith do?"

"He's a batter."

"A batter, eh? Well, that's nice. Did he tell you this?"

"Yes."

"Cathy," Paul said, "I know you wouldn't deliberately lie to me, but sometimes you get your facts a little mixed up."

He went on in this vein for some time but Cathy's story remained unshaken: Mrs. Smith was a night-club dancer, Mr. Smith a professional baseball player, they loved children, and they never watched television.

"That, at least, must be a lie," Marion said to Paul later when she saw the rectangular light of the television set shining in the Smiths' picture window. "As for the rest of it, there isn't a night club within fifty miles, or a professional ball club within two hundred."

"She probably misunderstood. It's quite possible that at one time Mrs. Smith was a dancer of sorts and that he played a little baseball."

Cathy, in bed and teetering dizzily on the brink of sleep, wondered if she should tell her parents about the Smiths' child—the one who didn't go to school.

She didn't tell them; Marion found out for herself the next morning after Paul and Cathy had gone. When she pulled back the drapes in the living room and opened the windows she heard the sharp slam of a screen door from across the canyon and saw a small child come out on the patio of the new house. At that distance she couldn't tell whether it was a boy or a girl. Whichever it was, the child was quiet and well behaved; only the occasional slam of the door shook the warm, windless day.

The presence of the child, and the fact that Cathy hadn't mentioned it, gnawed at Marion's mind all day. She questioned Cathy about it as soon as she came home.

"You didn't tell me the Smiths have a child."

"No."

"Why not?"

"I don't know why not."

"Is it a boy or a girl?"

"Girl."

"How old?"

Cathy thought it over carefully, frowning up at the ceiling. "About ten."

"Doesn't she go to school?"

"No."

"Why not?"

"She doesn't want to."

"That's not a very good reason."

"It is her reason," Cathy said flatly. "Can I go out to play now?"

"I'm not sure you should. You look a little feverish. Come here and let me feel your forehead."

Cathy's forehead was cool and moist, but her cheeks and the bridge of her nose were very pink, almost as if she'd been sunburned.

"You'd better stay inside," Marion said, "and watch some cartoons."

"I don't like cartoons."

"You used to."

"I like real people."

She means the Smiths, of course, Marion thought as her mouth tightened. "People who dance and play baseball all the time?"

If the sarcasm had any effect on Cathy she didn't show it. After waiting until Marion had become engrossed in her quiz program, Cathy lined up all her dolls in her room and gave a concert for them, to thunderous applause.

"Where are your old Navy binoculars?" Marion asked Paul when she was getting ready for bed.

"Oh, somewhere in the sea chest, I imagine. Why?"

"I want them."

"Not thinking of spying on the neighbors, are you?"

"I'm thinking of just that," Marion said grimly.

The next morning, as soon as she saw the Smith child come out on the patio, Marion went downstairs to the storage room to search through the sea chest. She located the binoculars and was in the act of dusting them off when the telephone started to ring in the living room. She hurried upstairs and said breathlessly, "Hello?"

"Mrs. Borton?"

"Yes."

"This is Miss Park speaking, Cathy's teacher."

Marion had met Miss Park several times at P.T.A. meetings and report-card conferences. She was a large, ruddy-faced, and unfailingly cheerful young woman—the kind, as Paul said, you wouldn't want to live with but who'd be nice to have around in an emergency. "How are you, Miss Park?"

"Oh, fine, thank you, Mrs. Borton. I meant to call you yesterday but things were a bit out of hand around here, and I knew there was no great hurry to check on Cathy; she's such a well-behaved little girl."

Even Miss Park's loud, jovial voice couldn't cover up the ominous sound of the word *check*. "I don't think I quite understand. Why should you check on Cathy?"

"Purely routine. The school doctor and the health department like to keep records on how many cases of measles or flu or chicken pox are going the rounds. Right now it looks like the season for mumps. Is Cathy all right?"

"She seemed a little feverish yesterday afternoon when she got home from school, but she acted perfectly normal when she left this morning."

Miss Park's silence was so protracted that Marion became painfully conscious of things she wouldn't otherwise have noticed— the weight of the binoculars in her lap, the thud of her own heartbeat in her ears. Across the canyon the Smith child was playing quietly and alone on the patio. *There is definitely something the matter with that girl,* Marion thought. *Perhaps I'd better not let Cathy go over there any more, she's so imitative.* "Miss Park, are you still on the line? Hello? Hello—"

"I'm here." Miss Park's voice seemed fainter than usual, and less positive. "What time did Cathy leave the house this morning?"

"Eight, as usual."

"Did she take the school bus?"

"Of course. She always does."

"Did you see her get on?"

"I kissed her goodbye at the front door," Marion said. "What's this all about, Miss Park?"

"Cathy hasn't been at school for two days, Mrs. Borton."

"Why, that's absurd, impossible! You must be mistaken." But even as she was speaking the words, Marion was raising the binoculars to her eyes: the little girl on the Smiths' patio had a straw curtain of hair and eyes as blue as the periwinkles along the creek banks.

"Mrs. Borton, I'm not likely to be mistaken about which of my children are in class or not."

"No. No, you're—you're not mistaken, Miss Park. I can see Cathy from here—she's over at the neighbors' house."

"Good. That's a load off my mind."

"Off yours, yes," Marion said. "Not mine."

"Now we mustn't become excited, Mrs. Borton. Don't make too much of this incident before we've had a chance to confer. Suppose you come and talk to me during my lunch hour and bring Cathy along. We'll all have a friendly chat."

But it soon became apparent, even to the optimistic Miss Park, that Cathy didn't intend to take part in any friendly chat. She stood by the window in the classroom, blank-eyed, mute, unresponsive to the simplest questions, refusing to be drawn into any conversation even about her favorite topic, the Smiths. Miss Park finally decided to send Cathy out to play in the schoolyard while she talked to Marion alone.

"Obviously," Miss Park said, enunciating the word very distinctly because it was one of her favorites, "obviously, Cathy's got a crush on this young couple and has concocted a fantasy about belonging to them."

"It's not so obvious what my husband and I are going to do about it."

"Live through it, the same as other parents. Crushes like this are common at Cathy's age. Sometimes the object is a person, a whole family, even a horse. And, of course, to Cathy a night-club dancer and a baseball player must seem very glamorous indeed. Tell me, Mrs. Borton, does she watch television a great deal?"

Marion stiffened. "No more than any other child."

Oh, dear, Miss Park thought sadly, *they all do it; the most confirmed addicts are always the most defensive.* "I just wondered," she said. "Cathy likes to sing to herself and I've never heard such a repertoire of television commercials."

"She picks things up very fast."

"Yes. Yes, she does indeed." Miss Park studied her hands which were always a little pale from chalk dust and were even paler now because she was angry—at the child for deceiving her, at Mrs. Borton for brushing aside the television issue, at herself for not preventing, or at least anticipating, the current situation, and perhaps most of all at the Smiths who ought to have known better than to allow a child to hang around their house when she should obviously be in school.

"Don't put too much pressure on Cathy about this," she said finally, "until I talk the matter over with the school psychologist. By the way, have you met the Smiths, Mrs. Borton?"

"Not yet," Marion said grimly. "But believe me, I intend to."

"Yes, I think it would be a good idea for you to talk to them and make it clear that they're not to encourage Cathy in this fantasy."

The meeting came sooner than Marion expected.

She waited at the school until classes were dismissed, then she took Cathy into town to do some shopping. She had parked the car and she and Cathy were standing hand in hand at a corner waiting for a traffic light to change; Marion was worried and impatient, Cathy still silent, unresisting, inert, as she had been ever since Marion had called her home from the Smiths' patio.

Suddenly Marion felt the child's hand tighten in a spasm of excitement. Cathy's face had turned so pink it looked ready to explode and with her free hand she was waving violently at two people in a small cream-colored sports car—a very pretty young woman with blonde hair in the driver's seat, and beside her a young man wearing a wide friendly grin and a baseball cap. They both waved back at Cathy just before the lights changed and then the car roared through the intersection.

"The Smiths," Cathy shouted, jumping up and down in a frenzy. "That was the Smiths."

"Sssh, not so loud. People will—"

"But it was the *Smiths!*"

"Hurry up before the light changes."

The child didn't hear. She stood as if rooted to the curb, staring after the cream-colored car.

With a little grunt of impatience Marion picked her up, carried her across the road, and let her down quite roughly on the other side. "There. If you're going to act like a baby, I'll carry you like a baby."

"I saw the Smiths!"

"All right. What are you so excited about? It's not very unusual to meet someone in town whom you know."

"It's unusual to meet *them*."

"Why?"

"Because it is." The color was fading from Cathy's cheeks, but her eyes still looked bedazzled, quite as if they'd seen a miracle.

"I'm sure they're very unique people," Marion said coldly. "Nevertheless they must shop for groceries like everyone else."

Cathy's answer was a slight shake of her head and a whisper heard only by herself: "No, they don't, never."

When Paul came home from work Cathy was sent to play in the front yard while Marion explained matters to him. He listened with increasing irritation—not so much at Cathy's actions but at the manner in which Marion and Miss Park had handled things. There was too much talking, he said, and too little acting.

"The way you women beat around the bush instead of tackling the situation directly, meeting it head-on—fantasy life. Fantasy life, my foot! Now we're going over to the Smiths right this minute and talk to them and that will be that. End of fantasy. Period."

"We'd better wait until after dinner. Cathy missed her lunch."

Throughout the meal Cathy was pale and quiet. She ate nothing and spoke only when asked a direct question; but inside herself the conversation was very lively, the dinner a banquet with dancing, and afterward a wild, windy ride in the roofless car …

Although the footpath through the canyon provided a shorter route to the Smiths' house, the Bortons decided to go more formally, by car, and to take Cathy with them. Cathy, told to comb her hair and wash her face, protested: "I don't want to go over there."

"Why not?" Paul said. "You were so anxious to spend time with them that you played hooky for two days. Why don't you want to see them now?"

"Because they're not there."

"How do you know?"

"Mrs. Smith told me this morning that they wouldn't be home tonight because she's putting on a show."

"Indeed?" Paul was grim-faced. "Just where does she put on these shows of hers?"

"And Mr. Smith has to play baseball. And after that they're going to see a friend in the hospital who has leukemia."

"Leukemia, eh?" He didn't have to ask how Cathy had found

out about such a thing; he'd watched a semi-documentary dealing with it a couple of nights ago. Cathy was supposed to have
been sleeping.

"I wonder," he said to Marion when Cathy went to comb her
hair, "just how many 'facts' about the Smiths have been borrowed from television."

"Well, I know for myself that they drive a sports car, and
Mr. Smith was wearing a baseball cap. And they're both young
and good-looking. Young and good-looking enough," she added
wryly, "to make me feel—well, a little jealous."

"Jealous?"

"Cathy would rather belong to them than to us. It makes me
wonder if it's something the Smiths have or something the
Bortons don't have."

"Ask her."

"I can't very well—"

"Then I will, dammit," Paul said. And he did.

Cathy merely looked at him innocently. "I don't know. I don't
know what you mean."

"Then listen again. Why did you pretend that you were the
Smiths' little girl?"

"They asked me to be. They asked me to go with them."

"They actually said, Cathy, will you be our little girl?"

"Yes."

"Well, by heaven, I'll put an end to this nonsense," Paul said,
and strode out to the car.

It was twilight when they reached the Smiths' house by way
of the narrow, hilly road. The moon, just appearing above the
horizon, was on the wane, a chunk bitten out of its side by some
giant jaw. A warm dry wind, blowing down the mountain from
the desert beyond, carried the sweet scent of pittosporum.

The Smiths' house was dark, and both the front door and the
garage were locked. Out of defiance or desperation, Paul pressed
the door chime anyway, several times. All three of them could
hear it ringing inside, and it seemed to Marion to echo very
curiously—as if the carpets and drapes were too thin to muffle
the sound vibrations. She would have liked to peer in through
the windows and see for herself, but the venetian blinds were
closed.

"What's their furniture like?" she asked Cathy.

"Like everybody's."

"I mean, is it new? Does Mrs. Smith tell you not to put your feet on it?"

"No, she never tells me that," Cathy said truthfully. "I want to go home now. I'm tired."

It was while she was putting Cathy to bed that Marion heard Paul call to her from the living room in an urgent voice, "Marion, come here a minute."

She found him standing motionless in the middle of the room, staring across the canyon at the Smiths' place. The rectangular light of the Smiths' television set was shining in the picture window of the room that opened onto the patio at the back of the Smiths' house.

"Either they've come home within the past few minutes," he said, "or they were there all the time. My guess is that they were home when we went over but they didn't want to see us, so they just doused the lights and pretended to be out. Well, it won't work! Come on, we're going back."

"I can't leave Cathy alone. She's already got her pajamas on."

"Put a bathrobe on her and bring her along. This has gone beyond the point of observing such niceties as correct attire."

"Don't you think we should wait until tomorrow?"

"Hurry up and stop arguing with me."

Cathy, protesting that she was tired and that the Smiths weren't home anyway, was bundled into a bathrobe and carried to the car.

"They're home all right," Paul said. "And by heaven they'd better answer the door this time or I'll break it down."

"That's an absurd way to talk in front of a child," Marion said coldly. "She has enough ideas without hearing—"

"Absurd, is it? Wait and see."

Cathy, listening from the back seat, smiled sleepily. She knew how to get in without breaking anything: ever since the house had been built, the real estate man who'd been trying to sell it always hid the key on a nail underneath the window box.

The second trip seemed a nightmarish imitation of the first: the same moon hung in the sky but it looked smaller now, and paler. The scent of pittosporum was funereally sweet, and the hollow sound of the chimes from inside the house was like an echo in an empty tomb.

"They must be crazy to think they can get away with a trick like this twice in one night," Paul shouted. "Come on, we're going around to the back."

Marion looked a little frightened. "I don't like trespassing on someone else's property."

"They trespassed on our property first."

He glanced down at Cathy. Her eyes were half closed and her face was pearly in the moonlight. He pressed her hand to reassure her that everything was going to be all right and that his anger wasn't directed at her, but she drew away from him and started down the path that led to the back of the house.

Paul clicked on his flashlight and followed her, moving slowly along the unfamiliar terrain. By the time he turned the corner of the house and reached the patio, Cathy was out of sight.

"Cathy," he called. "Where are you? Come back here!"

Marion was looking at him accusingly. "You upset her with that silly threat about breaking down the door. She's probably on her way home through the canyon."

"I'd better go after her."

"She's less likely to get hurt than you are. She knows every inch of the way. Besides, you came here to break down doors. All right, start breaking."

But there was no need to break down anything. The back door opened as soon as Paul rapped on it with his knuckles, and he almost fell into the room.

It was empty except for a small girl wearing a blue bathrobe that matched her eyes.

Paul said, "Cathy. Cathy, what are you doing here?"

Marion stood with her hand pressed to her mouth to stifle the scream that was rising in her throat. There were no Smiths. The people in the sports car whom Cathy had waved at were just strangers responding to the friendly greeting of a child— had Cathy seen them before, on a previous trip to town? The television set was no more than a contraption rigged up by Cathy herself—an orange crate and an old mirror which caught and reflected the rays of the moon.

In front of it Cathy was standing, facing her own image. "Hello, Mrs. Smith. Here I am, all ready to go."

"Cathy," Marion said in a voice that sounded torn by claws. "What do you see in that mirror?"

"It's not a mirror. It's a television set."

"What—what program are you watching?"

"It's not a program, silly. It's real. It's the Smiths. I'm going away with them to dance and play baseball."

"There are no Smiths," Paul bellowed. "Will you get that through your head? *There are no Smiths!*"

"Yes, there are. I see them."

Marion knelt on the floor beside the child. "Listen to me, Cathy. This is a mirror—only a mirror. It came from Daddy's old bureau and I had it put away in the storage room. That's where you found it, isn't it? And you brought it here and decided to pretend it was a television set, isn't that right? But it's really just a mirror, and the people in it are us—you and Mommy and Daddy."

But even as she looked at her own reflection, Marion saw it beginning to change. She was growing younger, prettier; her hair was becoming lighter and her cotton suit was changing into a dancing dress. And beside her in the mirror, Paul was turning into a stranger, a laughing-eyed young man wearing a baseball cap.

"I'm ready to go now, Mr. Smith," Cathy said, and suddenly all three of them, the Smiths and their little girl, began walking away in the mirror. In a few moments they were no bigger than matchsticks—and then the three of them disappeared, and there was only the moonlight in the glass.

"Cathy," Marion cried. "Come back, Cathy! Please come back!"

Propped up against the door like a dummy, Paul imagined he could hear above his wife's cries the mocking muted roar of a sports car.

NOTIONS

NOTIONS
Preface by Tom Nolan

Stories made by fiction-writers are often like the rumors described by the narrator of "Notions": they "start with a seed of truth which grows wildly in all directions but straight."

So seems the case with this brief tale in which little seems to happen but a good deal is revealed.

During World War Two, with Ken Millar on duty aboard the *Shipley Bay*, Margaret Millar sent her husband a newsy letter from the hotel in La Jolla, California, where they'd both been staying recently: "Scandal in the Cabrillo! Two young girls arrived last week—turned out to be Wanted by Detectives. They were runaway freshmen from U.C.L.A. & their poppas (from Iowa) had hired det's to find them. Upshot: they both sternly refused to return home or to college, & one of them already has a job at Morrie's Grill. What idiots!"

A few months later, Margaret bought a house up the California coast in Santa Barbara, where Helen Hunt Jackson had drawn inspiration for her 1884 novel *Ramona*. The heroine of that enduringly popular work was a woman of mixed Scotch and Indian blood, who eloped with a young Temecula Indian, who in turn came to a tragic end. The "legend" of Ramona, as written by Mrs. Jackson, was a key part of the myth of Old California around which Santa Barbara grew.

A droll modern Ramona is encountered in Ross Macdonald's 1973 novel *Sleeping Beauty* (a title, its author pointed out, which shares initials with Santa Barbara)—a half-Indian woman who asks the book's detective, "Where's your bow and arrow, Archer?" To which Lew replies, "Out in the back of the Pontiac."

Bits of the Ramona legend, mixed maybe with Margaret Millar's memory of those runaway girls and their two pursuing detectives, seem sprinkled into "Notions," whose Miss Porter, with her Pontiac radiator cap, all her life mourns (and takes pride in) her "lost" Ramon.

Miss Porter is proud too of another persistent presence: Blue

Boy, the jay she insists is devoted to her. Art lovers hearing the name Blue Boy will be reminded of the famous Gainsborough portrait of a dashing English youth, wellknown to Southern Californians for being on display from the 1920s at the Huntington Library in San Marino. Many fair copies of this painting were made over the years—a fact which plays into the humor of "Notions."

Also on view at the Huntington for decades, hung directly opposite the "Blue Boy," was a "sister" portrait (by Thomas Lawrence): "Pinkie." Is it mere coincidence that "Notions"' mock-Indian Miss Porter is described as "short and plump and pink"? And that the woman writing her story in 1987 was, like "Pinkie," less wellknown but, many said, equally as "good" as her blue-eyed, lifelong companion in art? And that Canada geese, even more devoted than bluejays, mate for life?

This oddly poignant tale, by an avowedly unreligious teller, draws attention to some of the ways (myth, fable, fiction) through which humans transcend such harsh realities as a killed bird or a vanished partner.

"Of course it's not likely we'll meet again. But it's a lovely notion, isn't it?"

Notes

" 'Scandal in the Cabrillo!' ": Margaret to Kenneth Millar, February 28, 1945, M Millar Papers, UCI.

"where Helen Hunt Jackson had drawn inspiration": See *Material Dreams: Southern California Through the 1920s*, by Kevin Starr (Oxford, 1990).

"a title, its author pointed out": Ross Macdonald interviews with Paul Nelson, UCI. Macdonald also once noted that Lew Archer shares initials with Los Angeles.

NOTIONS

Miss Porter had some strange notions. Many of us do: they wander in and out of our heads, leaving little or no impression. Miss Porter's were more persistent, impervious to time and reason. She was convinced, for instance, that a certain bluejay which frequented her feeding station at the rear of her townhouse followed her whenever she left the premises to go to the grocery store, the doctor, the bank, the library. It waited, she claimed, on the parapet of the library roof, on the telephone pole outside the doctor's office, on the water-maiden fountain in front of the bank, or on top of the oak tree planted in the center of the grocery-store parking lot. When Miss Porter returned to her old Lincoln, she would snap her fingers to alert the bird to her departure, and drive home using the same route every time.

I wasn't surprised that the jay or any other creature could recognize her car. The Lincoln was distinctive not only for its age and size but because the roof had been painted white to reflect the sun's rays and keep the interior of the car cool, Miss Porter having no use for air-conditioning. In addition to its rakish roof, the Lincoln carried an Indian radiator cap once used on Pontiacs. Miss Porter had gone to considerable trouble to acquire the Indian radiator ornament, corresponding with the main Pontiac officials in Michigan and, on their advice, canvassing various used-car lots and junkyards. She finally purchased one for fifty dollars at a swap meet, explaining to the swapper that the reason she wanted it was because she was one-ninth Indian. How she arrived at this unlikely figure no one knew, but to give it some authenticity she wore her hair long and black and straight. The rest of Miss Porter must have come from the other eight-ninths of her heredity. She was short and plump and pink.

There are always rumors about the very rich. Many of them start with a seed of truth which then grows wildly in all directions but straight. One of these rumors concerned Miss Porter's elopement at the age of fifteen with a Mexican gardener. Three weeks later she returned home in the company of a couple of burly men hired to find her. The fate of her lover remained in doubt. There were several versions: he had accepted a bribe to get lost; he had been killed by one of the two burly men; he was arrested after a bar brawl in Ensenada. The story Miss Porter told was different. She had repeated it to everybody she knew, swearing each to secrecy, without changing a detail. Her lover, Ramon, broken-hearted, had flung himself off a cliff into the sea and drowned.

"He was devoted to me," Miss Porter said. And I was, in spite of myself, rather touched, though it was long ago and far away and may never have happened.

The bluejay was also devoted to her, or so it seemed. There were numerous bluejays in the neighborhood, all of them the same size and shape and color, the same brashness of manner and loudness of voice. I couldn't tell if it was the same bird who came every day and perched on the railing of Miss Porter's deck, bobbing and weaving like a fighter at the sound of the bell. Its raucous demands brought Miss Porter scurrying out the back door with a handful of peanuts. She talked to the bird. If the air was still and my windows were open I could hear an occasional sentence.

"Now, now, is it nice to be so greedy? No, it is not nice. And that voice of yours. Why, it's enough to wake the dead and kill the living. Oh, oh, what a hungry boy you are."

Sometimes one of her sentences was punctuated by a little cry of pain when the bird's beak jabbed her flesh instead of a peanut. She was a good sport about it.

"Just a touch of blood-poisoning," she said when I met her one day in the library and inquired about her bandaged hand. "My little bird gave me a love peck."

"It was probably unintentional."

"My dear child, you don't know much about love pecks," she said with a little laugh. "They are always intentional."

About three months after I moved out from Chicago and rented the house next to Miss Porter's, she invited me to drive over the pass into the Santa Ynez Valley to pick olallie berries. I'd never heard of olallie berries but it was a pleasant day for a drive and I had nothing better to do.

Most short elderly women look overwhelmed behind the wheel

of a huge car, but Miss Porter seemed right at home and in full charge. She drove skillfully around the sharp precipitous road up the mountain, pausing every now and then to look over at a tree or shrub with the binoculars she kept on the seat beside her.

"Oh, dear," she said finally, "I feared this would happen, I really feared. But there was nothing I could do to stop it."

"Stop what?"

"Blue Boy is following us."

And so he was. Or so it seemed. Every time Miss Porter braked the car and pointed at a toyon, a manzanita, a scrub oak, a bluejay would be perched on top.

"He will be exhausted," she said. "The trip is much too long for him."

It had been a rainy spring and the valley was lush and green and the lake was blue as jays. We turned off the main road into a lane marked by a hand-printed sign, OLALLIES, PICK YOUR OWN, $4 PER BUCKET. At the ranch house, we were each outfitted with a plastic belt with a bucket fastened to it.

"We will just take our time," Miss Porter said. "That will give Blue Boy an opportunity to rest up for the return trip."

By noon, the day had turned hot and the sun was relentless. My head felt as if it had been put in an oven and taken out medium rare. Miss Porter filled her bucket before I even reached the halfway mark. My fingers were stained purplish red and covered with painful little scratches. We paid for the olallie berries, which were then transferred to plastic bags. On our way back to the car, Miss Porter stopped suddenly.

"Where's Blue Boy? I don't hear him. Do you?"

"No."

"I must find him and tell him we're leaving."

She plunged into a wild blue sea of sky flowers toward the place on the telephone pole where we'd last seen Blue Boy. He lay almost directly underneath in a tangle of burr clover.

Miss Porter turned away, covering her eyes with her hand. "Is he dead?"

"Yes."

"The trip exhausted him," she said. "It wore out his brave little heart. He loved me enough to die for me. He died of devotion."

I didn't point out the two small round holes in the bird's breast, nor did I draw attention to the boys with the BB guns we passed on the main road.

"There will be other birds," I said.

"No. Not for me. When Ramon died, people said there would be other men. But there never were."

"Birds are easier to replace."

There were other birds, of course, all the way home, many of them jays perched on scrub oak and toyon and manzanita, all exactly alike, the same color and size and shape, the same brash manners and raucous voices. Miss Porter did not acknowledge them.

When we reached home, she silently handed me both bags of olallie berries with an expression of revulsion on her face as if the berries had gone bad and she wanted to get rid of them.

This is how I remembered her during my month-long trip to Chicago on family business. When I returned home, my first job was the usual stocking up on groceries. Miss Porter and I met at opposite ends of the delicatessen counter. She waved at me merrily with her right hand. The left was heavily bandaged and supported by a sling made of a silk scarf.

"Another love peck," she said brightly. "Would you believe it?"

I said I would.

"What a surprise it was to come out on the deck and find Blue Boy waiting for me. He wasn't dead after all. He had merely fainted from exhaustion. When he regained consciousness we were gone, and it took him several days to get home without my car to guide him. But lo and behold, there he was, good as new." She took a step closer to me and lowered her voice. "It makes me wonder about Ramon."

"How?"

"Perhaps he didn't really die when he jumped over that cliff. Perhaps he is, right this minute, working in someone else's garden. He will have changed considerably by this time, but I would still know him—the way I knew Blue Boy." She shook her head as if trying to dislodge an idea. "Of course it's not likely we'll meet again. But it's a lovely notion, isn't it?"

I had to agree. It was a lovely notion.

Sources

"About the Author: Margaret Millar," *The Unicorn Mystery Book Club News*, vol. 3, no. 3 (1950)

"Mind Over Murder," *Street & Smith's Detective Story Magazine*, November 1942; reprinted in *All Fiction Detective Stories*, 1943 Edition

"Last Day in Lisbon," *Five-Novels Monthly*, February 1943

"McGowney's Miracle," *Cosmopolitan*, July 1954

"The Couple Next Door," *Ellery Queen's Mystery Magazine*, July 1954

"The People Across the Canyon," *Ellery Queen's Mystery Magazine*, October 1962

"Notions," *Ellery Queen's Mystery Magazine*, December 1987

THE COUPLE NEXT DOOR

The Couple Next Door: Collected Short Mysteries by Margaret Millar, edited by Tom Nolan, is set in 12-point Century Schoolbook. It is printed on sixty-pound natural shade acid-free paper. The cover painting and design are by Deborah Miller. *The Couple Next Door* was published in November, 2004, by Crippen & Landru, Inc., Norfolk, Virginia.

CRIPPEN & LANDRU LOST CLASSICS

Crippen & Landru announces a series of *new* short-story collections by great authors who specialized in traditional mysteries. Each book collects stories from crumbling pages of old pulp, digest, and slick magazines, and most of the stories have been "lost" since their first publication. Each volume is published in cloth and trade softcover.

The following books are in print

Peter Godfrey, *The Newtonian Egg and Other Cases of Rolf le Roux*, introduction by Ronald Godfrey

Craig Rice, *Murder, Mystery and Malone*, edited by Jeffrey A. Marks

Charles B. Child, *The Sleuth of Baghdad: The Inspector Chafik Stories*

Stuart Palmer, *Hildegarde Withers: Uncollected Riddles*, introduction by Mrs. Stuart Palmer

Christianna Brand, *The Spotted Cat and Other Mysteries from Inspector Cockrill's Casebook*, edited by Tony Medawar

William Campbell Gault, *Marksman and Other Stories*, edited by Bill Pronzini; afterword by Shelley Gault

Gerald Kersh, *Karmesin: The World's Greatest Criminal — Or Most Outrageous Liar*, edited by Paul Duncan

C. Daly King, *The Complete Curious Mr. Tarrant*, introduction by Edward D. Hoch

Helen McCloy, *The Pleasant Assassin and Other Cases of Dr. Basil Willing*, introduction by B.S. Pike

William L. DeAndrea, *Murder – All Kinds*, introduction by Jane Haddam

Anthony Berkeley, *The Avenging Chance and Other Mysteries from Roger Sheringham's Casebook*, edited by Tony Medawar and Arthur Robinson

Joseph Commings, *Banner Deadlines: The Impossible Files of Seantor Brooks U. Banner*, edited by Robert Adey; memoir by Edward D. Hoch

Erle Stanley Gardner, *The Danger Zone and Other Stories,* edited by Bill Pronzini

T.S. Stribling, *Dr. Poggioli: Criminologist*, edited by Arthur Vidro

Margaret Millar, *The Couple Next Door: Collected Short Mysteries*, edited by Tom Nolan

Phillip S. Warne, *Who Was Guilty? Two Dime Novels*, edited by Marlena E. Bremseth

The following books are in preparation

Gladys Mitchell, *Sleuth's Alchemy: Cases of Mrs. Bradley and Others*, edited by Nicholas Fuller

Rafael Sabatini, *The Evidence of the Sword*, edited by Jesse Knight

Michael Collins, *Slot-Machine Kelly*, introduction by Robert J. Randisi

Max Brand, *Masquerade: Nine Crime Stories*, edited by William F. Nolan

Julian Symons, *Francis Quarles: Detective*, edited by John Cooper; afterword by Kathleen Symons

Lloyd Biggle, Jr., *The Grandfather Rastin Mysteries*, introduction by Kenneth Biggle

Hugh Pentecost, *The Battles of Jericho*, introduction by S.T. Karnick

Erle Stanley Gardner, *The Casebook of Sidney Zoom*, edited by Bill Pronzini

Mignon G. Eberhart, *The E-String Murder and Other Mysteries*, edited by Rick Cypert and Kirby McCauley

For updates, please visit our website: www.crippenlandru.com